"Beginnings are magical times, don't you think?"

David's quiet voice floated through the gentle music.

"I don't believe in magic," Melody replied. "It's all done with mirrors."

"Not hocus-pocus magic. People think magic has to be out of the ordinary. They ignore the special times, the special moments that are the real magic. The magic of a flower. The magic of a newborn infant. The magic of getting to know someone new." His vibrant voice stirred waves of delicious tingling inside her.

"David, I'm not magic. Far from it."

"Maybe..." His hand slipped lightly from her neck to her cheek, leaving an invisible trail of fire on her sensitive flesh.

"David, I—"

"Shh. Don't say anything. This is a beginning. It's magical. Just sit and feel the magic...."

Dear Reader,

If you're looking for an extra-special reading experience—something rich and memorable, something deeply emotional, something totally romantic—your search is over! For in your hands you hold one of Silhouette's extremely **Special Editions**.

Dedicated to the proposition that *not* all romances are created equal, Silhouette **Special Edition** aims to deliver the best and the brightest in women's fiction—six books each month by such stellar authors as Nora Roberts, Lynda Trent, Tracy Sinclair and Ginna Gray, along with some dazzling new writers destined to become tomorrow's romance stars.

Pick and choose among titles if you must—we hope you'll soon equate all Silhouette **Special Editions** with consistently gratifying romance reading.

And don't forget the two Silhouette *Classics* at your bookseller's each month—reissues of the most beloved Silhouette **Special Editions** and Silhouette *Intimate Moments* of yesteryear.

Today's bestsellers, tomorrow's *Classics*—that's Silhouette **Special Edition**. We hope you'll stay with us in the months to come, because month after month, we intend to become more special than ever.

From all the authors and editors of Silhouette **Special Edition**,
Warmest wishes,

Leslie Kazanjian
Senior Editor

JUDI EDWARDS
The Perfect Ten

Silhouette Special Edition

Published by Silhouette Books New York

America's Publisher of Contemporary Romance

To all the Elizabeths,
and the rest of my patient family

SILHOUETTE BOOKS
300 East 42nd St., New York, N.Y. 10017

Copyright © 1988 by Judi Edwards

ISBN: 0-373-09470-1

First Silhouette Books printing August 1988

Printed in the U.S.A.

JUDI EDWARDS

once dreamed of being a professional oboe player but has long since been resigned to music as a hobby. She still plays in a Tucson amateur orchestra, but is *not* in love with the conductor. (Her spouse of nineteen years was her high school sweetheart, please note!) She spent many years teaching in remote areas of Canada but prefers writing at home, where she has only four children to contend with, rather than thirty.

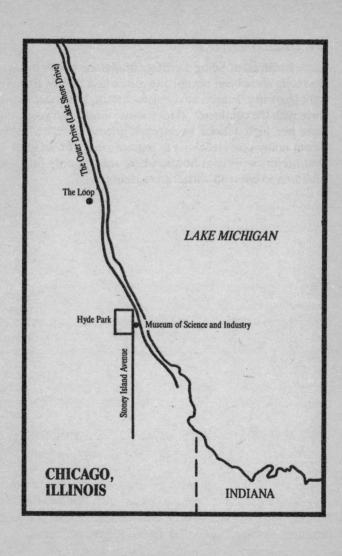

The Outer Drive (Lake Shore Drive)

The Loop

LAKE MICHIGAN

Hyde Park

Museum of Science and Industry

Stoney Island Avenue

CHICAGO, ILLINOIS

INDIANA

Chapter One

Mel, trouble!"

Melody Ross was so engrossed in the numbers on the computer monitor that Herbert Klein's shriek made no sense at first, as if he'd spoken in Japanese or Swahili. Her heart, however, heard his barely controlled panic and began to pound.

"What... Is it a holdup?" Klein's Hardware had never been robbed—during the daylight—in Melody's eight years there.

Mr. Klein's nervous grin etched additional wrinkles into his sallow face. A fold of skin under his chin swayed as he shook his head.

Melody let out her breath. Whatever the trouble, it probably wasn't worth the fright he'd given her. She should have learned by now. Lately Mr. Klein fell apart under the least pressure—leaving her to pick up the pieces, of course.

"No," he quavered, "it's nothing that serious. Lamarr's arguing with a customer."

"Rats. Uh, has Lamarr drawn a knife?"

"No. Your new boy is showing great restraint. He hasn't kicked, punched or even sworn. Yet."

Melody poked harder than necessary at the keyboard to save her current work to the disk drive. Mr. Klein had called Lamarr her new boy—which meant, obviously, that she was expected to handle the problem by herself. "Okay," she sighed. "I'll be there in just a second, Mr. Klein."

He nodded and shuffled down the short corridor to the store.

She didn't need this now, not at the end of a frustrating day. The bookkeeping output still didn't agree with her pencil-and-paper figures, and she dreaded the thought of facing this mess first thing in the morning. Well, she could stay late again and try to learn what she'd done wrong.

Melody slipped the large black wafer from the disk drive and placed it in its envelope. To her the brave new computerized world had so far meant long hours teaching herself bookkeeping menus, PC-DOS and spreadsheet commands—while at the same time she continued her other work. She waited on customers, worked the till and ordered stock. She even did the books manually, as well as on the computer, till she was sure she'd mastered the dumb bookkeeping program. Which might be never. This blasted machine would start saving work one of these days, or she'd wring its electrical cord till its chips went floppy.

A muffled shout from the sales floor jerked her from her reverie. No use putting it off. The argument didn't sound as if it would end of its own accord. Still, she didn't relish confronting an angry Lamarr Willington. Lamarr, the stockboy she'd hired this summer, was intimidating both physically and emotionally. His choice of shirts said it all. His T-shirts always had the sleeves torn off—not cut, torn—to expose his massive biceps. She wondered again why she'd given him a chance out of all those who'd applied. Her first, and maybe last, personnel decision had been to hire a high school dropout, a fugitive from a street gang. Why, oh, why?

Ancient floorboards creaked as she stepped across the threshold of the small office—Mr. Klein's office in theory, though not in fact—and toward the swinging doors that opened on the sales floor. Angry voices filtered through the doors.

"Better get to it." Her palms were damp; she wiped them on her slacks before pushing open the door. She ignored for once the creaking complaint of the outdated ceiling fans that symbolized Klein's uphill struggle against the slick air-conditioned hardware store down the street and that at the same time assaulted her illusions of being a successful business executive. She passed Mr. Klein, huddled at the back of the store. His eyes avoided hers. His frail body seemed to absorb like body blows each outburst of abusive language from the plumbing aisle. Melody hurried.

The shouting customer was Eric, the baggy-eyed, middle-aged janitor of the apartment building at the corner. He was complaining about the plumbing supplies Lamarr had tried to sell him—and in the process crudely questioning the youth's plumbing experience, IQ and ancestry. In a way Melody was glad the foul-mouthed customer was Eric. She'd always disliked him, even more than his lecherous eyes and hands warranted. Now she felt that her dislike was vindicated.

Lamarr was glaring silently at the janitor with more than his usual fierce expression. Lamarr wasn't always angry; the scar on his upper lip just twisted his mouth to look that way. But now his cheek muscles twitched, and his eyes were mere slits. His arms were crossed over his modest—for Lamarr—heavy silver necklace. To Melody he was obviously accentuating his biceps as a warning. If Eric had any sense, he'd shut up.

Without allowing herself time to think, Melody stepped between them—being very careful not to push or even touch the smoldering youth. Lamarr was by far the more dangerous of the two, so she deliberately turned her back to him. But how much longer would his veneer of civilization hold? Her back tingled as she forced a smile in Eric's direction. "May I help you with something?"

"Oh, Mel. Glad to see you." As he grinned at her, his breath nearly made her drunk. "Yeah, Mel, you can hire someone who knows what he's talking about. All I'm doing is putting a new trap in 304's kitchen sink. This jerk tells me I have to replace the pipe, when I know damn well I just need a new slip joint."

The stockboy's ominous voice rumbled from behind Melody. "That old trap you brung in is a piece of corroded garbage. You're gonna mess it up if you do it your way. You need a new pipe."

A man whose green work suit was the twin of Eric's limped up the aisle toward them. Melody was glad for the reinforcements. Al Jevaert was a levelheaded janitor, someone Eric would respect—and he was well over six feet tall. Of course, Al was also old enough to be her father, and his left leg arched like that of a bowlegged cowboy. No, she couldn't expect Al to break up a fight. It was still up to her to defuse things as best she could. She nodded to him. "Hello, Al."

"Hi, Mel." Al was his usual genial self, as if he hadn't noticed anything unusual. She observed that he stationed himself by Eric's side, though, just in case. "You're looking beautiful, as usual. But then, tall, sandy-haired ladies like you always remind me of my daughter and my late wife, so I guess I'm prejudiced. One of these days I'm going to carry you away from all this, my dear."

She was tempted to take him up on the offer—and not just to see his face grow red and hear his sputtered, though gallant, backtracking.

"Hello, Eric," Al said. He glanced at Lamarr but apparently decided against saying anything.

Melody resisted the urge to glance behind her. Instead, she took advantage of Eric's momentary distraction. "If you take your purchase over to the till, Eric, I'll write it up on your building's account."

But he ignored her. "You've got mighty rude help, Klein," he shouted toward the back of the store. "Maybe I ought to take my building's business to Strong Hardware. Do you know what this jerk said to me?"

Melody tried to gesture him over to the till, but he still ignored her. Her shoulders were tense, for she was half afraid Lamarr would suddenly lunge.

"Yeah," Al Jevaert interrupted, "he said you couldn't tell a drainpipe from a certain part of your anatomy. Absolutely shocking. By the way, Eric, do you have pipe-caulking compound this time?"

The smaller man wobbled and smiled up at Al. "As a matter of fact, I'd better get some. You'll be heading home soon, and I won't be able to pop over to your building to borrow any. Thank you." He turned to sneer at Melody and Lamarr. "That's the kind of help I expect in a store. And Al doesn't even work here!" He turned toward the cash register.

Melody smiled her thanks at Al, who winked. She tried to keep the smile in place when she saw that Eric was waiting with a crude leer for her to accompany him. She glanced back, but Al was trying to cool down Lamarr with an innocent question about a plumbing problem—a problem she was sure he'd understood for thirty years.

Taking a deep breath, Melody dodged Eric's arm as it snaked toward her waist. Lamarr hadn't noticed, or she was sure he would have charged like a one-man motorcycle gang. She stared at the janitor's back and whispered to herself, "Don't blow it, stupid, now that we've saved you from your own idiocy."

Eric stopped. "What'd you say?"

"Nothing."

He grinned and extended his arm in unsteady parody of a gentleman letting a lady go first. The look in his eye was lecherous; his fingers twitched in his eagerness to touch her. With a sigh of resignation, Melody crossed her wrists and stuck out her elbows as her brother had taught her in their childhood football games, then charged past him with nothing worse than a hand flitting against her derriere.

"I've been practicing for the Bears' defensive line," she said. "Think I'll make the team?"

Eric lurched after her. "Nah. They've got the Refrigerator. They don't need you. You have the height, maybe, but you're as skinny as the goal post."

"Gee, thanks." She reached the safety of the checkout counter and turned to face him from behind its battlement. But Eric merely tossed his plumbing onto the counter.

Now that it was all over, Mr. Klein hurried as fast as his bent-over gait allowed and helped her ring up the purchase. Eric didn't say another word, and neither did Mr. Klein. Big help her boss had been, thrusting her between a drunk and a juvenile delinquent, she thought. Usually she appreciated that he let her handle things by herself. But this was different. Darn it, this was his store, not hers....

Mr. Klein's hands were steady now, and the only outward sign of his previous panic was the way he tossed Eric's bag instead of handing it over. His eyes were back to normal, too: hard, shrewd, calculating. He neither praised nor thanked her, assuming as always that she could handle matters without help. The implied trust was nice; a pat on the back would have been nicer. And besides, if she goofed she heard from him endlessly, as with her hiring of Lamarr.

Together they rang up Al Jevaert's purchase. The tall janitor searched her face, then smiled at what he saw. Melody smiled back. Al was one of the few thoroughly decent men she'd met, and though she knew his flirting was only joking, she allowed herself a brief fantasy about what it would be like to date him. She couldn't keep a straight face, though, and Mr. Klein looked at her smile inquiringly. No. Al's daughter was old enough to be her big sister. Well, then, what if Al had been her father?

Now, that was a fantasy worth cherishing.

When Al left, it was still five minutes till closing, but Mr. Klein looked around for customers and then nodded toward the door. Melody, used to his silent mannerisms, sighed lustily. "I agree completely," she muttered as she flipped the Closed sign over. Mr. Klein dropped his keys, and she retrieved them before she even had time to think. He didn't look well, even less so than usual. When she gave him the keys she felt a tremor in his hand. "Your ulcer again? You really should see a doctor, Mr. Klein."

His blank expression dismissed her concern utterly. "Go see about Lamarr."

She wiped her own face free of emotion—the best way, she'd learned through hard experience, of dealing with her boss—and headed toward Plumbing.

Amazingly, Lamarr was standing in the same place, with the same defiant posture. Melody paused, disconcerted and at the same time impressed. This lad could sustain anger for a long time. Did she really want to confront him when he'd been sulking like this?

She wondered which of them had been right. Eric was an experienced apartment janitor, and janitors had to know how to fix almost everything. From working there she'd developed a healthy respect for their knowledge and industriousness. Unlike her, they had no boss directing their every move. They had to be self-starters, willing to endure low status and long hours made even longer by being on-call day and night in case of emergency. If a janitor got sick, no one covered for him; the work just piled up as a reward for his return to health. Still, some janitors—like Al—were bound to be better than others.

Lamarr, on the other hand, had spent just one month learning plumbing so he could help customers when he wasn't downstairs in the stockroom. Every Klein employee had a specialty: Roy and Ted, the two clerks who weren't on duty at the moment, had appliances and electrical, she had paint and Lamarr had agreed to learn about plumbing. He'd worked with a plumber for a month, going from job to job. At the end of the month the plumber had said he was so worried about Lamarr ripping off his tools that he'd never left the youth alone and that Herbert Klein could get someone else next time. But they'd never had complaints about Lamarr's plumbing advice.

"The jerk's wrong." The rumbling voice was still angry.

"I know." Melody walked slowly toward him. "It's over now."

"But he's wrong. He's trying to cut corners, save himself a little bit of work. But them pipes are too old for him to get away with it. I'm right!"

"Then he'll find that out for himself. Imagine the look on his face when he does."

The boy didn't laugh. He never laughed, rarely smiled. But his scowl grew fractionally less intense.

"Lamarr, there are some people you can't teach. Eric's one. When you come across people like that, just give them enough rope to hang themselves. It doesn't do any good to argue with them."

He fidgeted, and Melody wondered if he'd stood for all the lecturing he could take. Too bad. Lamarr needed to learn how to deal with people if he was going to survive in the hardware business—or any business. "You can't insult customers just because they won't listen to your advice."

"Say what?" His eyes narrowed in anger. "You people teach me about plumbing. You think I care about toilets?"

"Well—"

"Hell, no. But I keep at it, 'cause it's part of the job. I use what I learn and that yahoo jumps me for it. So what do I do? I keep my mouth shut. It's hard, too, because he was dishing out a lot of garbage."

"I'm sure. But Al said you compared Eric's knowledge of plumbing to—well, you know."

Lamarr's mouth angled into as much of a smile as it ever did, enjoying either her discomfort or the memory or both. "Oh, you mean to his—"

"That's what I mean," she interrupted quickly.

He turned solemn once again. "I guess this means I'm fired."

Melody's laugh covered her surprise. She hadn't even considered firing Lamarr; if anything, she felt more empathy for him now than ever before. "Of course not. Look, we both suffered from that fool. I just think you should work downstairs in the stockroom unless we really need you up here. And even when you're on the floor, stay away from Eric."

Slowly the boy's eyes relaxed. "Gladly. Man, that fellow is such a turkey."

"Don't I know it. At least you're a guy—all he does is yell at you. He pinches and pats me every chance he gets."

"Say what?"

A new gleam entered Lamarr's eyes as he stared openly at Melody's body from head to foot. She didn't like that look, especially the way it lingered on her torso. She restrained the impulse to cross her arms over her breasts, wishing she hadn't said anything to draw his attention to her as a woman, rather than as just his boss. Why, oh, why, had she hired this hoodlum?

She edged away from Lamarr, feeling the touch of his eyes, and concentrated on keeping her hips as still as possible when she walked. Not that she really believed he'd do anything to her, but her nerves were shaky. The idea of changing to her street clothes downstairs—Lamarr's turf— was suddenly daunting. She glanced at her faded jeans, spotted with at least a quarter of the 128 hues the store sold. No, she refused to let her imagination force her outside, dressed like a color sample chart. She steeled herself to walk down the creaky stairs, unconsciously marching to the whiny beat of the dilapidated ceiling fans, still sensing Lamarr's gaze on her backside.

But before she changed clothes, she double-checked that the washroom door was locked. And on her way home she took a roundabout route so she wouldn't have to walk past Eric's building.

The next day was Sunday. A day of rest. A day without the hardware store. A day, Melody thought as she drove a shovel into the soft dirt of her tiny garden, when she didn't have to handle drunken janitors. Only potatoes.

She had four paper bags lined up in the path between the growing beds. Two bags held good-size potatoes that would keep for a few months in the cool closet of the spare bedroom. A third held smaller potatoes for immediate use. A fourth held only a few potatoes, but each was a giant. Kennebec was a good variety for producing the occasional whopper to impress her father.

Papa approved of her garden. To his mind gardening was woman's work, because Mama had done the gardening back in West Virginia, before she died. Usually Papa's approval was enough to turn Melody against a project, but she liked gardening regardless. She even saved the best of her crop for him; not a peace pipe, but a peace potato. Besides, the potatoes would give them something to talk about when the tired old man came for his regular duty visit.

Last month it had been tomatoes.

The garden was only as wide as her town house, twenty-five feet. It wasn't long, either, but she knew she was lucky to have even this much ground in a crowded neighborhood like Hyde Park. A small garden like hers could be coaxed to produce abundantly with the proper planning and thought. The hardest thing was finding time, what with the long hours she put in at the store. But she puttered whenever she got the chance.

The six-foot fence gave her privacy as she worked, and the crab apple tree in the yard of the town house to the north helped, too. The only place anyone could watch her was from the second story of the two-flat on the south. She used to like that two-flat. The vintage brick building, with one apartment atop the other, was more typical of Chicago's older neighborhoods than her town house was. She hadn't minded the balcony overlooking her garden when Mrs. Talbot and her parakeets had lived there, either. But now that a man had moved in, she wasn't so sure. What if her new neighbor was snoopy? Melody wasn't crazy about physical work and spent as much time admiring what she'd done as she did working. He might think her lazy. Furthermore, she didn't look her best right now, in a streaked orange sweatshirt and with her shoulder-length hair uncombed. But who dressed up to dig in the dirt?

Just then she heard a noise in the alley. From the raised potato bed Melody could just see over the back fence. Well, speaking of exercise, she thought. Jogging toward her was none other than her new neighbor. She'd never seen him this close before. He might be fairly attractive when he wasn't sweating like a pig, she mused. His dark brown hair was long at the back, long enough so that with each step it bounced. Around his forehead he wore one of those ridic-

ulous sweatbands she considered such an affectation.
Though she could see only his head, she was suddenly certain his sweat suit was velour and his running shoes suede
and spotless—the very picture of the well-dressed jogger.

He nodded to her as he puffed past her yard. Belatedly she
nodded back.

On second thought, maybe the sweatband wasn't such an
affectation. Despite the touch of chill in the air, perspiration ran down his forehead and glistened on his neck. So, he
was a fanatical jogger rather than a jogger for appearances.

The latter type was easier for Melody to comprehend. She
could understand and even envy buying clothes to trot
around in so everyone would notice. But how could she
fathom someone who thought torture was fun? Oh, well,
her father's dog chased its tail. To each his own.

Melody recalled a game she had invented as an adoles-
cent. The game was born one summer rush hour as she'd
stood waiting for the light to change at Seventy-fifth Street
and Stony Island Avenue, where eight packed lanes of cars
whizzed by. Young Melody, still feeling alone and abandoned by her mother's sudden death months before, had
been abruptly aware of the people as individuals, all hur-
rying somewhere, all of them the centers of their own uni-
verses, all with their own stories, their own problems, their
own loves. She was new to Chicago back then, and this was
the first time she'd ever come close to realizing the true immensity of its crush of humanity. She'd stood, transfixed,
through three green lights, the heat and her growing appre-
hension combining to send perspiration running ever faster
down the long sleeves of her blouse. No matter how many
people passed, more always came. Stony Island seemed like
a road from infinity. As thirteen-year-old Melody Haakman watched the infinite street, she shrank to a mere insig-

nificant dot like all the other dots, hustling and bustling somewhere, from someplace, for some reason.

Shaken by the humbling experience, she'd invented the Face Game. She chose a face she liked from the teeming street and made it more than just one mote among many. She invented a name, destination and family, and felt less alone; the Face Game had helped her cope with the city's immensity and impersonality. Even after Papa had moved the family again, away from Stony Island Avenue to the southwest side, she'd walked a little taller, just in case someone chose her for their own version of the Face Game.

And now Melody turned her Face Game skills on her jogging neighbor.

Start with known facts, she thought. He liked to jog. He had just moved in. He played his stereo a shade too loud. He liked both pop and classical music.

Now for the fun part. A name. He had a cultured look to him, despite the sweat. Sort of an Alistair type. Okay. Alistair it was. In addition to jogging, Alistair was a health food fanatic, a vegetarian who cooked his food in a wok. He did his own mechanical and restorative work on his beloved old VW Beetle, which was red and always immaculate. The car was the true love of his life, though he was constantly cushioning the falls of women who threw themselves at his body.

Alistair had moved here to work on his Ph.D. in business. Was the University of Chicago's School of Business as prestigious as its other departments? It didn't matter. For Face Game purposes, it now ranked right up there with Harvard Business School. Anyway, he had a great job lined up for next year with General Motors—no, make that IBM. So he probably wouldn't be interested in women with high school educations who worked in hardware stores.

She frowned in the direction of the balcony. "Snob!"

Oops. She'd best lower her voice. Alistair was moving around in his living room, and the sliding glass door was now half open. Unless she was careful, he'd hear her.

She noted that she'd been wrong about his jogging clothes, or at least about the velour jogging pants. He wore ordinary gym shorts. She couldn't tell about his shirt, though, because he'd already taken it off. Maybe it was velour.

Melody bent to the potatoes again. Another ten minutes and she'd be done. She stopped once to consider whether she should add another whopper to Papa's bag. How many giant potatoes did a lonely widower need, anyway? It was such a beautiful spud, though.... In the end, she carefully placed it in the bag with her other prize potatoes.

Ravel's "Bolero" wafted out of her neighbor's open glass door. Melody smiled as she thought of the movie *10*. The girl in the movie, the one whose beauty was supposed to rate a ten on a scale from one to ten, claimed "Bolero" was great lovemaking music. Melody didn't think it was as sensuous as, say, "Afternoon of a Faun," but in a pounding, masculine sort of way she could see the truth of it. What was Alistair doing up there, anyway?

Ten. She had ten more years of payments on her town house—if she could keep up the payments, of course. Mr. Klein paid a good salary, but Hyde Park was a fairly expensive neighborhood and she had scarcely any surplus at the end of the month. It was worth it, though. Inside that town house she lived a quiet, safe and sane existence. She was proud of that quietness and sanity. In there she had rebuilt her life and her confidence after a disastrous marriage and a divorce that left her feeling insecure. The town house was the symbol of her survival.

"Ten more years." She spoke loudly, her words drowned out by the crashing climax of "Bolero." To own a house, mortgage-free, would be an accomplishment. Darned right. She tossed a potato straight up. "Ten!"

The last word rang in the air, alone. "Bolero" was over.

She was already facing the two-flat. She had only to glance up to see her neighbor, who wore only a startled expression and a jockstrap. He pulled a towel around his waist and came to the open door.

"Oh, Lord," she whispered.

"Excuse me, miss. Did you say something?"

Melody looked all around. No place to hide. "Who, me?"

"Yes. Did you say something just now?"

She tried to think, but nothing came. "Uh, yeah."

"What did you say?"

Her mind was hung up on the irrelevant fact that his towel was marked "Boston Villa Hotel." He took towels from hotels. "Ten."

He looked at her quizzically. "Ten? That's all, just ten?"

"Yeah. Ten."

He shook his head and was turning away from the door when suddenly his head jerked back to her. He looked down at his body, then back at Melody. "Thank you," he said self-consciously. "I guess."

Now it was Melody's turn to look quizzical, but only for a second. "Oh, no. I didn't mean... I mean, I don't even have my glasses on. Everything's just a blur. You're a blur, the bricks are a blur, your skirt's a blur. Blind as a bat without them. Really."

His chuckle wasn't angry. "Never mind. Let me put on something more than a towel, though, and I'll be right back."

As soon as he disappeared she kicked the ground in front of her. While the dirt was still spraying against the fence, she scooped up two bags of potatoes. If she hurried she wouldn't be here when he returned. This was one conversation she didn't feel like continuing.

He was quick, though, and reappeared in a shapeless plaid robe while she was on the way back for the rest of the potatoes.

"Hi down there."

Glancing up only briefly, she spoke while walking over to the bags. "Hello."

"I'm new in town, and I wondered if you could help me. Could you recommend a reliable dry cleaner?"

The two remaining bags were full, and she'd have to take them one at a time. She hefted one before turning toward the two-flat. "Well, not really. I don't have any wool outfits. I guess you could call me a wash-and-wear woman."

"My suits need pressing after being packed. The same place that does your husband's things would be fine."

With a terse shake of her head, Melody lugged the bag toward her kitchen. "I don't have a husband."

"How about a live-in lover? Fiancé? Steady boyfriend?"

Her heart sinking, Melody shook her head three times. Her new neighbor *would* have to be a ladies' man. From now on every time she went into her garden he'd probably come out to chat and make passes and generally intrude on her privacy. "No, no and no. Alistair."

"My name's not Alistair. You must have heard wrong about me. My name is David. David Halifax."

She wondered if he thought she'd been asking neighbors about him and had heard his name was Alistair. Probably. She'd known men conceited enough to believe women were that interested. "I'm Melody Ross."

"Glad to meet you, Miss Ross."

"It's Ms., not Miss. Ross was my married name."

"I stand corrected. Widowed or divorced?"

"Divorced." She was expecting the usual dreary inquiry into the gory details of her divorce, so his next question caught her by surprise.

"What are you working on, Ms. Melody Ross?"

"I'm taking my potatoes inside, and they're getting heavy, so you'll have to excuse me, Mr. Halifax." As she balanced the bag on one knee to reach for the doorknob, the bag suddenly began to tip. Though she caught it before it emptied completely, potatoes rolled across the patio in every direction. She briefly considered leaving them until David was gone, but she bent down to pick them up.

"Want help with those? I could be down in a minute."

"No, thank you."

"You've really got a lot of different vegetables packed into your garden, don't you? Tomatoes, cucumbers, potatoes. I can't see too well from up here. What else do you have?"

"Well..." The flip side of her privacy, of course, was that she never got to show off her garden. "I have a few strawberry plants here by the patio. The beans are all finished for the year, naturally. So is the cauliflower. Except for broccoli, lettuce and one or two tomatoes, the only things left are root crops like carrots and beets and onions."

"You grow all those things down there? Do you have enough room for the rows between plants?"

"No. But with the method I use, you don't need space between rows." He raised an eyebrow, and Melody needed no more encouragement to explain. "You see, I walk only on the paths between these three raised planting beds. In the beds themselves I plant things close together—carrots two inches apart, tomatoes eighteen inches apart, and so on. That way I can grow quite a lot even in this small space."

"Sounds good to me, Melody. You're self-sufficient, then."

"Hardly." She didn't quite succeed in keeping the pleasure out of her voice. Though she knew her garden could never grow that much, she liked the image of her town house, self-sufficient behind its high fence, impervious to the world's ills. "I'm a lazy gardener, I guess, but I still enjoy it." Then, remembering he was a jogger, she added, "It's good exercise, of course. All this digging and bending. The food is fantastic when it's fresh, too, and I don't have to worry about chemicals or sprays."

"You're making my mouth water. Bacon, lettuce and tomato sandwiches are my favorite."

"Really? Here, then. Let me find a good tomato for you. If there are any left. Ah, this one's juicy, even if it isn't very big. Are you ready to catch?"

"You aren't going to throw that thing at me, are you? What have I ever done to you?" But he stuck out his hands like a baseball catcher.

Taking careful aim, Melody tossed the tomato. She was wary of throwing it too hard, though, and ended up not throwing it hard enough. Reaching over the iron grillwork of the balcony, he snagged it with one hand just before it smashed against the metal. Red juice dripped down his finger.

"Got it."

"I'm sorry, David. I'll never make the White Sox, I'm afraid. If it's squished I can get you another one."

"No! That's quite all right, please. My fingernail punctured one end, that's all. Having people throw ripe tomatoes at me is one of my worst nightmares." He chuckled, taking the sting out of his last words.

He had a pleasant laugh, Melody decided. So many people had strange laughs, but his was deep and warm. She liked his eyes, too. They were large, giving him a look of innocence. She walked to the next bed and bent down.

"Now for some lettuce. I hope you like leaf lettuce. It's the only kind I grow."

"Leaf lettuce won't go splat in my hands, so it's fine. How are you going to get it up here, though—by making paper airplanes out of the leaves?"

"No, silly. I'll throw you the whole plant. Be careful of flying dirt." She shook the roots thoroughly before trying an underhand toss. The plant sailed over her fence, barely, and swished against the bricks of the first-floor apartment.

"Not even my arms are long enough to catch that, Melody. Or is this a clever murder plot to make me fall off the balcony, diving for your lettuce?"

"Give me a second chance. I misjudged the air resistance that time. Are you ready? Here goes, then."

As soon as the plant fluttered out of her hand, she was afraid she'd pitched it too hard. David was tall, though, and caught it over his head amid a shower of soil. Shaking the dirt from his hair, he placed the lettuce on the balcony floor. "Thank you very much, neighbor, although I must say, it's easier to get food from the grocery store."

"My tomatoes and lettuce are cheaper, taste better, and you don't have to wait in long checkout lines. Store-bought tomatoes can't begin to match the garden-fresh kind."

"So I've heard. Say, you wouldn't happen to have some bacon growing down there, would you?"

"There's a bit of pigweed. Is that good enough?"

"No, thanks." Again, that deep, warm chuckle. "On the topic of food, though, maybe you can help in another way. As eager as I am to try your food in a BLT, I have to admit that frying bacon taxes my cooking skills. Since I've just moved here from Boston, I don't know many decent restaurants, and I'm in danger of wasting away to a mere two hundred pounds if I don't get a square meal soon."

Two hundred pounds? He didn't look that heavy, and he certainly didn't carry any excess fat. She'd noticed that much before he grabbed his towel. "How tall are you, David?"

"Six four. What about it? Do you know any nice restaurants?"

"There's the Peppermill, on Fifty-third Street."

"Yes, I've been there. Not bad. Anyplace else you can recommend, maybe a bit nicer? I have a car, so it doesn't have to be in walking distance."

Melody had to search her memory, since she wasn't a regular restaurant-goer. They were too expensive for her budget, and the men who took her to dinner usually thought places like the Peppermill were the epitome of haute cuisine. On top of which was the fact that the closer she got to age thirty, the fewer dates she seemed to have. "Do you like pizza?"

"I love it, especially the kind with thick crusts."

"Then you'd like Uno's. It's a local landmark, along with the Water Tower, the Sears Tower and the Tribune Tower."

"It sort of towers over other restaurants, right?"

"Ouch."

"Anyway, it sounds like the kind of place I want. Where is it?"

She spread her hands. "I don't know the address. I just know it's somewhere north of the Loop. It's in the phone book. I'm sure."

"Never mind. You can show me yourself. Tomorrow night I'll pick you up at seven."

"What?"

"I said, I'll pick you up at seven."

"I heard you, David."

"Is there a problem? If you're busy, we can make it the next night."

Melody wiped her hands on her already dirt-streaked sweatshirt, unsure whether she wanted to date the boy next door. He'd be hard to avoid if things didn't turn out well.

But what the heck—this was the city, and she scarcely ever saw any of her other neighbors. She took a deep breath. "I'm not busy tomorrow night. Just one thing, David. I'm not a vegetarian."

He raised an eyebrow. "Neither am I. Seven o'clock it is. Thanks again for the veggies."

He didn't see her wave, because she waited till he had gone inside to do so.

Chapter Two

Ten to seven. Now what?

Melody hated waiting the last few minutes before company arrived. It was even worse when the company was another awkward first date that led nowhere.

A brief smile tugged at the corners of her mouth. On the other hand, David was tall, an important consideration for a five-foot-ten woman like her. He might be rather handsome when he wasn't dripping with sweat. Besides, she was too young to give up on the male half of the human race.

She killed five minutes dusting the furniture, but Sunday had been cleaning day, and dusting was the only chore that was even vaguely required. She hustled around regardless, fluffing up a throw pillow, straightening the pictures on the wall behind the couch, restacking a slouched pile of magazines. She had thought she'd stopped striving for housekeeper of the year, though. Why was she doing this?

She took a deep breath, sat and picked up a magazine. The article on designing data base files sailed over her mind, but her eyes were kept busy with the words till the doorbell rang.

She stopped by the hall mirror to check her clothes and had just gotten out her comb when the chimes sounded again. She squeezed her lips together as she glanced at the door. "Hold your horses," she muttered. She checked the curl of her hair at the sides and back, then finally laid a hand on the doorknob.

"I'll let you in on one condition," she whispered so there was no chance of her date actually hearing. "You've got to promise that this evening won't end up as a wrestling match."

The door remained stubbornly, silently unresponsive. With a sigh she pulled it open.

"Hello, Melody. I hope I'm not late."

She stared at David for a moment before answering. She'd been wrong about him. She had thought he might be fairly attractive, but he was gorgeous—especially his large eyes, with their fascinating, interlinked patterns of brown, hazel and green shifting and dancing like a kaleidoscope. *Iridescent* was the word that popped to her mind, but she wasn't sure if that described their shimmering clarity. She felt the urge to look up the word. If iridescent didn't describe the hazel windows into his soul, it should.

David's clothes were striking, as well. The gray herringbone sport jacket fit him so perfectly it must have been tailored just for him. That cost money—probably more than her entire fall clothes budget. Yet the impression was more one of good taste than of ostentation. "No apologies necessary, David, believe me."

He had been appraising her, too, she realized. If nothing else, her dates in the six years since the divorce had flattered her till she rediscovered that men found her attractive. But all the compliments in the world couldn't overrule the evidence of her eyes. She wasn't in the same class with this man, as he'd surely see.

"You look nice, Melody. That dress goes well with your hair."

"Thank you." Nice. She thought of beautiful words like *iridescent* and he came up with *nice*. The pattern for the evening was set, she was afraid.

Hmm. Why not? "Excuse me, David, but I just remembered something. Won't you come in for a minute?"

She left him sitting in the living room while she went upstairs to her bedroom. The TV table beside her bed creaked under the weight of books and magazines, most noticeably the leather-bound unabridged dictionary she'd gotten last January with the birthday money her father had given her for a new dress.

"Characterized by a rainbowlike play of colors, as in the soap bubble, mother of pearl, etc." Melody closed the dictionary with a gentle whoosh. At least she'd learned something from this date, even if her escort was wishing he'd never asked her out.

David was on his knees by her record collection when she returned to the living room. "Interesting selection you have here," he said. "Prokofiev sandwiched between Charlie Parker and Ann Murray. Dolly Parton. The Beatles. Debussy. Mantovani."

"I guess you can blame my mother." She sat on the chair nearest him and watched as he flipped through her records. It was a bit embarrassing that the records rested on the floor, between the wall and the stereo console, but since her friend Judy, owner of a Chevy, had remarried, Melody didn't have much chance to search garage sales and secondhand stores for a record stand. "When she named me Melody she made it inevitable I'd like music, all kinds of music. Either that or hate it."

He pulled a record from the collection and skimmed the back cover. "Nice apartment you have here," he said absently.

She bristled at the word *nice* but managed to bite back the words that came to mind. "It's a town house actually, not an apartment."

David must have noticed something in her tone of voice, for he looked up at her apologetically. "I'm sorry." He held up the record, which was Mahler's First Symphony. "I was trying to make small talk while reading, and I guess I'm not up to doing two things at once. Your apartment really is quite nice, though. I meant it."

"Oh, then, that's different," Melody said in a flat voice that she hoped was free of sarcasm. She was mentally reassessing her image of David. Just because he looked sophisticated didn't mean he actually was sophisticated. Or even intelligent.

"I have the Boston Symphony recording of this piece," he said. "I'm not fond of Mahler, but this symphony is nice. Not as bombastic as some of his later works."

"Oh, I wouldn't say that." Melody's current musical interest was the classics—last year it had been country and western—and Mahler was one of her favorites.

David looked at her and chuckled. "You mean this symphony is just as bombastic as all the rest, then?"

"That's not what I meant and you know it." Mahler was certainly not worth arguing about at the beginning of a date with the most handsome man she'd ever gone out with. But David spoke so confidently that she felt a great urge to show him she wasn't about to swoon at his feet just because he was handsome and spent money on clothes and knew one piece of classical music. "When I performed Mahler's Fourth Symphony," she said, "I was impressed with how much the tunes were like folk songs. He even uses 'Frère

Jacques' in one of his symphonies, for heaven's sake. He isn't like, say, Wagner."

"I take it you don't care for Wagner. Okay, I'll agree with you. Compared to Wagner, Mahler is a pussycat." He put the record back and faced her, sitting with his legs folded. "You're a musician, you say. What do you play?"

"I didn't say I was a musician. Not really." She faltered, feeling the hot warning of a blush creep up to her neck. "I used to play the oboe in school, a long time ago. That's all."

David studied her with a new interest. "Was this back in college?"

The warmth spread from her neck to her cheeks. "High school. When I was a senior I played in the all-city band for a while. That's when we did one movement of Mahler's Fourth."

"Mahler arranged for band. Ugh. Do you still play?"

"Well, I pick up my oboe from time to time—mostly to dust the case, if you must know. It's frustrating, trying to play. I remember what I used to be able to do, but I don't have any reeds that are playable."

"Hmm."

That was about as noncommittal a comment as possible, she mused, yet David still watched her with an irritating intensity. Those big, soulful eyes of his were glued to her. He *looked* as though he was really listening, but she doubted he was; if this were after dinner she would suspect he was doing a "look how interesting you are" number on her, to be followed shortly by a wrestling match. Melody's embarrassment congealed into impatience. What did this pretty face know about oboes—or care? Probably nothing at all. Playing the unusual instrument had been her one badge of uniqueness at a time of her life when she had ached to blend in with the upper-middle-class crowd, and she was still mildly proud of her arcane knowledge. Well, she had learned something this evening. So could he. Whether he wanted to or not.

"You see," she said in a schoolteacherish tone, "the oboe is a small instrument that looks a lot like a clarinet. It uses a tiny double reed carved from a cane that grows along the Riviera. The reeds are delicate and incredibly fussy. An oboist can play worse than her reed, but not better. Good reeds have to be handcarved, too, because the manufactured ones are terrible. I used to get good handmade reeds through my band teacher, but now I'm out of luck."

She stumbled then, surprised she still had David's rapt attention. "Uh, I'd like to play again. Not that I was good, mind you." She ended with almost a whisper. "It was fun."

David nodded. "You must have been good to be in the all-American band."

"All-city band," she corrected him. Why had she brought any of this up? "You didn't have to be a great musician to get in. They had five oboists."

"Still, being judged one of the five best high school oboists in a city this size is an honor. Even if you haven't done anything with music since, you had your moment of glory."

Thankfully she watched as David stood to get ready to leave. She looked at him in the hall mirror as he helped her on with her coat. He'd let her escape her bragging with grace. Maybe there was a real person under the tailored clothes and soft eyes.

Parking spaces were an endangered species in Hyde Park, so Melody could understand why David kept his car in the garage behind his two-flat. However, she didn't like the narrow, poorly lit passage between buildings they had to walk through to get to the garage. With Hyde Park surrounded on three sides by decaying neighborhoods, she'd taught herself to avoid such places as this.

As he put his key in the garage door, she asked, "What kind of car do you have? A Volkswagen Beetle, by chance?"

"Please. Beetles were made for gnomes, not people my height."

She thought he was being a bit unfair. The ones she'd ridden in had seemed roomy enough. And when he flipped on the garage light, she knew he was being unfair. "You complain about the size of a Beetle, yet you drive this toy?"

"This toy, as you call it, is my brand-new Nissan 300ZX, one of the fastest production cars available." He chuckled, filling Melody's senses with lighthearted, rumbling music. "Let's have a little respect, please."

Her Face Game had been at least partly correct. Oh, she'd guessed the wrong make of car, but his tone told her that the car was indeed his baby. She patted the burgundy roof as he bent way down to unlock her door. "My apologies, little car. I mean, *fast* little car."

"That's more like it. Climb in, milady."

The interior smelled of the rich leather seat that fit her body like a glove. As David edged the car out of the garage she ran her fingers along the baby-soft leather. The vehicle reeked of quality and money. "This is some car. What do you do for a living, print your own money?"

"I'm a conductor."

"A conductor?" A queasy feeling began to stir in Melody's stomach. "You don't mean a conductor on the Illinois Central, do you?"

His laugh was deep and musical. "No. I'm a symphony orchestra conductor." He got out to close the garage door, leaving Melody alone with her thoughts.

Her first reaction was anger, which quickly decayed to chagrin. She, whose musical education consisted of reading record jackets, had disputed the musical opinion of a conductor. Not only that but she had lectured him about oboe reeds and had supported her opinion of Mahler with her personal experience in a high school band.

The garage door slammed with a metallic clang. Melody pounded her palm against her forehead, then settled her face into a pleasant, noncommittal expression just as David slid into the driver's seat. Glancing furtively at his dimly lit profile, she vowed not to express another opinion for the entire evening. Get him to talk about himself, she thought. That way he'd think she was charming.

She sighed. It shouldn't be too hard to keep a low verbal profile. What in heaven's name could she say to a conductor, anyway? The car purred down the streets and came to a smooth halt at the stop sign at the Outer Drive. "What do you conduct, David?"

"An orchestra."

"Very funny. I mean besides just an orchestra."

"A choir."

When she heaved a theatrical sigh, he elaborated. "Well, if you must know, next summer I'll be taking over as the director of the New England Pops—that's an up-and-coming clone of the Boston Pops."

"I've heard of it. I think."

"I'll be in Chicago till March, off and on. Long enough to bother leasing an apartment instead of renting a hotel room. Long enough, too, for me to enjoy getting to know people here." He turned to fix her with a brief, penetrating stare that was openly speculative. He stretched his arm across the console, and his finger grazed her thigh before settling innocently atop her hand. "Like you, perhaps. Who knows where tonight will lead?"

Melody turned in confusion to look at the passing lights. It was natural, for her at least, to wonder if a relationship might develop from a first date. That was the charm of first dates; the first fifty of them, at least. Even men must wonder about that sometimes. But she'd never been with a man who acknowledged his speculation so openly, and she wasn't sure how to respond.

Or did he just mean sex? Probably. And yet just now his eyes hadn't lingered on her breasts and legs. His stare hadn't felt insulting or leering. Just confusing. Melody propped her best unconcerned smile in place before turning back to him, but by then his eyes had returned to the Outer Drive ahead of them.

"You say you'll be in Chicago off and on, David. Where will you be when you're off?"

"Well. I have guest appearances lined up in Boston. Pittsburgh, Detroit, Cleveland, Toronto, London, Brussels, Paris and even here in Chicago. In my spare time I'm teaching at the university and conducting the Rockefeller Chapel Choir."

"Oh."

London. Boston. Paris... The only one of those cities she'd even been to was Pittsburgh. Yes, she was definitely out of her class. This could be a long, boring evening for poor David.

Things didn't get any better, either. David had expected that she would lead him to the restaurant, and she had expected him to look up the address in the phone book. It wasn't really her fault—more a failure of communication—but the upshot was that they couldn't find the restaurant. After half an hour of cruising through the congestion of the near north side, she was relieved when he finally decided to stop at a restaurant on Michigan Avenue. Though he didn't say a word of blame, her chagrin grew.

They didn't have a reservation, but of course David persuaded the hostess to give them a table. Melody could understand how the woman was charmed and intimidated by his aristocratic handsomeness; that was how she herself felt. She didn't know the inner David, only his facade—but what a dazzling facade. When he put his hand on her arm to lead her to the table her knees felt like jelly. If only she weren't afraid to open her mouth...

The silence between them was broken only by the tinkling of other people's silverware. Darn. David was watching her, not seeming the least disconcerted by the silence that was driving her insane. "Uh, this is excellent wine, David."

"Not bad." He smiled, then regarded her openly, as if he expected something from her. What? She covered her uncertainty by sipping from her glass. Yes, the wine was excellent. It should be, at these prices.

Rats. David was still looking at her. She avoided his eyes by glancing around. All the other people in the restaurant were chatting easily, their words merging into a pleasant background hum of sociability that contrasted sharply with how she felt.

"Tell me about your career," she managed to say at last.

He chuckled. "That could take all night. Not because my career is so wonderful but because it's my favorite topic."

Good. "Oh, I'm sure you're a wonderful conductor. I mean, you'd have to be, to conduct orchestras all over the world."

"Thanks. Actually, my career is right on schedule."

His voice was rich with a quiet satisfaction that Melody envied. Conducting a symphony, directing a hundred dedicated professionals, must require a large dose of self-confidence. At what point, though, did justifiable pride become unbearable egotism? Melody didn't know, but David was on the humble side of that point and she admired him for that. "On schedule?"

"Yes. I wanted to have my own orchestra by the time I was thirty-two, and I'll take over the Pops two weeks before my birthday. I wanted to have at least one European tour before I settled down and come January I will. Give me five years with the Pops and then another five with an even better orchestra to solidify my reputation and get some records out, and I should be in enough demand to go into full-time guest conducting by the time I'm forty-two."

"Wow." Melody tried to hide this gauche remark by lifting her crystal goblet for a sip of wine. She noticed that David held the stem of his goblet between his fingers while cradling the cup part from underneath; she decided to hold hers the same way. "I mean, it sounds like you have everything planned."

"True. Now I just have to make sure my musicianship continues to grow in sync with my schedule. That's why I'm in Chicago. I had to mark time anyway, till Carlo Vontti—he's the current conductor of the New England Pops and a friend of mine—steps down. I heard that the Rockefeller Chapel conductor was taking a sabbatical to write a spy novel, so I decided to come here, make a few contacts in Chicago and hone my choral directing at the same time."

She sipped again at her wine. She could never plan out her life the way he seemed to have done. Life just happened—to her, at least.

Well, that wasn't quite true. Since her divorce she'd begun to nudge the future in the general direction she wanted, and that seemed like a big accomplishment. Next to David, though, it was nothing. "It seems to me," she said thoughtfully, "that one of the hardest things about planning your life would be knowing what you want. I have no idea what I want to do in ten years, and even if I did, something new would come along to change my mind."

Oops, she thought. That sounded suspiciously like an opinion. She'd have to watch how much she drank.

"I see your point," David replied. "I know quite a few people who don't seem to know what they want out of life. So they drift along, just doing a job. I realize how lucky I am that I know what I want and am willing to pay for it."

"Pay for it?"

"'Take what you want, says God. Then pay for it.' That's an old Spanish proverb I stumbled across while I was in college, and it seemed as if it was written just for me. One of the prices of reaching the pinnacle of a profession like conducting is a certain rigidity. I can't allow myself to be sidetracked, not even by things other people take for granted, like a home and normal working hours and fun and new interests—and a family.''

"You're dedicated, in other words."

He shrugged. "I guess you could put it that way. I want a lot—I want to be the best conductor alive—so I have to pay a big price.''

Melody's pulse began to gallop. What must it be like, she wondered, to have a goal worthy of such dedication? Compare that to the hardware store. "I'd be scared," she mused. "What if you choose the wrong thing?"

"Then," he said so softly she almost missed the words, "you pay an even higher price." He leaned back and stared at her with a lazy smile. "I wonder what you'd cost me."

Her mouth opened, then closed. She looked down at her lap, wishing there were some way for her to control the flush that was threatening to spread across her neck. She didn't know what to say. Of course, she could pretend to misunderstand and protest coyly that her body wasn't for sale. Or she could voice the pat answer that would have sufficed before now: "My price is love and a longterm commitment, with a powerful preference for a gold band."

But those profound, iridescent eyes held her speechless.

She was saved by the appearance of the waiter. The tantalizing aroma of veal parmigiana teased her back to the normal world. As they ate she tried to steer the conversation back to safer territory. Namely, him. "Do you want to become famous?"

"Definitely not. I abhor the thought of losing my privacy by being turned into a media celebrity. Can you imagine this face on the cover of *People* magazine?"

Melody rested her chin on her hand and studied him for a moment. "Yes."

"I can't. I don't care if the general public knows me, as long as my peers and audiences do. On the other hand, some amount of fame is inevitable, I suppose—another price I have to pay for my ambitions."

"Your life sounds very glamorous. Also very demanding."

"Anything worth doing is demanding, whether it's conducting or raising children. Anyway, don't be too overwhelmed with how hard I work, because this year should be a bit of a lark for me."

"In what way?"

He pierced her with a look of amused interest. "I have time for fun this year."

Melody's lips opened in anticipation; she couldn't quite help herself. "And what is your idea of fun?"

She couldn't believe she'd asked that.

David stared at her, then broke into a broad grin. "I can tell what you expect me to say. For once you're not the enigma you think you are. Actually, though, I'm going to conduct an amateur orchestra."

Her, an enigma? "Kind of a busman's holiday?"

"Exactly. It's a community group, the Hyde Park Orchestra. By the way, we could use another oboe. I'm told there's only one."

Melody laughed delightedly, her constraint punctured by the absurdity of *her* playing in a symphony, especially one conducted by someone like David. "I'm glad to be able to say I don't have any reeds. It gives me an excuse."

"Okay," he said easily. "Just thought I'd mention it."

Eventually the evening came to an end. Melody was partly relieved and partly sorry when they headed south on the Drive, with the dark, brooding presence of Lake Michigan on the left contrasting sharply with the glittery lights of high rises on the right. When David asked her to choose some music for the tape deck, she was surprised that nearly a third of his tapes were contemporary, rather than classical. Still, the familiar yet classic New World Symphony seemed a safe choice. From nowhere and everywhere low strings began a lonely tune. She could feel the deep vibrations of the basses as if she were sitting in the middle of the orchestra.

"I think I've fallen in love with your car, David."

"Well, you can't have it. This is a case of love my car, love me. A Porsche would be even better, but this beast will do till I become rich and famous."

Melody laughed, but the sound held a touch of sadness. It figured that this car, which was superbly fast and sleek and desirable—a new standard of excellence for her—was his second choice. "The bank is the actual owner, eh," she said sympathetically. Finally she'd come across something they had in common. Bank loans.

"No, it's all mine." He pressed on the accelerator and the car zipped effortlessly past a bus. "Besides my conducting, I have outside income from my share in the family business. The Halifaxes are manufacturers from way back."

Melody paused for a moment. "Oh."

"I've learned hardly anything about you, Melody. All we've done is talk about me. Tell me about yourself, mystery woman."

"There's nothing much to tell. I married too young, for the wrong reasons, then stayed married too long. I work in a store over on Fifty-third. Dreadfully ordinary stuff."

"Which store?"

"Uh, Klein's. David, which person has influenced you the most in your career?"

Did he look a bit annoyed with her? In the dim light from the dashboard, she wasn't sure. Annoyed or not, he took the bait and the subject was safely changed. "My older brother, Martin."

"Is he a musician, too? Somehow I'd expected you to name a person like Bernstein or your friend Carlo Vontti."

"No," David said with that dry chuckle of his. "Martin knows nothing about music." He was silent for a while, then turned to her decisively. When he continued talking his voice grew quiet and confidential. She was sure that if the light were better his eyes would have opened to his soul again. "Martin gave me the courage to break out of the family mold. Or maybe I should say the family straitjacket. The Halifaxes, you see, have a tradition. Namely, making money."

"Sounds like a great tradition."

"Oh, money is all right. It bought me this car and the education and opportunity to pursue my career. The problem is what money does to people when they feel they aren't making enough."

"David, are you saying your family is greedy?"

"Not really. Not the way you mean, at least. Actually, it's all my great-grandfather's fault. He was a penniless cobbler who built the family fortune around a shoe factory in Concord." He paused, then continued in a still softer voice. "Martin helped me realize that old John haunts the Halifax men. He was just too damned successful. My grandfather, my father, my uncles, all were driven to prove they were worthy descendants of the steely-eyed ghost whose picture hangs over the fireplace. But how could mere mortals match a myth? The ghost started from nothing, from poverty, and they were already rich, thanks to him. Even if they doubled the fortune, they still owed it to *him*, because without *him* there wouldn't have been a fortune to double. So they all tried to live up to an impossible ideal, measuring their worth by the bottom line of the profit ledger. But they were doomed to failure before they even started.

"As a youngster," David continued, his words coming harder, "I wondered at the haunted sense of failure I saw in my father's face at precisely those times when he'd scored a big success. Why, I wondered, should a rich, powerful man feel like a failure? Martin was smarter than me. He understood and he explained. Martin made it possible for me to escape while there was still time." His voice died away into a thoughtful silence.

Melody didn't know whether to be flattered or embarrassed by such a soul-baring confession from a near stranger. The quiet, unbroken except for the melancholy loneliness of an English horn solo on the tape, stretched thin. She timidly broke into his thoughts. "I'm glad you felt you could talk to me about your family."

David drew himself back to reality with a laugh. "It's all a ploy, you realize. I take you into my confidence so you'll open up to me and feel you can trust me."

"No," she said with a shake of her head. "I don't believe you're the calculating type."

He arched his eyebrows in a way that could have meant anything—denial, agreement, surprise. When he said nothing she continued. "Tell me about Martin. What's he doing now?"

"Ah, there's a sad story. He helped me escape the family ghost, but he himself couldn't escape. He thought that by leaving the family business he'd get away from old John, but he got mired in the mediocrity of middle management in a New York PR firm. Dad had to rescue him with a position with Halifax Enterprises. Charity, Martin thinks. He goes through the motions, feeling like a failure in his own eyes as well as the ghost's. His bottom line's red, all right."

"I'm sorry."

"Sorry, for a poor little rich boy?" David pressed on the accelerator, and Melody was pushed against the seat by the sudden surge of speed. He swung past another vehicle, then slowed once more.

"Anyway, only my little sister has succeeded with Halifax Enterprises. Jennifer's a vice president now, and she's done quite well by getting us into making snowshoe bind-

ings and aerospace vinyls and heaven knows what else. Her
bottom line looks a healthy black. Who knows? Maybe
she'll beat old John's ghost. She's a woman, after all. She's
already accomplished more, in a business sense at least, than
any of the other Halifax women. Do you think Jennifer will
consider herself a success?''

"Yes," Melody answered immediately.

"That's the most definite you've been about anything all
evening. Well, I hope you're right. I also hope she doesn't
establish a new set of impossible standards for the women
in the family.''

After that there didn't seem to be much to say. Maybe it
was the darkness, which shielded her from his eyes, but this
silence didn't feel strained or uncomfortable. Still, she felt
the pressure of words unsaid—not on his part but on hers.
All evening she'd hidden behind questions. David knew
mercifully little of her life, a life that seemed dull and banal
when contrasted with the brilliant strivings of his. Not only
was he dedicated and ambitious; he was sincere and open
and self-knowledgeable and handsome.

As the burgundy sports car turned off the Outer Drive,
Melody wondered what a woman like her could possibly
have to offer a man like David Halifax. Only one thing came
to mind.

Sex. A quick roll in the hay. A one-night stand. And if she
was outstanding in bed, she might even manage to hold his
interest for a few weeks.

She turned her head away from him. The idea of herself
as someone's sex kitten was absurd. It had never even occurred to her before tonight. To some of the men she had
dated, certainly, but not to her. No, even if she wanted to
play that role, she was constitutionally incapable. It took her
too long to feel comfortable with a man. By the time she'd
begun to lose her inhibitions, David would be long gone.

Nonetheless, her skin felt unusually alive when they pulled into the cool darkness of the garage. Dread or anticipation? Ordinarily it would be dread, because most men's idea of a first date with a divorced woman seemed to be dinner and bed. They credited her with sophistication and experience far beyond the reality, and this was the time the pawing would begin. David sat silently after he turned off the headlights. Goose bumps rose on her arms.

"Melody," he said at last, "thank you for an interesting evening. I don't remember when I've met someone so easy to talk to. I just want you to know I appreciate that."

Her laugh was too loud and too long. Men. Play dumb, keep them talking about themselves, and they'll think you're wonderful. Even an intelligent man like David was taken in. She felt unexpectedly disappointed, rather than relieved. "You're welcome."

As they walked through the black intimacy of the passage between his two-flat and her town house, a pounding pressure grew in her temples with every step closer to her front door. She had no idea whether she should—or would—invite him in. Or should she try to get away with a hasty goodbye at the door? How would she react if he put his arms around her and kissed her? And if he did more than that? Her temples pounded still more.

The rough material of his jacket brushed against her hand as he held the door open for her, and she jumped. Then somehow—she wasn't exactly sure how—they were inside, and the gentle thud of the door made her jump again. She swallowed in an effort to moisten her dry mouth. She wished she had another glass of wine, then abruptly wished she hadn't drunk as many as she had. It was an effort to turn to face him, even more of an effort to lift her eyes to his.

He watched her with amusement. Of course. She must be acting strangely. Not that he was laughing at her, exactly, but his eyes twinkled merrily. He just stared at her till her knees grew weak.

Why didn't he say something or do something? Even a pass would be more welcome than this soul-searching scrutiny. Come to think of it, why didn't *she* say something? She swallowed again.

But when at last he moved she was as startled as if a statue had come to life. He took her limp hand in his, shook it, thanked her again for the evening and left her—alone except for the nervous ticking of her cuckoo clock.

Chapter Three

Dark and lifeless. Empty.

Melody tore her gaze away from the balcony. She wandered down the short garden path, pulled up two carrots and then searched in the shadowy light from her kitchen window for the brown and shriveled leaves of an onion. As she squatted to yank out a cool, gritty bulb, a faint oniony smell reached her.

She looked up again, but the glass doors still showed only darkness. It had been five long days since her date with David. And with every day her mood had slumped steadily.

"Oh, this is ridiculous," she lectured herself aloud. "Dinner's late already. You don't have time to waste out here." But she remained sitting, rocking precariously on the balls of her feet.

Dinner was late because she'd stayed late at the store again. Finally the computer had agreed with her manual bookkeeping. But now it was dark and her stomach wouldn't allow her the patience for sitting around in the garden.

"He's not going to ask you out again. Face it, girl; you're from different worlds." A shiver spread from her spine to her arms. She hugged her elbows. The air must be turning cool.

The last time she'd worked out there in the garden, the life she'd made for herself had seemed safe and sane. The hardware store, her house and a few potatoes—this was the sum total of her life, and it had seemed enough. And now? Well, maybe tomorrow she'd buy as many daffodil and tulip bulbs as her budget allowed. She'd plant them, instead of potatoes.

Or maybe not. Flowers wouldn't be enough.

"Oh, snap out of it," she said to herself. "You're just envious because he's rich and talented."

But it wasn't just envy. What did she feel, anyway? It wasn't even how she felt about David; it was more how he made her feel about herself. She searched her mind for a label. No word came and she was too tired to think anymore. Even the effort required to balance was too great, and she sprawled backward from her squat to an awkward sitting position on the cool dirt. She quickly pulled her skirt around her raised knees, but another glance at the balcony assured her that her unladylike posture didn't matter. She could do whatever she wanted and no one would care, because no one could see past the walls of her fortress.

She'd had such marvelous success today, too—which perversely made her feel worse. When she'd finally gotten the computer to agree with her manual bookkeeping, it confirmed that September profits were up over the previous two years. Even better, they were up—marginally— over September of three years ago, before a national hardware chain had threatened Klein's existence by moving in two blocks away. The store was over the hump. It would survive.

Still, only she knew, and maybe that was her problem. Mr. Klein had long since made it clear that his unlisted home phone was off-limits except in a dire emergency. Melody doubted he'd consider her excitement an emergency. She even thought of calling her father, though she hadn't shared anything important with him since Mama died, seventeen years ago. No. They'd forgotten how to communicate.

All right, Klein's Hardware would survive, thanks to her. What now? Ten, twenty more years of marginal survival? She should be feeling great, but she felt lousy, and she might as well not be feeling anything at all, like Mr. Klein, because no one cared. Not really. Not her father nor her brother, nor Mr. Klein nor Lamarr. Nor David. The darkness of his window mocked her. She listlessly removed her hand from her knee, and the soft material of the skirt slid down to her lap. It didn't matter, because no one could see.

"If a tree falls in the forest," she whispered, "and there's no living thing there to hear it, does it make a sound?"

An answer to the old conundrum echoed through her bones. *No.*

She sat for what seemed ages. When she rose she wasn't sure if it was because of the cold seeping into her buttocks and hands or because of the sudden realization that she almost wished David were up there now, watching her, excited by her careless pose and the sight of her slender calves and exposed thighs.

Back in her kitchen, Melody splashed cold water on her face. Enough of this. During her marriage she had sometimes felt sorry for herself like this, and she didn't like it. Work was the best antidote. If David Halifax was part of the problem, well, she was bound to see him again. After all, he lived next door.

She should plan the data fields for the inventory data base rather than waste time wondering when David would return. If she decided on a format tonight, she'd go in early tomorrow to try it out on the computer. She had better choose her data fields carefully, too, because after she'd entered the inventory it would be too much bother for her to change them.

The computerized inventory wouldn't help immediately, but she hoped to spot sales trends more quickly after a few months. Not that she expected the computer to deliver a revelation about the type of merchandise Klein's sold. She already knew—she should know, since she'd talked Mr. Klein into it—that the store had mostly abandoned the "pots and pans" consumer-type hardware. They simply couldn't compete with Strong Hardware's mass purchasing power. Instead the store specialized in what she called nitty-gritty hardware: plumbing and electrical supplies, appliance parts, that sort of thing. Janitors and maintenance men frequented Klein's because if the part they needed wasn't in stock, Melody would get it quickly. It was a smaller market niche than Strong's, but dependable.

The carrots burned while she scribbled data base formats on paper towels.

It was a week till she saw David again.

She worked six full ten-hour days that week—an increasingly common occurrence. Her work week depended on Mr. Klein's ulcer. If it was acting up, he wanted her around and clung to her, even if he appeared well enough to be at the store.

Years ago she'd fussed and commiserated until he'd snappishly and repeatedly declared his health none of her business. Melody sometimes wondered if the ulcer wasn't just a convenient excuse to hide creeping old age and a loss of interest in his business.

She'd never learn the truth from him.

Friday afternoon Mr. Klein started complaining again. He didn't come out and ask her to work Saturday, her scheduled day off. He didn't have to; by now she was trained to volunteer. And anyway, she didn't have anything special to do Saturday except shop for groceries. She could leave an hour early to do that.

So Sunday was her only day for working in the garden. It was a cool fall day, and she worked more quickly than usual, to keep warm.

"Hello, Melody."

She jerked her head in surprise. David leaned against the balcony's iron railing. He'd been nowhere around the last time she'd looked.

"Hi, stranger." Her voice was even and unemotional. She'd had plenty of time now to get over the shock of her date with him, yet she wiped her hands on her jeans and brushed a strand of hair out of her eyes.

"What are you working on today?"

"Oh, I'm clearing the rest of the carrots out of this bed so I can dig in compost and plant winter rye."

"Really? I'm surprised you can grow anything in the winter here."

Was he putting her on? Or was he naive enough to think *anything* could grow during a Chicago winter? She decided to play it straight and hope she didn't make a fool of herself. "Winter rye is a cover crop. I plant the seeds in the fall and they sprout before winter. The ryegrass starts growing again in the spring. When I'm ready I turn the rye under so it'll rot."

He looked at her blankly, and she was relieved. Not only wasn't he kidding, but she'd found something she knew that he didn't. "When things rot, they improve the soil. Winter rye is like a fertilizer."

"Gardening sounds complicated. I thought you just shoved seeds in the ground and got out of the way. I never realized it was so cerebral."

Cerebral—that meant something to do with the brain. Was he saying she was brainy? He really was naive, then. He wouldn't say that if he knew about her senior year.

"Gardening also sounds like a lot of work," he said. "Want some help?"

"No, thanks." The polite response fell from her lips before she even had a chance to think of a graceful way of accepting. "Uh, I'm sure you're much too busy," she finished lamely.

"Nonsense. I was going to go jogging. If you promise to work me hard, I'll get my exercise in your garden instead."

"In that case I promise to let you do all the hard work. Girl Scout's honor."

"Sounds wonderful. I'll be down in a couple minutes, after I've changed."

Melody had time to put away a bag of carrots, wash quickly, brush her hair and bring lawn chairs onto the patio before he came through the back gate in sweatpants and a tank shirt with the number one on it. "David, you give me the shivers just to look at you."

"Understandable. Some of us affect women that way."

"I mean you make me feel cold even to look at you in that shirt. Brr!" As if to emphasize her point, goose bumps rose on her arms at the sight of his smoothly muscled arms and shoulders.

"Is that all? You really know how to make a guy feel good."

"You're here to exercise, not feel good. The two things are mutually exclusive." As she turned from him to get a shovel, she grinned to herself. She wasn't having trouble talking to him this time. Maybe this situation was more natural and personal than the date, or maybe she was simply so glad to see him. Who cared why, as long as she continued? "Here's a shovel. Put a two-inch layer of compost on the potato bed. Come on—hop to it. I expect to see you work up a sweat."

He did, and the next half hour's labor was interrupted only by light conversation. "I must admit," Melody said at the end of that time, "I admire your energy."

He grinned at her as he flung shovels of compost onto the garden. "I needed a break from studying scores. When I sit too long I begin to go quietly crazy. And if I continue sitting, my insanity grows louder."

"I can sit for hours." She sometimes thought the real reason she'd coerced Mr. Klein into buying the computer was the excuse it gave her to work sitting down.

"You're lucky. Back when I was in school I'd get in trouble for squirming all the time. I can't take inactivity, and that's a problem, because music is a pretty sedentary occupation."

"I'll bet you conduct very vigorously, then."

"My arms flail away like a windmill."

"You're lucky you enjoy exercising, though. I wish I did."

David thrust the shovel deep into the soft soil. "I don't know if I really enjoy it or if it's something I need to do. And after a week like this one I need a lot of exercise."

"Rough week?" She hoped so; if he'd simply been too busy to phone her...

"Rough trip to Boston and Toronto. Too many scores to study, too many rehearsals to attend, too many university meetings to squirm through. I'm supposed to take over the Hyde Park Orchestra next week, and it's the straw that's breaking my back. Aside from the Unfinished Symphony, I've never conducted the music they're working on."

"So much for having time to enjoy yourself this year."

David leaned on the handle of the shovel and gave her a frank yet innocent look. "Oh, I still intend to."

"Yes. Well, I feel for you. I know what it's like to work too hard."

He snapped his fingers. "Speaking of the Hyde Park Orchestra reminds me of something. I have a present for you up in my apartment. I'll be right back."

As he dashed out the back gate and through the alley to the two-flat, Melody couldn't keep herself from grinning. She conquered the urge to do cartwheels, but the grin she couldn't squelch. Not only did David seem glad to see her, but he had something for her. He hadn't forgotten about her. Amazing.

Her foolish smile was still in place when he returned. She couldn't help it.

Almost apologetically, he held out three plastic tubes about the size of a pencil sawn in thirds. "I talked to the principal oboist in the Chicago Philharmonic, but he doesn't make reeds for sale. He referred me to a lawyer who's a frustrated oboist. The guy sells reeds of different hardnesses, so I got you one of each. Here's his card if you need more."

Melody took out and examined each of the delicately carved pieces of cane tied to a metal tube. Three presents: a gift of music; an offering of potential, hers to develop as far as she would; and an invitation to enter his world of music. "Thank you, David. It's very thoughtful of you to remember." Well, it seemed she was committed to an attempted musical comeback. She looked into the warm beauty of David's face. That was fine with her. Just fine.

"I don't mean to pressure you," he said. "I got you the reeds because you said you'd like to play, not because I need an oboist in the orchestra."

All of a sudden Melody couldn't wait to try out these precious reeds. At that moment anything seemed possible.

"I'll be pretty terrible till I get my lip back, but you know, I'd enjoy trying out for the Hyde Park Orchestra."

Though his expression didn't change he sounded relieved. "I'd like that, too."

She was pleased but a little puzzled. Why would a man like David seem apprehensive about a gift of music? If it were her, of course, she'd be apprehensive because some people might be intimidated by classical music or great competence—another price of dedication. But would that bother David? Whatever the reason, this hint of shyness touched her, and she suppressed an urge to hug and comfort him.

David smiled and was back to his usual self-assurance. "I can't guarantee you a seat in the orchestra till I've heard you play of course. Why don't you come to a couple of rehearsals and we'll decide after that."

"Sure."

"The rehearsals are Wednesday nights. Do you want to wait a while or come next Wednesday?"

"Next Wednesday."

"It's from seven to nine-thirty, at Mandel Hall, on campus. Do you know where that is?"

"That's the auditorium. I know where it is."

"Great, you can show me. Can you be ready by six-thirty?"

Melody pursed her lips. "I get off work at five-thirty. It'll be a rush, but I think I can make it." If Mr. Klein's ulcer would cooperate she'd let him close up so she could leave early. No, let him close up in any case. It was his store, not hers.

"Fine. Well, your gardening is about done. I'm afraid I have to get back to work now."

"Oh." The bed was neatly raked and seeded, and there didn't seem to be any other reason for him to stay. She kept her eyes away from the lawn chairs on the patio. "Thanks again for your help."

"Think nothing of it. Just don't expect me to do all your digging from now on."

"Rats. That's precisely what I had in mind."

"I'd better get out of here while I still have the energy to move. See you Wednesday."

"Bye."

When he was gone she ran into the house, dusted off her oboe case and played till her lips ached—for all of ten minutes.

During Melody's Monday lunch break she hurried over to the small open-air shopping center at Fifty-fifth Street. She could have stopped there on her way home from work, but she was taking no chances on everything being closed by the time she got out of the hardware store.

Of the shops in the mall she knew the record store the best—aside from the grocery store, of course. She pushed open the door of Hyde Park Records and waved to the precisely dressed, willowy woman behind the counter. "Hi, Lou."

The older woman peered at her over the top of her glasses. "Hello, Melody. What brings you here in such a rush?"

"Schubert."

"Still into the classics," Lou commented as Melody headed for the back of the store. "Interested in the Unfinished Symphony, I bet."

"Yes, I am." She was tempted to blurt out that she needed to study the record because she was going to be playing the oboe part in an orchestra, but that would have been presumptuous. After the horrid sounds she'd wrung from David's fine reeds she'd last five minutes of the rehearsal before he threw her out. Ten minutes, tops.

The record might help, though. She wouldn't have much time to become familiar with it, because she was planning to do a lot of practicing tonight and tomorrow night, but she needed every bit of help she could get.

"It's a beautiful piece of music," Lou commented. "I have three versions here."

Melody would rather have found the records without help. She couldn't really blame Lou, but the store owner always tried to push the expensive recordings, while Melody's budget dictated the cheapest. If *she* ran this store she wouldn't pressure the customers. For appearances, since she knew at a glance which copy she'd buy, Melody asked, "Which is the best version?"

"They're all quite good. This digital recording has by far the best sound quality, though, so I'd suggest it."

"I see. What about this one with Fritz Reiner and the Chicago Philharmonic?"

"It's a re-release of a recording from the fifties or sixties. The sound is dated, but musically it's fine."

Sound quality meant little when she considered her cheap console stereo, which was left over from her marriage. "I'll take it. Hometown loyalty and all that."

As the woman rang up the record on the register, she asked if Melody had heard that Lou wanted to move to Arizona now that her husband had retired. "I'm hoping to find a buyer for this place soon so we won't have to endure another Chicago winter. Know anyone who wants to buy a record store?"

"Sure." Melody counted the bills in her wallet. "I'll give you twenty-three dollars for it."

Lou laughed. "We aren't quite that desperate yet. Here's your record."

Melody left, feeling a sense of loss. As much as she loved the large record stores downtown, she couldn't get to them very often. If this store closed she'd miss it.

* * *

"I don't want to go into the orchestra as a friend of the conductor, David. No special favors, please."

"All right, then," he responded as he pulled the car out of his garage. "If your playing lowers the quality of the orchestra, you're out on your ear."

"Couldn't I just walk out with dignity?"

"Nope. On your ear, Melody. But," he added, "I'll take into account that you've been playing for just three days after a layoff of . . . how many years?"

"Eleven."

He looked at her in surprise. That got his attention. Melody was rather pleased to have gotten a rise out of him, even if the only way was by shocking him with the depths of her incompetence. "How good is the Hyde Park Orchestra, David?"

"I have no idea. They've rehearsed three times this season with the former conductor, though, so at least the music isn't new to them."

Melody leaned her head against the cool leather of the bucket seat, suddenly struck by a sense of unreality. "This is weird. Here I am, going to play in an orchestra led by a world-class conductor. I can't quite believe it's happening." She studied his profile speculatively. "David, you say you want to be the best conductor in the world. Why are you, of all people, conducting a small-time community group?"

"To recapture my youth," he answered promptly. "Being an amateur is a matter of attitude, really. I remember the enthusiasm we had back when I was in college, and I feel sad when I compare that with most of the professionals I work with. Oh, the professionals are more polished and businesslike but they've lost something."

"What?"

"Well, if you get a bunch of symphony musicians together, they'll discuss baseball or politics or sex or even the weather—anything but music. They like music, of course, but it's become a job to all but those rare few. When I played violin in my university symphony, music was all we talked about. There was excitement, eagerness. One time when we toured on a chartered bus, the brass players began singing their parts. The strings joined in, then the woodwinds and percussion. I tell you, Melody, you've never heard music till you've heard Beethoven's Fifth sung by a busload of enthusiastic amateurs."

"It does sound different." She didn't bother telling him that he wasn't talking about the kind of amateur she was—unskilled, *amateurish*. He'd find out soon enough.

They had reached the university, and David began the hunt for a parking space. "How did you hear about this conducting job?" she asked.

"A stroke of incredible luck. Andrew Blankhurst, the business manager of the Chicago Philharmonic, has a son who plays cello in this group. The former conductor is a violinist with the Philharmonic who's facing a stiff challenge for her seat. She wanted out so she could practice eight hours every day or something like that. Andy was asked to find a replacement. When he learned I'd moved to Hyde Park, he didn't quite ask me to take over, but he let out some broad hints."

David chuckled. "The beautiful thing is that not only do I get to conduct the H.P.O., but Andy is delighted his son gets to work with a top conductor. Besides, it's a feather in his cap that he could get a 'name' for the job. Andy's tripping over his tongue with gratitude, and he's a fairly powerful man."

"I see," Melody said. "You're a politician, too."

"Hey, don't insult me." But his look of pain quickly melted into a smile. "You should see me charming the money out of rich widows at a fund raiser...."

The University of Chicago had character, especially the older buildings such as the auditorium where the H.P.O. rehearsed. With massive limestone blocks and carved griffins and gargoyles, the building was straight out of a gothic fantasy. Melody well knew the mood the gray campus could evoke on a gray winter morning when even the snow seemed, and was, gray; a mood not so much of gloom as of anticipation, as if something great and important was about to happen, a new day about to dawn.

She tried to hold that reassuring thought as she walked into Mandel Hall, several steps behind David. He seemed to understand her desire to be accepted on her own merits, and went off on his own business.

A few people were setting up chairs on the stage in a large semicircle. Never having played in a symphony, Melody had no idea where to sit until a red-haired clarinetist took pity on her and directed her to the center of the group, next to where two flutists were warming up by playing scales. She tried to catch their eyes so she could say hello. The closer of the flutists, a thin-faced man with a receding hairline and swatches of gray at his temples, responded by waving his whole torso, flute and all, without ever missing a beat.

More players were trickling in every minute. Melody assembled her instrument, curled her lips around her reed and blew a few tentative squawks. The trumpet players were warming up, too, so there was little danger of her timid notes being heard, but she wished the other oboist would show up for moral support.

Someone whose name Melody immediately forgot introduced himself as he dropped a wad of sheet music on her stand. The notes seemed to blur together into a jumble of unreadability, just as the sounds of the musicians warming up blurred into a mellow yet foreign ritual. "What in heaven's name am I doing here?" she muttered through clenched teeth.

At quarter after seven people were still straggling in and socializing loudly. One group of brass players was discussing the perennial disappointing finish of the White Sox. The two viola players in front of her were wondering how long the Indian-summer weather would last. David stood at the podium, seemingly undismayed that they weren't the dedicated amateurs he'd expected. He rapped his white baton against his music stand, and slowly the musicians settled down.

"For those of you who haven't heard," he announced in his fine baritone, "my name is David Halifax, and I'll be your conductor till the March concert. And now, since I know we're all here to make music rather than talk—" which was, Melody thought, a fairly broad hint that he wasn't as unaffected by the chaos as he appeared "—would you please take out the Beethoven overture?"

A last-minute surge of insecurity made Melody miss her first entrance, and she was surrounded by a burst of sound she wasn't part of. After that everything blurred together again. Except for the occasional half note or whole note, the music whizzed by before she'd figured out exactly where to play. And when she did manage a few notes, she was dazed to learn that orchestral oboe music wasn't like band music. Instead of being just one of many instruments playing the same notes, Beethoven expected the oboe to play by itself or with only a few other instruments. There wasn't much place to hide.

Melody was panting by the time the overture was finished. Taking a much-needed breath, she stretched her stiff, exhausted lips. She wasn't ready for this.

Neither, it seemed, was David. He was trying to keep his expression neutral, but she thought his eyes looked dazed.

"Let's take it again from letter A," he said calmly, "and look at your music this time. Be careful. Listen to one another."

Melody had seventeen bars' rest at A, so she tried to relax. She studied David as he started and stopped the cellos several times. She hoped to notice something about his conducting that she could comment on intelligently, but all she noticed was that his hair swung and his arms waved flamboyantly. His arms were long—like an ape's, she thought with a surge of rebellious mischief—but then, a lot of his height was from the waist up. A very graceful ape, she amended with a grin that reminded her how tired her lips were.

Somehow she didn't think ape's arms would impress him. So much for sounding intelligent.

Finally David let the orchestra continue past the first few bars of letter A. The balding flutist leaned across the empty chair between them to whisper, "What's the count?"

"Ten bars," she whispered back, then sat straighter. He had played a beautiful solo near the beginning of the overture, full of sixteenth-note runs, yet she'd been able to help him. There was hope for her yet. At least she could count to ten.

Just then a noise at the back of the orchestra distracted Melody. Not just her, either. The music ground to a halt as musicians turned to see who was talking so loudly.

A late arrival, a pudgy young woman with orange-red hair, was talking to a double bass player whose embarrassed glance darted from David to the orchestra and back again. The redhead looked familiar, and hair like that would be hard to forget. More important, the woman carried a small black case: an oboe.

With an obvious effort, David kept his voice neutral. "If you're quite ready, we're taking the Beethoven from letter C, miss."

"Fielding," the redhead said as if he'd asked. "Noelle Fielding. Glad to meet you, Mr. Halifax. I'm your oboist."

David drummed his baton against the palm of his hand. "If you'll get your instrument out, Miss Fielding, we'll begin at letter C."

Waving to various people, Noelle pushed through the brass section to the empty seat between Melody and the flute player. Either Noelle was oblivious to the disruption she'd caused or she enjoyed grand entrances. As she put her oboe together, David began conducting.

"Hi, I'm Noelle," she said to Melody a trifle too loudly.

The cellos played a succession of horribly out-of-tune notes just as the flutist leaned toward Melody again. "What's the count?" Melody held up five fingers.

This could be a long night, for David as well as herself, she thought.

Halfway through the rehearsal David called a fifteen-minute break. Melody needed it. Her lips felt like soggy toast and even her shoulders were tight from tension. She wondered if David felt this weary. Probably not. He was used to conducting.

Well, look on the bright side, she told herself. After Noelle arrived she'd had someone to play with and occasionally hide behind. As first-chair player, Noelle had all the solos. But Melody was still appalled at how exposed her own, second oboe parts were.

As she stretched she realized she'd waited too long to catch David. Not surprisingly, he was surrounded by a crowd of players eager to meet the new conductor. She would have to wait till after the rehearsal.

Noelle was studying her. "You look familiar. What did you say your name was?"

"Melody Ross."

The girl's freckled face scrunched into a look of concentration. After a moment she laughed. "Well, either I'll remember where I've seen you or I won't." She pointed to the balding flutist. "Melody, have you met Greg Defosse, our eccentric first flutist? He seems a bit weird at first, but he's just shy."

Greg smiled—the first emotion he'd displayed. "Compared to you, Noelle, everyone is shy. Hello, Melody."

A laugh bubbled out of the redhead. "Do you want to know the best thing about Greg?" She lowered her voice mysteriously. "He's a professor of mathematics."

A professor. At first Melody was impressed—she'd never actually met a professor face-to-face—but then she recalled his frequent questions. "Mathematics? But—" She stopped before she put her foot in her mouth.

Noelle, however, was undeterred. "That was my first reaction, too. He can't count a three-bar rest, yet he's a math professor."

"But you're good, Greg," Melody said quickly. "A lot better than me." And then, realizing that wasn't much of a compliment—almost a put-down, instead—she smiled awkwardly.

"Thanks," he answered. "I'm well aware that counting rests is my fatal musical flaw even as the noble Achilles had one weak spot."

Noelle put one hand on Greg's shoulder and pointed at him with the other hand. "See?" she said to Melody. "I told you he was a professor."

Greg winked at Noelle as he dried the inside of his flute, then stood up. "And now, ladies, if you'll excuse me. Mother Nature calls."

Noelle was studying her again. "I've got it," she said suddenly. "You used to be Melody Haakman."

"Yes, that was my maiden name, but I'm afraid—"

"We went to Morgan Park High together. You don't remember me, I see, but then there wasn't much reason for you to. You were a senior and a big shot and gorgeous and popular, and I was just a bubble-brained, flat-as-Chicago freshman.''

"That doesn't sound like me." Melody laughed. "It must have been a different Melody Haakman."

"Oh, sure. It's such a common name. I'm amazed I didn't recognize you earlier. I played in junior band, and then I replaced you in senior band partway through the year."

Melody felt her face stiffen at this mention of her senior year. "I remember you now. You were the one who'd been taking private lessons since you were eight."

"Nine. That's ancient history, I'm afraid. Till I joined the H.P.O. last spring, I hadn't played in years."

"Same here. I just started again three days ago, and I am *not* ready to play in an orchestra."

Noelle raised her eyebrows. "Three days? I'd better start practicing, or you're going to beat me out for first chair in no time. You always did have more on the ball than I did."

Melody was surprised by this last remark. From the little she remembered of the younger woman, Melody knew she'd been typical of their high school. Noelle's father was a doctor or dentist or some such, and her family had things Melody could only dream of. Gorgeous clothes. Music lessons. Someone to do the cooking and housekeeping. Noelle had been precisely the sort who had intimidated her throughout high school.

"Strange, meeting you again," Noelle continued. "You were one of my idols. A role model, you know? I got serious about music, for a little while at least, after hearing you play. I remember we were at the same party once. I guess it was the band Christmas party. The boys flocked around you. You and your boyfriend, the one you married, danced so well everyone stopped to watch. You were wonderful. When I got home I plopped in front of the mirror and tried to make my face light up when I laughed, like yours."

Melody began to laugh, then stopped self-consciously. "That's not quite how I remember the party. Jason was the dancer, not me. I just tried to avoid tripping him. And the boys didn't flock around me. Believe me, I would have remembered that. Oh, maybe one or two, but that was because I joked around a lot. They liked my jokes, not me."

Noelle's freckled face looked skeptical. "I think you're wrong."

"I don't. Why would they have been interested in me? I wasn't that pretty, and all I ever had were hand-me-down party dresses."

Noelle shook her head and laughed—and her face did indeed light up. "I don't quite believe this. I'd have to revise all my freshman memories. I even used to imagine what it would be like to be you. I never imagined you felt insecure, though, and I'd hate to think I was so far off the mark."

Now it was Melody's turn to laugh. "I used to play a game like that. I pretended I knew all about a person, and sometimes I wondered if anyone else pretended the same about me."

"Well, I did. I realize I don't really know you, but I feel like we're old friends. You live here in Hyde Park?"

"Just west of the IC tracks."

"I live in a high rise just *east* of the tracks. Hey, we're neighbors. Gosh, this makes me feel fourteen again, God forbid. Are you still married to Jason?"

Melody found her eyes wandering over to the crowd surrounding David. "Not for six years. You're divorced, too?"

"Is it that obvious?"

"Well, usually only a divorced person makes the assumption a marriage might be over." David caught her eye and smiled.

"Say," said Noelle, "do you know our new conductor?"

"He's my next-door neighbor. He coerced me into coming." Which wasn't strictly true, but why she felt compelled to explain, Melody wasn't sure. "Actually, the only reason I was willing to make a fool of myself like this is because David's here."

"Are you and he an item? Oops. None of my business. Just tell me to shut up if I get too personal." But when Melody said nothing right away, Noelle leaned forward in her eagerness to hear an answer.

"I don't mind you asking," Melody admitted. This rehearsal had driven home the truth, which she'd realized before but not faced. "David and I went out once, but nothing is going to come of it. We're too different."

Just then David clapped his hands to call the musicians back for the second half of the rehearsal. "Here I go," Noelle groaned as she pushed her reed into the top of her oboe, "once again displaying for everyone's amusement my musical idiocy. Hey, I'll have to tell David we went to high school together. Maybe he'll have mercy on me."

Melody's face froze, though her mind raced. Mindlessly she managed to go through the motions of putting her instrument together. During a passage where she rested while Noelle nervously misplayed a solo, Melody's gaze flicked from the redhead up to David.

Don't do that, Noelle, she pleaded silently. Please don't tell David about high school!

Chapter Four

Finally the rehearsal ended.

A lone oak leaf zigzagged to the sidewalk, a ghostly flutter in the unreal amber light of the streetlamp. It crackled under Melody's foot and was gone. That was the only sound. The smoldering remains of a leaf bonfire added a wistful tang to the air. The only witness to their silent progress down the empty sidewalk was a gray lion crouching atop a campus archway.

After half a block, David chuckled thinly as he shook his head. "That was quite a rehearsal. I feel silly about what I said to you about how wonderful and dedicated amateurs were, compared to professionals." He laughed again, and this time the sound had its usual depth and resonance. "This evening opened my eyes to reality. I guess I have a tendency to idealize things like my memories of college. I'll have to watch that, or I'll get myself into more situations like this."

Melody remained stubbornly silent, but she doubted he would even notice. He was so concerned about his music, his all-important music....

"Well," he continued, "they're not totally hopeless. Some of them seem to want to strive for excellence, even if they aren't sure how. But I'll have to go back to the very basics."

Out of the corner of her eye she saw him studying her, but she kept her eyes from his.

"Something wrong, Melody? If you're worried about your playing—well, my only comment is that almost no one could lower the quality of that bunch of dilettantes."

Dilettantes. That's all she could ever be to him, a person to be dismissed with a scornful word. What about Noelle, who tried but lacked David's talent? What about Melody herself? Her lips thinned and her darting glance raked at his rugged, self-assured face, seemingly so full of concern yet so contemptuous of people like her. Superior. That was David. The differences between them were deeper than money or talent; there were fundamental differences in how people were treated....

He was talking again, his baritone soft with superficial honey. "If you'd like to talk about something, I'd like to listen."

"Sure you would." Melody was pleased at the calmness in her voice. "Look, David. I like you. But—"

"But?"

A sudden heaviness thrust the breath from her in a long sigh. "But I don't belong in your orchestra."

He put his hand on her elbow. The contact fizzed along her nerves, making her want to push him away. "We can discuss that better in a few weeks, though I already told you what I thought. When your lips get strong enough to stay curled over your teeth, your tone should be decent and you'll stop sounding like a wild duck. But if you insist, I can arrange a formal audition to determine whether you stay."

"That's not what I meant! I'm not what you think I am."

For a breathless moment he riveted her with a gaze, his features motionless as they studied her. Finally he shook his head. "I don't know what you are, aside from attractive, shy, intriguing and easy to talk to. You haven't let me find out."

"That's precisely it."

He dropped his hand from her elbow. "*What's* precisely it?"

"You don't understand me." He still looked confused, and she groped for words to explain what felt so obvious. "I know almost nothing about classical music. I got interested in it just last year. The only piece you played tonight that I know was the Schubert, and I only know it because I bought the record Monday. David, I'm an ignoramus."

"Well, if you insist, you're an ignoramus. So what?"

Melody pivoted to confront him, burning to wipe the amused crinkle from the edges of his eyes. "So, I'm trying to tell you why I'm not right for you, if you'd just listen."

"This is getting tiresome. As a matter of fact I've already decided you are right for me, and I'm not wrong. Not about this."

"Of course not. Your kind of person never makes mistakes."

She stomped off toward the car, forcing David to hasten along to continue the conversation. But he would catch her in a step or two; she spoke hurriedly, without looking back, before he did so. "But this time you're wrong. I don't sound like a wild duck, and we're from different worlds. Your world is filled with money and tradition and class. You've had all the advantages in life."

"I see." His voice came from beside her, not behind as she'd expected. "And now I suppose you're going to tell me you're from the wrong side of the tracks, and that's why you want to dump me before we even have an affair.''

"An affair? That's a laugh. And I'm not from the wrong side of the tracks, the bottom of the hill. But then I don't suppose you know about such things. Where I went to high school there was actually a hill, maybe the only one in Chicago, and the rich people lived on the slopes so they could look down on the likes of me. The whole time I went to school I had my nose rubbed in the fact that those kids were from a separate world. No matter how I tried to lose my accent, it was still another world.''

"What accent?''

The mildness of his tone sent the blood roaring through her temples. She flung her next words at him as if they were poison-tipped darts. "A hillbilly accent.''

David's eyes grew rounder, and she could see her words bounce off him—but not without denting his placid calm, at least. Her voice filled with more bitterness than she knew she felt about her childhood. "We moved here from West Virginia right after my mother died. From the time I was twelve I cooked, laundered, mended and picked up dirty underwear. My papa was a coal miner turned steel mill worker struggling to find work and raise two kids by himself, not a millionaire industrialist—'' her voice grew thick with sarcasm "—whose biggest problem was an asinine family ghost.''

Too far, too far! Melody sucked in her breath as if to suck the words back. She stared at David, appalled.

He was silent, his face unreadable. He had trusted her with intimate, unhappy details of his family life and she'd returned the trust with an insult. Well, this just proved she didn't deserve him.

He held the car door open for her. She slipped into the lush, alien interior. A station wagon had parked close to them, so David had to maneuver back and forth several times to get onto the street. He swore softly at the wagon's absent driver, then sped down the street.

"David, this isn't the way home. Where are you going?"

"I don't know. For a ride. We're not finished talking."

She wished she could interpret the thick emotion in his voice. Anger, probably. She stared sightlessly out the side window. After a few blocks of heavy silence the scenery registered on her preoccupied mind. On both sides of them abandoned apartment buildings loomed, dark and windowless. A sudden fear stabbed at her. He wouldn't let her out here to walk home, would he? "Let's not drive this direction, David. Head back toward Hyde Park. Please."

"Why?"

"You're going into a bad neighborhood. Someone might kill us for your hubcaps."

"From what you were saying, I thought this was your world we were entering."

"David, I didn't come from the slums. Look, maybe I exaggerated a bit."

He laughed, but she felt it was more a laugh of relief than one of mockery. The sports car screeched into a dramatic and highly illegal U-turn.

"Better?" he asked.

She looked around for flashing lights and sirens. "I guess so."

He headed toward the lake, and soon the car purred through the always-heavy traffic of the Outer Drive. Still he said nothing, though every instant she expected him to break into angry denunciations. When his iron self-control failed, it must explode like Mount Saint Helens....

Well, tough. His anger would make it easier for her to say what she had to say, the words necessary to drive away the most remarkable and exciting man she'd ever met. She didn't waste energy analyzing her lemminglike determination to fling herself off the precipice of her past. Better now than later. That was reason enough.

Why didn't he say something, though? If his strategy was to wear her down with silence, it was working. When her arms and legs grew sore from bracing for his expected outburst, Melody realized she'd have to say something or explode from sheer tension.

"Look," she said defiantly, "I'm sorry for making fun of what you told me about your family. I shouldn't have done that."

"Apology accepted," he answered cheerfully as if he wasn't even aware of the steam bath of silence she'd sweated in for the last fifteen minutes.

And the anger she'd so carefully nurtured hissed from her as from a leaking balloon. Even her voice sounded deflated. "I guess I'd better tell you everything. Even the main thing I don't want you to know about."

"Sounds absolutely fascinating. What is it?"

"Something I'm ashamed of, from back in my high school days. Something that makes me feel we're not right for each other." She fiddled with the air-conditioning louvres in front of her on the dashboard. "You have a university degree, right?"

"Yes. And a master's and a Ph.D."

Worse and worse. She laid a hand on his arm. "David." She paused. Squeezing his arm, she stared straight ahead. "I never even finished high school. I dropped out with three months left, to get married."

Only a tiny pause admitted to his surprise. "Pregnant?"

"No," she said wearily. Some things were beyond explaining. Like the look in Papa's eyes when she announced, not requested, marriage. A sad look that promised punishment, a fierce look that made her advance the date of her escape so as to destroy the diploma he wanted for her....

After a brief silence David inverted his arm to hold her hand. "I hate to say it, but after such a big buildup your revelation is something of a disappointment. It doesn't rank with Watergate or a juicy sex scandal."

Though she didn't move, all her muscles tightened. "Don't make fun of me, David. Oh, on second thought, go ahead. I deserve it."

"I wasn't making fun of you. Just trying to put things in perspective. And for what it's worth I would never have guessed about your education. You seem not only intelligent but well educated."

"I don't need condescension." She removed her hand from his.

"Melody, Melody." He reached out for her. His hand whispered through her hair. "Don't put yourself down. I meant what I said about your intelligence. You say you don't know much about classical music, but you know more than most. Some people look at me as if I'm from outer space when I tell them I'm a conductor. You're not uneducated. Self-educated, perhaps, but not uneducated."

A single laugh escaped her lips. It sounded more like a snort, though, and the noise struck her as funny. Her shoulders shook with silent chuckles.

"Please don't cry, Melody."

"I'm not crying, silly. I'm laughing. At myself."

His hand slipped under her hair and stroked her nape. Her dark thoughts of incompatibility melted under his touch, and though she still knew they were from two different worlds, it somehow didn't matter. For the moment, at least.

"Thank you," he said.

"For what? For laughing at myself? You're welcome."

"No. For finally letting me get to know something about you. You've been so busy trying to impress me that you've hidden the real you."

"Don't get cocky, young man. You still don't know everything about me. For example, I exaggerated. I have my high school diploma now. I got it through night school five years ago."

"See. I knew you were educated. And now I know not only that you finished high school but that I shouldn't believe a word you say, because you exaggerate."

Melody leaned her neck into his caresses like a cat rubbing against the hand that pets it. "You're very nice."

"Exaggerating again, eh?"

They shared the intimacy of a laugh. She opened the console and bypassed the classical recordings in her search for a tape. Soon Kenny Rogers's mellow voice whispered softly through the car.

"David, have you been to the Museum of Science and Industry yet?"

"No. Should I?"

"Well, we live just a couple blocks away, and it would be a shame for you to miss it. I'd be glad to show you around."

Eyes on the road, he shook his head. The swaying of the hair at his neck mesmerized her. "I thought we'd gotten past your trying to impress me. It may surprise you, but even though I'm well educated, moderately wealthy and incredibly intelligent, touring museums isn't my favorite pastime."

"This museum's different. It's a fun place. You can go into a German U-boat and down a coal mine. There's a great dollhouse that used to belong to a movie star. Really, I think you'd enjoy it. Of course, if you'd rather not go..."

He grinned at her. "If you recommend this place so highly, who am I to refuse your offer? I'm afraid I have to leave tomorrow for a couple of guest-conducting gigs, and I won't be back till Tuesday. Next week sometime?"

"Sure." She carefully hid her disappointment at the delay. He was a man, after all, and might be tempted to capitalize on her eagerness. "Let's see. Next week I have Friday and Sunday off. How does that fit your schedule?"

"Friday afternoon would be fine. A lot of my work is in the evenings."

"Great."

After a while David's quiet voice floated through the gentle music. "Beginnings are magical times, don't you think?"

"I don't believe in magic. It's all done with mirrors."

"Not hocus-pocus magic. People think magic has to be the out-of-the-ordinary. They ignore the special times, the special moments, that are the real magic. The magic of a flower. The magic of a newborn infant. The magic of getting to know someone new." His vibrant baritone stirred waves of delicious tingling in the skin of her neck and arms.

"David, I'm not magic. Far from it."

"Maybe." His hand slipped lightly from her neck to her cheek, leaving an invisible trail of fire on her sensitive flesh.

"David, I—"

"Shh. Don't say anything. This is a beginning. It's magical. Just sit and feel the magic."

After a while she let herself relax into the softness of the leather seat. There was a special feeling to this moment, but it wasn't coming from any magic. It came from his touch. His hand rested on her shoulder; his musician's fingers strumming a delicate tune on the harp of her neck. The silence that stretched between them grew tense with anticipation.

His fingertips began to trace intricate circles on her throat, and she was certain he must feel the quickening of her pulse. With an effort she kept herself calm during this unaccustomed intimacy and let her mind drift on the lazy pulse of desire that spread through her body from his gentle, undemanding caress. The butterfly softness of his fingertips asked not surrender to his virility but acceptance of the mutual attraction between them, an acceptance she was powerless to refuse even if she'd wanted to. Her uncertainties and inhibitions evaporated in the half-floating euphoria of his gentleness. Only when his hand moved down her chest did silent alarms ring inside her, and her muscles automatically stiffened. As if in response to her unvoiced fears, his fingers stopped their downward voyage at the material of her modest U-neck. They ran lightly along the skin and the cloth, back and forth, his fingertips tracing the boundary between decorum and desire. Only on the final pass did one finger slip inside to tease an extra inch of her flaming skin, leaving the beginning swell of her bosom yearning for more.

"Where's a good place to turn around?"

His voice jarred her brain after the prolonged silence. His hand left her heaving chest and returned to the steering wheel.

For a frozen moment the scene outside the car felt like a jumbled, alien landscape, but she readjusted quickly to the sensations of the ordinary world. Ahead she saw the McCormick Place convention center and the overpass that crossed the Drive. "Get off at the next exit. Turn left, and on the other side of the overpass you can turn south onto the Drive again."

He turned, letting the incline slow the car. He stopped at the side of the overpass.

"David, what are you doing?"

Instead of answering, he leaned toward her. The way he looked at her made her breath stop and her lips part. His first kiss was on her cheek, his second at the corner of her mouth. Only then did his lips begin a soft, probing discovery of hers that swept her away from the car and the traffic and into a moment of startling ecstasy. It was as if she'd never been kissed, as if kisses had never been invented prior to that breathtaking instant, as if she and David had discovered a level of communication never before experienced, and together they explored the joy of discovery and creation and sensuality.

A blasting horn and screeching tires ended the kiss prematurely. Melody struggled to keep her voice from betraying the depth of her amazement and confusion. She'd expected his kiss to be pleasant, but not so shattering as to completely redefine what a kiss could be. "I don't think we're supposed to park here, David."

His swirling eyes glowed, burrowing into her as if seeing her for the first time. "I haven't parked in a car since I was a teenager. Too cramped for someone my size." He had trouble keeping his voice level, too.

The corner of her mouth crawled upward of its own volition. "You know what I mean," she said breathlessly.

He smiled before turning his attention once more to the car. The burgundy flash screeched away from the curb and into traffic. The Burgundy Flash. She liked that name.

And him, too.

Was it possible for a week to be *light*? Melody wasn't sure that word could make sense to anyone else, yet it was how she felt about the seven days till the next rehearsal. The time rested lightly on her hands. The usual spate of minor store emergencies seemed light and frivolous. Al Jevaert even commented that she had a new light in her eyes.

It was definitely a *light* week, in every sense of the word.

Melody knew what infatuation was, knew she was infatuated with David; she knew she'd been infatuated with Jason, too, knew it was an unsuitable basis for a long-term relationship. Yet somehow all that self-knowledge didn't matter. She gloried in her feelings while at the same time she vowed not to let herself get hurt.

A return to earth was inevitable, and the next rehearsal did it. David worked the orchestra mercilessly. The easygoing, patient man she knew vanished when he picked up a baton. His eyes took on an inner glow, and his jaw clamped into a position of barely controlled eagerness. Oh, he wasn't a tyrant. He didn't badger or blame anyone, but he had obviously set a goal for this rehearsal—everyone would start *together* on the beat—and he tolerated no exceptions. The cellos and, unfortunately, the oboes, seemed destined for the roles of dunces, constantly making ragged entrances for which David stopped everyone to "take it one more time." Melody wondered what Andrew Blankhurst's son in the beleaguered cello section would tell his father about the new conductor after tonight. For herself, she found the rehearsal tiring and nerve-racking. But the group sounded marginally better at the end of it.

Noelle glared in David's direction as she put her oboe in its case. Despite the redhead's chattery frivolity, Melody had noticed that when an important oboe solo came up, Noelle's eyes darkened into the same smoldering intensity as David's, though the musical results were only tentative. Noelle snapped her instrument case shut and then, when David wasn't looking, stuck out her tongue at him. The impish smile she turned on Melody took the sting out of the gesture.

Melody found it impossible to dislike the younger woman, and she smiled back. They chatted for a moment and even made vague plans to get together sometime soon. Melody's membership in the orchestra had something going for it—a possible friendship with Noelle, an undeniable sense of musical accomplishment mixed in with the frustration and, of course, David. Despite her exhaustion, she hoped she'd be able to make the grade.

The final musician finished her question, leaving David alone at the front of the stage. He found her with his eyes— eyes that lost their intensity as she watched, eyes that grew warm and easygoing. Eyes a woman could get lost in.

* * *

Melody frowned at the mirror. Nope. The white-collared, violet dress was too fancy for a place like the Museum of Science and Industry. She glared at her closet. She wore jeans at the store often enough to last her a lifetime. Of the remainder of her meager wardrobe, the maroon corduroy pants and blazer were probably the best, such as they were. She sometimes wished she had more interest in clothes, and this was one of those occasions. She rummaged through a drawer, hoping something would catch her eye.

Maybe the whiteness of her loose-knit cardigan could lend some life to the blazer. She surveyed the effect of the outfit with a sigh. It wasn't quite right, not for a date with David. She got out the shoe box that held her jewelry and sifted through it till she found her silver pin in the shape of sixteenth notes. When the pin raised the sweater's plunge to a more demure depth, she shrugged at her reflection. Well, it would have to do.

She went downstairs to the living room, where the Unfinished Symphony played softly. Should she leave it on? She didn't want David to think she was trying to impress him by playing one of the orchestra pieces, even though that wasn't why she was playing it. Or was it? David Halifax certainly made life complicated.

Her cuckoo clock and the doorbell sounded in unison. One-thirty on the dot. Time to go.

As they entered the garage, David paused before unlocking the car door for her. "I thought you looked familiar today. You and the ZX are twins."

Leaning against the cool metal, she could see the similarity of the colors of her cords and the Burgundy Flash. "This goes to show how much I identify with your car, David. That's the real reason I agreed to go out with you again, you know. Your car."

"If you're trying to insult me, you've failed. Cars like this are supposed to attract beautiful women. That's why men buy them. The ability to attract women is even part of the fifty-thousand-mile warranty."

"Oh? And is the warranty invalid if a woman buys one?"

"I'm not sure about that. I'd have to check the papers, but I think the actual wording is 'members of the opposite sex.'"

"That's better. I'm glad the Japanese auto makers aren't sexist."

"Say, would you like to drive? The few blocks to the museum would give you the feel of the beast."

Melody darted her eyes to her lap, then covered her action by searching through her purse for something—anything. "No, thank you."

"Come on, Melody. I know you lust after my car. Indulge yourself in an orgy of vehicular sensation."

"I don't think so."

"You don't have to be afraid of it. It's just a car, faster than most you've driven."

She glared at him. Why wouldn't he drop the subject?

He sat back in his seat and studied her, his forehead wrinkled in puzzlement. "You do know how to drive, don't you?"

She hesitated fractionally before nodding. "Yes."

"But you don't have a license." He stated this as a fact, not a question.

Even more annoyed because he could read her so well, she nodded wearily.

"It's hard to imagine you as a wild driver, so I don't suppose the police took your license away because you were a menace to the driving public."

"If you must know, I've never had a license. There, are you happy?"

"I'm impressed. Not driving makes you as rare as a violinist who doesn't dream of being Isaac Stern."

Melody sighed. "It's not impressive; it's embarrassing."

"I don't understand. If it bothers you, why don't you have a license?"

"When I was a teenager my father didn't think women needed to drive. My brother gave me a few lessons, but nothing came of it. Then I got married, and my husband tried to teach me."

"Couldn't you learn?"

"For a long time I thought I couldn't. I thought I was too nervous. I flunked the driver's test twice, the only test I ever flunked in my life. Jason was insulted that I'd failed despite his help, and he loudly proclaimed me unfit to drive."

"You don't seem the nervous type."

"I was back then, believe me. After our divorce I began to realize it was Jason who made me feel nervous and inadequate, and about more than just driving. I don't mean he tried to make me flunk the test, and he wasn't a bully. It's just that . . . well, if I learned to drive he'd lose just a bit of control over me, and for him that meant he'd lose a bit of his masculinity. So he didn't try too hard to teach me."

David's face showed just the right amount of sympathy, enough to show her words mattered, yet it was tempered by the understanding that she'd weathered the marriage and come out whole. "He sounds like an immature jerk."

"Definitely immature. A jerk? I'm not so sure about that anymore. Every time I run into him since the divorce, he gets nicer and more mature. We just weren't good for each other. Our relationship helped to keep him immature." She shrugged and buckled her seat belt. "Anyway, I'm used to not driving. Between buses and commuter trains I can get anywhere I want easily enough."

"Still, don't you miss the freedom of a car?"

"Can't miss what I've never had. A year or so ago a friend of mine, Judy, gave me a few lessons, so I feel I can drive a bit. She got married and moved to Calumet City before I took the driving test, though."

"There are driving schools."

"I have to be realistic. I can't afford a car. My priority at this point in my life is paying off the town house."

"I didn't realize you owned it. Very impressive."

Her face grew warm, but her voice was light and mocking. "I'll bet. You're very easily impressed, then. With all your money, you're impressed with a two-bedroom town house that's exactly like twelve other adjoining town houses."

"But it's solidly built, not cheap-o cardboard. Besides, if your mortgage is anything like my rent, that place is an accomplishment."

"Well..." She looked out the side window so he wouldn't see the smile on her face. "Actually, I arranged for higher payments and a shorter term mortgage than usual so I'll own it sooner, and I'm a year ahead in my payments."

"You'd better not tell that to all your dates, or they'll be wanting to marry you for your money."

"I figure my secret is safe with you."

"Oh, I don't know. I personally am no millionaire, despite what you may think. Besides, how do you think rich people get that way if not by marrying other rich people?"

The music of her laughter echoed through the car. "By being born to rich parents, of course."

"Ouch. That's hitting awfully close to home. So what about it? Shall I teach you to drive?"

Her laughter died. She studied his profile before answering, "Are you serious?"

"Sure. We can get you a learner's permit when we're finished at the museum."

Melody reached out to stroke the cool metal of the steering wheel. He was generous, overwhelmingly generous, to offer his brand-new car to a novice driver. She must be careful with this man, for his sake and hers. Very careful. "Okay."

He must have read her mind, because he did exactly what she hoped. He leaned over and kissed her.

"You told me you didn't park," she whispered into his cheek when his lips left hers.

"I lied." But as if she had reminded him, he squirmed in his seat. He turned the key and the motor roared to life. "We could have walked to the museum and back by now. I guess we should be going."

"I guess so."

David was a jogger and she wasn't. Maybe that was why he walked her legs off at the museum. He hurried from exhibit to exhibit, calling her to look at something new before she had finished with the last thing of interest. He was disappointed he couldn't touch the antique airplanes that were hung by cables from the vaulted ceiling but was mollified by strolling the turn-of-the-century thoroughfare, complete with horseless carriage parked at the side of the brick street. When they went into the old-time street's Nickelodeon theater to watch the Charlie Chaplin short, David put his arm around her. The warmth of his touch sent swarms of pleasure through her shoulder.

Melody was disappointed the coal mine was closed for repairs. She pointed to the tall, inelegant metal framework rising twenty-five feet from the center court. "When it's open you take this elevator down to a replica of a coal mine. It's always been one of my favorite exhibits. I guess because when we were kids Papa took us down there and told about his days as a miner. They even have the type of machine he operated, a coal drill."

David switched to a dreadful Southern drawl. "That must have been when you all lived in the South."

She poked him in the ribs with stiff fingers. "Stuff it, Yankee. I suffered enough put-downs like that in school to last me a lifetime. If I never hear the word *hillbilly* again it'll be too soon."

Eventually, however, they trudged down the massive stairs of the Greek-style museum into the brisk lakeshore breeze. Traffic noise from the Outer Drive roared over the sound of the wind. Melody pulled her blazer closed.

"Chilly?" David put his arm around her and held her tight. "It looks like rush hour is starting. We'd better hurry to get you a learner's permit."

She leaned into the warmth of his body. "Are you certain you want me practicing in the Burgundy Flash?"

"The *what*?"

"The Burgundy Flash. It's a name I made up for your car. Nissan 300ZX is such a mouthful."

David's face grew stern. "Melody, you can drive my car. You can listen to music in my car. You can even make out in my car, as long as it's with me. But don't call it names. Understand?"

His face was scowling, but his eyes flashed and the skin at the corners was wrinkled. "Amazing," she commented.

"Don't change the subject. Uh, what's amazing?"

"Your eyes. They're smiling. I've never seen anyone smile with just his eyes. I'd like to play poker with you sometime. I'll bet I could win your family fortune away from you. You're not Irish, are you?"

"Wasp, through and through. Why do you ask?"

In reply she hummed the beginning of the song "When Irish Eyes Are Smiling." He joined her with a rhythmic counterpoint that skillfully changed it from a ballad into an upbeat rock tune.

Getting a learner's permit took a while. Afterward Melody insisted on treating David to dinner at a place that she told him had great food. He was surprised, then, when she directed him to a fast-food restaurant. As they entered the spotless white interior of the building, she turned to him. "How many hamburgers do you want?"

He looked at her, one eyebrow raised. "One will be plenty, thanks."

"You're certain? It's my treat, after all."

"I might eat two, but I'll start with one."

"French fries or onion rings?"

"Such difficult decisions. Oh, what the heck, make it French fries. You only live once."

"A hamburger and French fries, coming up. Find us a table while I get the food."

A few minutes later she put a paper plate in front of him. It held French fries and a tiny square hamburger. He lifted the plate and looked underneath. "You ate my hamburger," he accused, though his eyes twinkled and danced.

"I did not!"

"Well, you ate most of it." He opened the bun. "And most of the meat, too. Though how you managed to scrape the meat away to leave a patty a quarter of an inch thick, I'll never know."

"Don't exaggerate. The meat's thicker than that. And remember, I asked you if you thought one hamburger would be enough."

"That was before I knew the burgers were for midgets. Is this some kind of cruel joke you're inflicting on a hungry man?"

"You poor thing. I got four hamburgers for myself." She allowed a smile to escape to her lips. "And by the way, this proves my poker face is better than yours."

His first bite demolished half his hamburger. She watched his face anxiously. "Very good," he said. "Unique, even. I trust I may have seconds, though."

A relieved smile played at the corners of her mouth. "I'll have to think about that. I'm glad you like them, though. I didn't know if conductors ate hamburgers."

He froze with a French fry halfway to his mouth. "That's the most ridiculous thing I've ever heard. What do you think we eat, cellos?"

"Nope. Pâté de foie gras, three times a day."

He stood. "I'm going for seconds."

She rose quickly and nearly pushed him back into the booth. "I'll get them. Please, David. This is my treat, remember. How many do you want?"

As he stared intently into her eyes, she felt a warm flush rising to her cheeks. She was about to apologize for bringing him here and joking around too much when his gaze left hers and traveled slowly and deliberately down her body. The buzzing warmth of her blush spread through her veins and settled with an almost painful heat into her breasts. His gaze lingered there possessively, and she knew that even through her sweater he could see her nipples swell in response to his bold, sensuous survey.

"Ten," he said.

She exhaled, and only then did she realize she'd stopped breathing. "Ten?"

"Definitely. Ten."

Oh, yes, she recalled their first, embarrassing meeting at his balcony. She glanced down at her body before she could stop herself. "Uh, right. Ten hamburgers it is." As she walked to the counter she pulled the blazer closed over the telltale evidence of her arousal.

He ate all ten hamburgers.

When at last their evening out was over, he held her gently in the vestibule of her town house. She wasn't used to leaning her head back to kiss, and at first she felt awkward.

David didn't say anything, merely held her softly, as if she might break, while he brushed feathery kisses on her forehead, cheeks and nose. A slight shiver rippled down her back, but she wasn't cold. The raw desire evident in his earlier visual ravishment of her body was there, but it was restrained and cushioned by an incredibly gentle, reassuring tenderness. She'd never been held and kissed and *treasured* in quite this way. His touch was cozy, pleasant, demanding nothing and offering much. His velvety lips caressed hers as he tasted sparingly, delicately of the nectar of her mouth. She felt she could stand like this, safe and comforted in the envelope of his arms, forever.

His gentleness and restraint defused her nervousness. Without conscious thought she found herself reciprocating, trailing her open lips over his chin and neck. Hormones too long denied sent an unfamiliar surge of breath-quickening desire coursing through her body wherever he touched her. She opened her mouth wider to taste his exquisitely masculine chin, and with a muffled groan he responded by cupping her bottom in his hands in an embrace that was no longer delicate, no longer safe, no longer comforting. When he lifted her chin his kiss was different, passionate and demanding, and he forced her suddenly cautious lips open with urgent probings of his tongue. After the kiss he drew back to look her in the face. What did he expect of her now?

Silly question.

No longer feeling secure and protected, Melody glanced down the hall at the darkness that hid the kitchen. "Uh, do you want to come in for a coffee? Or something?"

She sucked in her breath. She could kick herself for those last two words. The liquid fire of her passion was rapidly congealing into a gelatinous mass of reluctance and doubt, even sooner than usual.

His dreamy eyes smiled at her. "Sure. I'd like that." As she led the way down the hall, he pressed his hands possessively on the small of her back as if to proclaim the *something* he'd like.

To get to the kitchen they had to pass the living room and then the stairs leading to the bedrooms. When they were even with the stairs she involuntarily slowed to glance upward. She swallowed and pressed her lips together, praying he hadn't taken her hesitation as invitation. But then, if it was a choice between going to bed with him tonight—even though the fire inside would build, then die—and losing him, well... Why did relationships have to be so confusing?

Her answers to his compliments about the house were mechanical. In silence she put fresh grounds into the filter and poured water through the coffee maker. He was standing close behind her when she turned from the counter.

He gazed at her with those wonderful eyes. At first she enjoyed watching their kaleidoscope of color, but soon she looked away in confusion. Hesitantly she put her hand on his waist and tried to pull him into an embrace, but his body had become stiff and immovable. She couldn't stand the hard inscrutability of his face. Why didn't he speak? Surely he'd want the *something*, even if not the coffee. She reminded herself that he was one of the nicest men she'd met and she'd had a wonderful time and she didn't want to take chances on losing him and this was the real world where sometimes a woman had to...

"No thanks."

She looked quickly into his face, expecting to find she knew not what, but his eyes were expressionless blanks. Her heart sank.

His face and voice were carefully controlled and emotionless. "I'd like to play poker with you. I think I could win the town house from you."

He brushed her cheek wistfully. She felt a brief return of the warmth his touch could generate.

He was already in the hall when he spoke again. "I think I'd better go."

She stood rooted to the same spot, eyes closed, listening to the sound of his footsteps, the slam of the door and then the endless, angry bubbling of the coffee maker.

Chapter Five

Quarter to seven the next morning. Melody had waited as long as she could force herself to wait; she reached out of the covers and got David's number from directory assistance. Too early to make amends for last night—she'd only worsen matters if she phoned now. So she lay sleeplessly till seven-thirty before she called him.

David sounded groggy but not noticeably unhappy to hear from her. Relieved, she decided to avoid any mention of last night. He readily agreed to meet at noon for a picnic lunch, followed by her first driving lesson.

On the far side of the museum was a wind-rippled lagoon that was bordered by manicured parkland. As they crackled through brown and yellow leaves along the shore, Melody watched the easy sway of the picnic bag and the thermos in David's hands. If his hands were empty, would they twine around hers? She hoped so.

The park acreage was private except for a few strolling couples and a football game at the far end. Remembering the ten hamburgers, she'd made extra tuna fish sandwiches. By the time he reclined on her blanket all of them were gone.

And still they hadn't discussed his abrupt departure from her town house last night. She wanted to ask him how he felt, but the words hid in her throat. Finally, an apology in her eyes, she leaned down to kiss him. Then, with her cheek resting on his chest, she savored the pounding of his heart. A languid comfort began to seep from his flesh to hers. They stayed like that for a long time, speaking in whispers that added to, rather than interrupted, the mood of the moment.

David held up a tiny white flower he'd picked from the grass. "Do you know what this is? It's pretty."

"It's just clover. Very common."

"It's still pretty. Look how petals crowd around the center in perfect symmetry."

She leaned over for a better look. "You're right. I guess I never looked closely."

He rested his head on the blanket and fixed her with a penetrating stare. "Beauty is all around, if you look for it." His eyes were suddenly stripped of civilization and restraint, forming instead such clear windows into his inner fires and passions that she stared in fascination.

Warmth and confusion rippled through her. How could he affect her this way with a mere look? And did he really mean he thought she was beautiful? She held her eyes level with his for as long as she could before turning away. She nonchalantly studied a nearby tree trunk, but she still felt the invisible pressure of his eyes. "There's a grasshopper over there," she said lamely.

She was totally aware of how he brushed against her thigh as he turned to look at the tree, and then of how he gently braced his hand on her hip as he rose. He went over and knelt at the trunk. Something was cupped in his hand when he returned. His eyes, she noted with relief, were back to normal.

"It's not really a grasshopper," he said as he studied his palm. "It seems to be hollow." He puzzled over it some more, then finally shook his head. "I wonder what it is."

"It's just a grasshopper's skeleton."

"You've seen them before?"

"Sure. Haven't you?" He looked at her blankly. For someone with a Ph.D., he had gaps in his knowledge. She couldn't remember when she'd learned about such things, but it seemed she'd known all her life. "Bugs have shells, you know, rather than bones. To grow larger they have to molt. The only unusual thing about this skeleton is that we found it so late in the year. Somewhere around here is a bigger grasshopper."

He looked at her, then back at his hand. "That's fascinating."

"Maybe. But I pity the poor grasshopper." The shell struck her as unaccountably sad and pathetic. Silly of her, she thought. "It must hurt terribly. And then it takes a while for the new shell to harden. Imagine how vulnerable the poor thing is."

A vivid image of the bewildered creature's comfortable old shell splitting asunder sent a shiver down her back. Sensing her mood, David respectfully placed the grasshopper back on its tree.

In an atmosphere of growing trust and wonder, conversation flourished as they explored the differences as well as the surprisingly numerous similarities in their outlooks. They talked of matters small and large: their childhoods, books, her marriage, Chicago's expressways, the weather, people they admired.

"You never say very much about your family," David said. "Tell me about your brother."

"Not much to tell. Clay's three years older than me, has four kids and drives a truck for a beer company. He's very involved with his work, if you get my meaning. The cargo, not the truck. I guess I don't talk about him because he's irrelevant to my life."

"What about your dad?"

She was lying on her back, snug in the crook of his arm, but now she turned her face to study the quickly drifting clouds. "He's irrelevant, too."

"That's too bad. Family shouldn't be irrelevant."

"Maybe yours shouldn't be. Besides, I have my work."

"I see." He tightened his grip on her shoulder. "So you're one of these career women who live for their jobs."

She laughed, and the brittle sound was quickly carried away by the lake breeze. "My job. You know, I sometimes get the feeling that if I mess up once, just once, all my years of hard work will be forgotten." An image of Lamarr's snarling, scarred face drifted through her mind. Would he be the mistake that did her in? She shook her head to drive away the image. "I used to think the job could be a stepping-stone to something better, but it appears more and more like a dead end." The corners of her mouth curled in to a self-deprecatory smile. "Besides, who wants to work in a hardware store?"

He didn't smile back. "It's honest work."

"Listen to the rich, dedicated musician, talking about honest work. Would you like to work in a hardware store?"

"No, but that's beside the point. The fact remains that there's nothing wrong with it. Besides, it's your career."

"Oh, sure, my career." She was silent for a moment as she focused on an indefinable something beyond the rippling waters and the gray museum. "I wanted to be a career woman, and for a while I thought there was a small chance

"Watch it—the car's moving!"

She straightened up and stomped on the brake. "Sorry again."

"Lesson two will be stopping the car without putting your passenger through the windshield." He clicked his seat belt on. "Now, try again."

She did, and the tires didn't screech at all. After a few more tries she was maneuvering with wary ease and stopping on command. The tires protested on only one of her turns.

"You're pretty good at this, Melody. I'd say you basically knew how to drive already. What you needed most was a chance to get used to the power of the Flash."

"You noticed." She felt her face grow warm as she recalled her first try. "I must admit, your car is nothing like Judy's tame Chevy."

"We'll have to see how you do in traffic, of course, but you must be nearly good enough to have your license. I'm amazed you never got one."

"Thanks. But I still have to pass that silly test." He moved his hand to cover hers, and she responded with a firm squeeze. "The test covers parallel parking, too, and I haven't done much of that." She gave him a leering wink just in case he missed the awkwardly intentional double meaning of her next words. "I'll need *parking* lessons, as well."

A smile tugged briefly at his lips, then his face grew serious. He touched her shoulder and neck as he spoke in a quiet voice. "When you tell me you're ready, Melody." He moved his fingers to her cheek, and her skin tingled under his touch. "When you're ready."

She was the one who finally broke off the stare. Surprised to find she was breathing heavily, she busied herself by setting the emergency brake. "What I need is time, David. Time to develop confidence. Time to adjust. Time to get to know and become comfortable with new relationships. I can't jump into things. It takes time for me." Her voice took on a note of wonder. "But you already understand that without being told, don't you?" She gazed at him with a sly grin. "I'm talking about learning to drive of course."

His eyes were soft, and the corners of his mouth twitched. "Of course."

Slowly she and David leaned toward each other. In fascination she watched the gradual approach of his lips, whose pliant flesh was slightly parted and already puckering outward in readiness. He got closer, and his lips blurred as her eyes went pleasantly out of focus. Closer still, and she lost herself in the breathtaking sensations of his lips on hers, his arms around her, his mouth drinking deeply of the honey of her tongue. Just as their kiss ended she darted her tongue boldly into his mouth, and she felt a warm glow at his sudden intake of breath.

When the stampede of her heartbeat had eased, she asked quietly, "Why?"

So in tune were they that he understood. "Why? Oh, I guess because casual sex isn't worth the effort. Because you're not that kind of girl. Because I like you and I think I could learn to like you a lot more. Because I think no one ever took the time to wait for you before, and with half a chance you could be awe-inspiring. Because good things are worth waiting for."

She turned back toward the steering wheel, as happy as she'd ever been. If they were alone right now, instead of in a public parking lot... No, he was right. Good things were worth waiting for, and when she made love to him, it wouldn't be out of gratitude.

Strange. David told her he wouldn't rush her into bed, yet the very denial committed her to becoming his lover. And of course once she made a commitment, she kept it tenaciously. *When she was ready.* A light-headed, devil-may-care euphoria bubbled out of her in a laugh. "May I try the Burgundy Flash on the street?"

"Are you sure you haven't had enough for one day?"

"I'm sure." She grinned. "This is fantastic."

And it was only the beginning. The magical, mystical beginning.

Over the next weeks she grew to treasure David's patience and empathy more and more. Together they explored a Chicago that was new to Melody: the Chicago of elegant restaurants and social graces. Together they entered each rehearsal of the Hyde Park Orchestra, then later discussed the evening's work to give each other the benefit of their viewpoint. Together they talked and laughed and shared intimacies that went beyond sex: intimacies of the mind. Together they spent tired, quiet hours watching TV— or sometimes ignoring the TV, concentrating instead on the gradual, evolving exploration of each other's bodies.

Together they lived the best month of Melody's life.

"Thank you for shopping at Klein's."

No more customers at the till. Good. Melody looked at her watch impatiently. Rats. Where was Mr. Klein?

She had agreed, reluctantly, to work this morning, even though it was her day off. Since David had entered her life, she'd begun to jealously guard her time off, living for the rare hours they both had free. Still, she felt guilty about her sudden cutback in working hours, and Thursday Mr. Klein had played shamelessly on that guilt with complaints about invoices and ulcers. She pursed her lips as she thought about her boss. Here she was, still in the store despite his promise to relieve her immediately after lunch, and David would be picking her up soon for her driver's test.

She dashed to the side of the store and halfway down the narrow stairs to the basement. "Lamarr? Where are you?"

His head popped up from behind a pile of crated merchandise. He didn't stand straight, but hid in a half crouch. His gaze shifted from Melody to the floor behind the crates.

"Lamarr, go upstairs on the sales floor for a minute. Roy can't handle all the customers himself. It's time for me to leave and Mr. Klein's not back, so it looks like I'll have to pry him out of the lunchroom."

Lamarr studied the floor again, then looked at Melody as if waiting for her to leave. He was up to something, obviously. How, she wondered, had he avoided jail if this was how he reacted to getting caught? And caught he was; he must have a girl down there, right in the middle of working hours. How dared he? "Move it, Lamarr," she said harshly.

"All right, all right." Slowly he moved around the crates and into view. She let out her breath. At least he was dressed.

After he'd edged up the stairs past her, she investigated behind the boxes. She expected a naked girl, perhaps a marijuana cigarette or a porno magazine.

She certainly didn't expect a toilet. It wasn't the whole thing, just some old pipes and valves from a toilet tank, lying in a jumble with some tools from the store. What was the kid up to? She looked at her watch again. She didn't have time to fathom Lamarr's clandestine activities, and at least a toilet was legal.

She dashed over to the washroom, changed from jeans into beige slacks, freshened her face and combed her hair. Back upstairs, she sternly reminded Lamarr that the crates had to be unpacked by closing time, then headed to the back of the store to get Mr. Klein.

A handsome black man in a blue suit intercepted her before she got to the swinging doors. "Hello, Ms. Ross. I wonder if you could help me. I need a fifteen-amp Wokawski breaker. I'm putting in a dishwasher for my wife."

Melody chuckled and folded her arms. Despite her hurry, this sale was too good to pass up. "What's the matter, Ted? Doesn't your store carry all brands of circuit breakers?"

Ted Gleason, the manager of Strong Hardware, winked at her. "As a matter of fact, no. But we do have a great preseason sale on snow throwers."

"Uh-huh. Well, we have Wokawskis in stock—but even if we didn't, I could get you some by tomorrow morning. This way, please." With a flourish she waved him down an aisle. She dangled a brown plastic part in front of him before plunking it in his palm. "I can't tell you what a pleasure it is to be able to sell this to you."

"You don't have to, Ms. Ross. You're grinning like the Cheshire cat."

She eased the smirk from her face. Ted Gleason was a pleasant enough competitor. She suspected he wouldn't forget to relieve an employee who had to leave for a driver's test—especially when that employee had worked the morning of her day off as a favor to the boss.

As if reading her mind, Ted switched subjects abruptly. "You're making me look bad, Ms. Ross. My employer expected our store to wipe Klein's out of Hyde Park within three years. We're behind schedule, but I think we could still succeed—if you'd join us."

The last traces of Melody's smile vanished. His thin, neatly trimmed mustache didn't curl up as if he was joking. "What are you trying to say?"

"Simply that Strong Hardware could use a woman of your caliber. If you're tired of this dump, well, I think I could find a position for you down the street. A responsible position."

Rubbing her moist palms on her slacks, she searched for a reply. "Thanks, Ted. Your offer means a lot to me. But this place isn't a dump, and I don't think you'll wipe Klein's out of Hyde Park."

"Too bad. Keep the offer in mind, though. Oh, you can keep this, too." He tossed her the circuit breaker. "My house has Square D breakers, and we do carry those at Strong."

She watched him till he was out of the store. *He knew.* He knew that she, Melody Ross, had his chain beaten! She'd heard of raiding practices in big corporations, but she'd never dreamed she'd be a target. Buoyed by Ted's offer, she floated past her office toward the lunchroom.

When Mr. Klein had moved the stockroom to the basement, he hadn't intended the old room to become a gathering place for janitors and tradesmen. It just happened. The men appreciated a spot to eat their brown-bag lunches, though, and Mr. Klein didn't object, because it was good for business.

Melody didn't object either, but she rarely ate there. With its pipe-lined ceiling, bare brick walls and girlie calendar from a tool company, the place was a bastion of working-class male chauvinism. Oh, they'd be polite, almost gallant. They'd even watch their language, except for occasional slips, followed by sidelong glances to see if she'd heard. But they'd also expect her to wipe the table and pour their coffee.

Forget that. She ate in the office instead.

Right now the lunchroom was empty except for Mr. Klein and Al Jevaert. Al waved at her, his long face breaking into a mass of smiling wrinkles. "What's gotten into you, Mel? You're grinning like you just won the lottery."

She raised her eyebrows as she nodded to him. "Wouldn't you like to know?"

Mr. Klein looked at her sourly, as if he resented the interruption. What was so important that it kept her from leaving? she wondered. Mr. Klein never talked about anything important, only hardware. No, that wasn't fair. Maybe he saved the important things for Al. The big janitor was the closest thing to a friend the old man had.

"Mr. Klein, it's time for me to go," she reminded him. He said nothing, didn't even move a muscle. "David will be picking me up any moment."

"What!" Al slapped his thighs and glared at her in mock agitation. "Do I have competition?"

"Don't worry, Al. He won't replace you in my heart."

He looked at the wall clock with its bent minute hand. "Kind of early for a date, though, isn't it? Things must be pretty serious between you and this David."

"It's not actually a date. He's taking me for my driver's test. He buys me dinner only if I pass."

"Oh, you'll pass," Al assured her. "Your problems are only beginning, though. Next you have to find a parking place." He turned to Mr. Klein, who continued to sit on the bench, rigid, unmoving, his back hard against the brick wall. "Isn't that right, Herb?"

Mr. Klein stared at her till she felt uncomfortable. She had a horrible premonition of what he would say.

"My ulcer is bothering me, Mel."

Her smile vanished. Not again. Not today. How much of her life would this man demand? "Mr. Klein," she whispered in a tightly controlled voice, "I give up my days off with great regularity. I agreed to come in this morning—the morning only!—even though I already had plans for the day. It's too late for me to cancel my plans now, even if I was willing to. Which I'm not."

Though his face remained impassive she noted his body's telltale signs of emotion. His back grew stiff. He began to sway ever so slightly from the waist up. As he ran a bony hand through what was left of his hair, he looked stronger than he had in years. Anger was the one thing that could still animate him. Well, too bad if he was angry with her. If her job and her relationship with Mr. Klein didn't allow her to think of herself at least once, then—then... "If your ulcer's so bad, why don't you see a doctor?"

He just scowled at her, his mesmerizing, snakelike swaying growing stronger.

"I know why not," she said. "You'd rather just sit back here and let me do all the work."

He muttered something in German. Casting a brief look of suffering to the ceiling, he spread his hands in a placating gesture. "You leave doctors out of this, Mel. Maybe I've been working you hard, but it's for your own good."

"My own good," she whispered. Further harsh words—bottled up inside her from every unexpectedly long work day, every nonrecognition of work well done, every time her extra care and effort were taken for granted—words rolled and writhed inside her and threatened to burst forth. Her face red from the effort, she somehow stifled them. Not in front of Al. Mr. Klein was her employer, and more than that, he truly needed her. "Okay. I'm sorry I blew up. But I still have to go."

Al cleared his throat. "Mel, I'm not sure you..."

Both Melody and Mr. Klein glared at him. He looked from one bristling face to the other, shrugged and concentrated on a seemingly fascinating crack in the cement floor.

Mr. Klein painfully got to his feet, then quickly looked over at her. Oh, no. She wasn't going to be taken in by that look-at-poor-me act. Not again.

He saw her determination, and his face hardened. "What's the matter with this guy, Mel?"

"Who?"

"Donald, or whatever his name is."

"David. And nothing's wrong with him."

"Sure there is." His words were oiled with sarcasm. "Is he married? Are you positive? Maybe he's divorced because he beat his wife. Or maybe he's a born loser. There must be something wrong with him."

Al interrupted with a polite cough. "Excuse me. I'm heading back to work." He rose to leave, but Mr. Klein clung to his arm like a flea attaching itself to a mastiff.

"Al, this woman is a human magnet. Put her in a room full of men and she'll point out the one who's guaranteed to hurt her the most."

Melody stared around the room as if the walls had suddenly, inexplicably turned hostile. He was *trying* to hurt her. "Mr. Klein," she said with the last of her self-control, "stop."

"Did I ever tell you about her husband, Al? A real loser, that one. Got booted out of college after one year. Couldn't hold down a job, at least not till he found another woman who inspired him. Messed around right under Mel's nose. Used to drink, as I recall. That's the kind of man she goes for. Yeah, Mel sure can pick 'em."

A dam inside her burst. A palpable red wave of anger flooded her head with such an intolerable pressure that she thought her skull would split. Rage and tears almost blinded her, but she could still make out his frail face, twisted by an evil directed—impossibly, unfairly—at her.

"No!" She wasn't aware of sweeping a cup from the table to smash against the wall but it must have been her. "No, no, no! I don't have to take this from you!" She probably just imagined his ephemeral look of surprise and regret, but nonetheless her remaining angry words froze painfully in her throat. At the door she turned and shouted with a voice full of ice, "I won't be in tomorrow, either. You owe me a Saturday off." As she stormed past her office she shouted without looking back, "Maybe I won't be back at all!"

She ran blindly through the store, not bothering to pick up the box of copper pipe fittings that scattered to the floor with a sound like tiny cymbals crashing. Avoiding other pedestrians through instinct, she reached the no-parking zone near the corner where David was parked. The car reverberated when she slammed the door.

When he asked what the problem was, she nearly snapped his head off.

Melody had calmed by the time they went to his apartment after dinner. The apartment always bothered her, but never more than today; it was airy and spacious but sterile. His furniture was functional but not particularly high quality. Only the baby grand piano dominating the living room fit his usual standards of excellence. Worse, the place was barren of the small touches that made a home—memorabilia, pictures, clutter, books. This was a hotel room with a piano. The apartment rubbed her nose in how temporary he viewed his time in Chicago. Just four more months...

"Cheers," he said as he handed her a long-stemmed glass full of clear bubbly liquid.

"Cheers." The champagne tickled her nose as she drank.

He studied her over top of his wineglass. "A toast—to the newest and best driver in the city."

"And to the best driving instructor in the city." After one sip she moodily studied the broken fragments of the room reflected in her glass.

"You're awfully quiet for someone who just passed a driver's test *and* got the sincerest of all business compliments from the competition."

She smiled up at him ruefully. "I was just thinking about that grasshopper molt we found in the park that time. Do you remember?"

One eyebrow rising in surprise, he nodded.

She spun the glass lightly by its stem. "Imagine the pain that poor thing felt as its old shell broke." And, she thought, how vulnerable it was. She pursed her lips as she swept her gaze through the stark room. Vulnerable.

He waited, expecting her to continue, his jaw set in a line of concentration and concern. When she said no more he gently placed his arm around her shoulders. "Are you trying to tell me something, or are you just waxing philosophical?"

She swallowed a mouthful of champagne before speaking. "David, were you ever married?"

Surprised by the question, he removed his arm from her shoulder and leaned forward with his elbows on his knees. "No, of course not. I would have told you if I had been." As if deciding that her mood called for total openness, he continued quietly. "I came close once, but the lady in question seemed to feel I was already married to my career." He cocked his shimmering eyes at her. "That was years ago. Many's the time I've been glad she didn't accept. She wasn't the right one. The closest I'd come across, but still not the right one."

Somehow she didn't find his words reassuring. "I see."

"Since we're both being so serious, it's my turn to ask a question. Why didn't you have any children?"

"Oh, that. Well, remember when I told you I dropped out of high school to get married and you automatically asked if I'd been pregnant? Well, I knew that was how everyone would react, even though I was a virgin when I got married, and I was determined not to give people any excuse for gossip. Even at the time I guess I was embarrassed about dropping out of school. So I made sure I didn't get pregnant. After that Jason said he wasn't ready to be tied down. He'd married me, but he didn't want to be tied down."

David touched her again and drew her cheek against the delicious warmth of his shoulder. "I'm sorry if I brought up painful memories."

She smiled, even though he couldn't see it. Dear David. Always polite and considerate. Nothing was wrong with him, no matter what Mr. Klein said. If only he were *hers*.

"No need to apologize. Those memories are too old to be painful." Her hand went to his chest, and she slipped her fingers through the opening between shirt buttons to toy with his mat of hair.

His lips sought hers with a passion that drove away the last shreds of her blue mood. When the kiss ended, he held her to him and spoke in a voice that was already laced with desire. "One more question before we get too involved in important matters. Do you want to have children?"

"Yes." Unconsciously copying his dry humor, she looked at him as solemnly as she could manage, but her eyes danced. "However, if you're asking if you can get me pregnant tonight, I must decline your generous offer."

"You silly goose, that's not what I meant." He reached for her playfully, and she immediately fell backward on the couch, pulling him with her.

He paused to stroke her cheek and stare longingly at her face. She wound her arm around his neck to guide his mouth gently to hers. She never got tired of the time they spent kissing; each kiss made her feel closer to him. She gloried in the solid pressure of his legs against hers, his abdomen against hers, his chest against her breasts. She knew he liked it when she ran her fingers roughly through the hair on the back of his head like this. He found and caressed the sensitive spot between her shoulder blades, causing her to dart her tongue ever more passionately against his in kiss after wonderful kiss.

Delicate shivers of pleasure rippled across her skin as his fingers traced the line of her jaw and the softer tissues of her neck. As he slowly moved his hand lower, her heart began to race. With each newly opened button cool air blew wisps of anticipation across the skin of her chest. The heavenly warmth of his lips drove the coolness away and replaced it with darting pangs of ecstasy. She inhaled the clean smell of his hair as she laid her chin on its sleek smoothness.

When at last he pushed aside the modest fabric of her blouse and sought the front clasp of her bra, she felt as if her heart would explode. Surely he could feel its pounding as his lips drove her wild with their voluptuous circling of her sensitive globes. Her own caresses of his neck grew weaker as her energy was siphoned into her pressing herself fervently against his uninhibited, pleasure-giving mouth. Time lost meaning. She existed solely for the sensation of his exquisite touch and the passion it aroused. Her taut, saturated nerves carried the message of his fluttering caresses throughout her body in bursts of tingles that stirred her shimmering passion to a boil. Her hips began to move involuntarily against his, and he responded by nipping gently at the swollen centers of her twin peaks, driving gasps from the core of her being. Through the steamy haze of her desire she saw her hand roam from his shoulder to his side, lower still to his hip, and then between their bodies.

At her touch he sucked in a lungful of air and raised his head to dazzle her with the pristine clarity of his eyes. He placed his hand on hers to still her hesitant caresses. Breathing deeply, he whispered in a voice of sultry desire, "Milady, if you do that we'll be past the point of no return—or I will, at least—whether you're ready to make love or not, so be sure. Be very sure." His eyes still pinned her, utterly serious in their demand. "Are you ready?"

Her body cried out *yes*! How she wished she could let her body rule just this once and let her mind sort things out later, but his words forced her to face up to the step she'd be making. Her mind was a spectator, ready to pounce the moment the desire hesitated, ready to declare the limit to her arousal, ready with sad eagerness to feel her desire wane while his still waxed. In having gotten married so young she'd gone directly, unpreparedly, from innocent fumblings to her marriage bed. Maybe if Jason had taken his time with her . . .

Unfair. He'd been nearly as young as her. No, it was her.

David wanted more than just the acquiescence of her aroused body; that knowledge was glorious and yet was a burden. He wanted all of her, her mind as well as her body. *When you tell me you're ready.* How hard it would be to say those words with confidence, to acknowledge what she yearned to do. A flush of embarrassment crept into her cheeks, and she lowered her eyes, her reply catching in her throat.

After no time and forever he sat up, his face mirroring his struggle to regain control of his emotions. He delicately traced the outline of her breasts with a teasing fingertip. "Have I ever told you that you have a perfect figure?"

The fascinating music of his deep voice poured golden dizziness through her nerves, and between the sounds and the touches she had to swallow hard to enable herself to speak. "Feel free—"

"Oh, I do." And the squeezing pressure of his hand matched his words.

"I mean," she gasped, "feel free to tell me as often as you want. Who knows? I might begin to believe you."

His voice grew husky, and his hazel eyes flashed with both amusement and desire. "You have a beautiful figure. Your breasts are aesthetic marvels, so petite and delicately rounded, so perfectly shaped, with big, blatantly erotic nipples peeking upward impishly...."

Blushing and giggling at the same time, she put a finger to his lips. "Hey, stop that, David!"

"Well, do you believe me now?"

She looked at him for a few seconds, then burst into laughter. "No."

Mostly pleased but partly embarrassed, she sat up and pulled her blouse together without buttoning it. An amazing man. Though he must find her incredibly frustrating, he was never other than patient and considerate, yet at the same time he left no doubt of his desire for her. Even now, as he allowed their passion to cool, he did so in a way that affirmed her feminine allure. She laid her cheek on his shoulder, listening to the gradual slowing of his breathing.

He stroked her face with gentle, loving fingers that comforted rather than aroused. "I still think something is bothering you tonight. Is there something you haven't told me?"

Mr. Klein. She hadn't told him about her fight with Mr. Klein.

Melody heaved a sigh. She felt her muscles tense just from the thought of that spiteful old man. At least she could think straight now, more or less. Maybe she'd calmed down enough to discuss this afternoon's altercation. Maybe. She was slow to anger, but once roused, she stayed furious. "I had a fight today with Mr. Klein."

"Did you punch him for making you late?"

She sat rigidly straight, worry tightening her features into a frown. "This is serious, David. I've never told Mr. Klein off, though I've certainly felt like it often enough. Today I did it. I even announced I was taking tomorrow off."

"Good for you. You should have done it ages ago."

"You don't understand. I've worked for that man for eight years. The pattern of our relationship is set, and it doesn't include my flinging coffee cups at him. I wonder if this will ever heal over. Mr. Klein isn't a forgiving man."

"If he fires you, he'll regret it. You'd be better off working for Strong Hardware anyway."

"Yeah," she muttered, "and I'd feel like a traitor."

David stroked her hand soothingly. "I forgot, you're loyal. Well, if that's how you feel, then call and say you'll be at work tomorrow."

She scowled. He still didn't understand. "David, are you busy tomorrow?"

"During the day, yes, but I've kept the evening free for our date. Why?"

"Because," she said darkly, "I don't want to be around in case he phones me tomorrow."

"How about this one? You'd be a knockout in it."

"You've got to be kidding, Noelle." The dress the carrot-haired oboist had taken off the rack featured a skirt slit to mid-thigh and a neckline that plunged beyond daring. "I'd be afraid to be seen in public. How would I look, standing like this all night?" Melody stood stiffly with one arm across her chest and the other against her thigh.

Noelle winked and held the dress up to herself in front of the mirror. "You said you were looking for something feminine and alluring for tonight's date with David, and you must admit this is alluring. I wonder if they have it in a size thirteen."

Melody shook her head in amusement. Asking Noelle to come downtown shopping today had been a stroke of genius. Besides getting away from the telephone, she also squeezed in some girl talk. Since she lived and worked in a masculine world, she needed to talk to another woman to keep her sanity.

She lifted a dress off the rack. It was decidedly more feminine than anything else in her wardrobe. From the middle of the hips to the low neckline, soft crepe would cling to her figure. The pleats on the skirt would accentuate her height—something that she usually avoided but was acceptable around a giant like David. She carefully avoided the price tag. She'd be going over budget no matter how much it cost, but she didn't care. In a perverse way she even hoped it was expensive. "I think I'll try this one on."

"I could never wear that dress," Noelle said, "not with my baby fat. On you it'll look great, though, especially if you leave three or four buttons undone on the bodice."

Shaking her head at her friend, Melody laughed. Leaving three unbuttoned might not get her arrested for indecent exposure, but *four*? "You're determined to turn me into a Siren. Two buttons—maybe three at the most." She draped the dress over her arm and headed toward the changing rooms.

"Melody, they have the dress in my size. Wait for me!"

A short while later they emerged from the store with their new dresses and began to weave with the subconscious skill of city dwellers through the crowds on State Street. A sudden twinge of guilt pricked at Melody as they jostled their way across the sidewalk and into a restaurant for lunch. She wondered how Mr. Klein was doing.

The rush of guilt was easy to ignore, however. She had only to think of David's finely chiseled features and it was gone.

"Your playing's coming along pretty well," Noelle said after they had ordered. There was a note of challenge in the younger woman's voice. "Soon you'll be passing me up."

Melody tried to shrug off the comment, but it made her think. Sometimes she agreed. Sometimes—when her reed was cooperating and her lips weren't too tired and her tone was almost as smooth and mellow as a *real* oboist's—Melody felt cocky about her returning skills.

It never lasted, though. Besides, she knew that despite Noelle's shortcomings, the redhead was proud of playing first oboe, and Melody's fleeting images of superiority seemed disloyal. The first chair was prestigious. Before, she'd always thought of violins when she thought of symphony orchestras. Now—though she might be prejudiced—she realized that the most crucial individuals were actually the first flutist, the first oboist and perhaps the first horn player; no one else had so many exposed passages. But the first chair was Noelle's, and rivalry over the position wasn't worth the only woman friend she had. "It's hard to find time to practice" was all she said.

Noelle clicked her tongue. "Don't I know. As soon as I got away from my parents I stopped taking lessons and vowed never to practice again. I even sold the Lorée they'd given me."

"You had a Lorée oboe and you sold it?"

"Yeah." Noelle's rueful smile made her look like a teenager again. "I bought a closetful of clothes with the money. Then when George and I split last year I found I missed music. So there I sit on Wednesday nights, ogling the most gorgeous guy in the orchestra—"

"David?"

"You're hopelessly prejudiced, so I'll ignore that. Chris Adelson, the bass player with curly blond hair. Anyway, I sit there making a fool of myself, yet it's too discouraging for me to practice. I'm not even as good as I used to be, and I was never as good as you."

"You're too modest."

"No. You are." Noelle paused while her eyes followed the torso of a man in a sleek brown suit as he walked across the restaurant. When she saw that Melody was watching, she laughed self-consciously. "My weakness. Since my divorce I've discovered the joy of men. What about you? Are you and David just good friends, or are you going at it hot and heavy?"

Melody laughed to cover her initial burst of embarrassment, then leaned forward to speak in a confidential hush. "I guess I'd have to say we're just *very* good friends right now. I think that's going to change soon, though."

"Congratulations. Maybe even tonight, huh? Where's he taking you?"

"To a harpsichord recital at the university. It's being given by one of the men he teaches with."

"Harpsichord? You're kidding." Her freckled face creased into a skeptical frown. "Doesn't sound very romantic. Maybe tonight won't be the night after all. Still, I'm sure you two will make beautiful music together—especially with you in that dress. It fits you like a dream. I sure wish I had your figure."

"Oh. Well, thank you." Melody became dreamy-eyed, recalling David's praise of her figure yesterday, and she had to force herself to listen when Noelle resumed talking.

"A harpsichord recital, you say. It sounds like a two-button affair. Maybe even one. But promise me that as soon as you're out of there you'll open another two buttons—three if you're not in public. And forget a bra. With your figure you don't need one, you know."

Melody's mouth twisted into a lopsided grin. "Maybe. I'll think about it."

"Good. Women our age can't afford to be too subtle."

"Noelle, I don't think you have to worry about being too subtle."

"I know. It's the secret of my charm." She winked knowingly. "Good luck tonight."

Melody was amazed to realize that just thinking about tonight made her breath quicken. A warm glow was spreading throughout her body, and she hoped Noelle couldn't see the flush creeping upward from her chest.

"Yes," she murmured. "Tonight."

Chapter Six

The ethereal notes of the harpsichord danced around the dark paneling of the book-lined university drawing room. David and Melody sat alone in an alcove that was given a sense of privacy by an arch. She could almost imagine herself a princess from another, grander age. As she snuggled comfortably into her overstuffed chair she admitted to herself that the music was perfect for this room and this audience.

She glanced at David, then stared openly when she saw that his eyes were closed in enjoyment of the music. Everything about his posture declared his oneness with this environment. If it weren't for the rhythmic swaying of his index finger she might think he was asleep. The soft lighting showcased his square jaw and the gentle yet masculine cleft in his chin. In his cream-colored shirt, corduroy pants and blue sport jacket he was the very picture of an aristocrat at leisure.

Melody pursed her lips. No, the word *leisure* didn't capture his relaxed yet intense absorption in the music. She wished she had the words to describe the marvel that was David Halifax. But that would take a poet laureate.

A warm glow seeped through her, melting her body into the soft contours of the chair. "Tonight, David," she murmured.

Her eyes darted to the two dozen people sitting in comfortable chairs and couches, but only David seemed to have heard her. He opened one eye, only to close it again when she shook her head. Living alone must be getting to her; she'd have to guard against talking to herself.

On the other hand, talking to herself had led to meeting David. So it had to be a good habit.

She clapped when the heavy, dark-haired soloist finished the sonata. The man seemed impossibly huge to have coaxed such sparkling, bell-like tones from the harpsichord. He began another piece, making sound float around the room, to land on her ears with intimate delicacy. Noelle was wrong. This refined sensuousness was very romantic. She smoothed the pleats over her knee with one hand, rested the other on the brushed wool of David's sport jacket and was content.

Afterward they went to her town house for coffee. David walked behind her as they carried their cups to the living room. She imagined his gaze on her bottom, and she accentuated the mild swagger of her hips. A feathery whisper of anticipation tickled her insides. With David in her life even the simple act of walking was erotic.

Too soon they reached the living room. He sat on the couch with a pantherlike grace that somehow proclaimed that this was *his* territory. Their eyes met, sparking an unbearable yet delectable tension between them.

As usual she was the first to break that overpowering connection. "Would you like some music?"

"Sure," he replied lazily. He slipped off his shoes and stretched his legs on her round coffee table, resting his cup and saucer on his lap. "Anything but harpsichord. I apologize for subjecting you to such a boring evening, Melody. I think I fell asleep there at one point."

She stared at him in surprise. "I enjoyed it. I thought you did, too."

"Give me a lively jazz band anytime."

She wasn't in the mood for a jazz band, and mere background music wasn't good enough for tonight. If only she had "Bolero," sinful "Bolero." She settled for the most sensual music she owned, "Afternoon of a Faun." As she walked back to David a cool, graceful flute poured forth lush beauty. She held his gaze as she crossed the room, right until she snuggled against his arm.

"Careful, milady."

She pressed her face onto his shoulder.

"Hey," he insisted. "You'll spill my coffee."

"Then put it down, because in three seconds I'm going to kiss you." She moistened her lips. "One."

Coffee sloshed over the lip of his cup and settled into a round brown puddle in the saucer as he laid it on the table.

"Two."

He turned to her and threw his arm behind her on the back of the couch.

"Three."

And then he was ready for her. His tongue probed the recesses of her mouth with alternate softness and strength, his fingers cushioned her cheek with loving delicacy. She tasted the heady wine of his lips. The intoxication of his love slid down warmly and settled in her abdomen with a fiery glow. Her mind was spinning with uninhibited delirium. When the kiss ended, her head wobbled slightly, so drunk had his kiss made her.

She was nibbling at his nose when he began to speak. "I have a surprise for you."

And I have a surprise for you, she wanted to say. Her mind roamed lustily over the delights her body would offer him this evening. But a last, unexpected vestige of shyness bottled the words inside her, where they rankled like an attack of indigestion. "Hmm?" That was the best she could do. She let her lips do her talking as they moved to taste his cheeks and temples.

"Yes, but ... I can't concentrate when you do that." He cushioned her jaw in his hands and moved her face away, then chuckled at her pout. "I promise this won't take long, but I'm dying to tell someone. I got a phone call from Andy Blankhurst today."

Her mind still blurred by his kiss, she wondered who Andy Blankhurst was.

"Andy," he explained, "is the father of Art, the young cellist in the H.P.O."

"Oh, yes. The business manager of the Chicago Philharmonic."

David nodded. "He called to pay back the debt he thinks he owes me for taking over his son's orchestra. It seems the assistant conductor of the Philharmonic tendered his resignation, effective next fall. Andy wanted me to be the first to know the position was open. He assured me confidentially I'd have the inside track if I wanted the job."

"David, that's wonderful!" She threw her arms around him, the weight of the deadline for his departure lifting from her subconscious in an explosion of delight. Four months was too short for a love like hers. Even a lifetime might be too short.

He kissed her, but with as much amusement as passion. "Slow down, girl. I'm not going to take the job."

She released her arms and, knowing she couldn't erase the disappointed curl of her mouth, kept her cheek pressed to his chest. "Oh? Is this your good news, that you're not going to take a job you hadn't known was available?"

"Yes." His voice was flat and guarded, as if he was surprised at her lack of enthusiasm, but his deep baritone quickly regained its vibrancy. "Even if I don't accept, it's an honor to be considered. You may not realize it, but the orchestra here is the best in America, perhaps the world. This is one of the greatest honors I've received."

Her emotions under control once more, she studied him with scarcely a hint of exasperation. "Then why won't you even apply for the job?"

He returned her appraising look, and she realized she'd let some of her disappointment slip. "I must admit I'm surprised, Melody. I thought you'd be happy for me. You have to understand that my plans don't include being an *assistant* conductor. I'd do a few concerts a year and spend the rest of my time preparing the orchestra for big-name guest conductors. Probably the most exciting thing I'd do is lead the Civic Orchestra—that's the Philharmonic's amateur training orchestra—and with the H.P.O., I'm getting my fill of amateurs. No, my career schedule calls for me to have my own orchestra by next year.

"Put yourself in my shoes," he continued. "Yesterday when that man from Strong wanted to hire you, you were ecstatic. Well, this is an equivalent thing for me."

She dropped her eyes, embarrassed by her selfishness. He was right, completely right. With that realization came another; for all his self-confidence, even David needed an occasional pat on the back to reassure himself that his lofty goals were indeed within reach. Nailing a bright smile in place, she shook his hand vigorously. "Congratulations."

"Thanks. And by the way, I intend to apply. Andy said my guest-conducting slot in December could serve as my audition."

"Huh? You've lost me again. Why apply if you don't intend to accept?"

A satisfied grin flitted across his face, and for a heartbeat he crossed the line from self-confidence to arrogance. "Because," he said, "how many conductors can say they've turned down the Chicago Philharmonic?"

"I see." Melody's smile was genuine now. David sometimes seemed almost too controlled, too good to be true. But he was human after all.

Her own magnanimity in the face of his arrogance came easily. She had only to remember how both Ted Gleason and Al Jevaert had said she was gloating. Who was she to object to a moment of well-deserved gloating? She gazed into the kaleidoscopic brilliance of his eyes, slowly coming to terms with the disappointment of his "good news." What had she expected, a guarantee about the future? Anything might happen in the months remaining to them, but he was worth a risk.

Still, it was time to return to more important matters—namely, the seduction of David Halifax. But despite her resolve, the romantic mood had dissipated. The role of the aggressor was an unfamiliar one for her, and now she had to psych herself up all over again. She sighed, wishing David could read her mind.

"What about your career, Melody? Have you reconsidered taking the job at Strong Hardware?"

She leaned forward and planted her elbows on her knees. "You sure know how to make a woman feel romantic."

"I take it that means you haven't decided."

"How can I make a decision like that?" She paced over to the stereo. If he was going to bring up sloppy subjects like this, then she'd change the record. A grim Mahler symphony might be appropriate. "What do you think I should do?" The words fled from her mouth before she could yank them back. How *could* she?

"Leave me out of this," he protested. "It's your decision, not mine."

"Rats." The word just plopped out. Why did she sound disappointed? Shocked and wary, she clamped on her voice before it could betray her further. No. She wasn't going to seek another man to make all her decisions for her. Never again. This was her decision. Hers alone. She glowered at David before reminding herself she'd asked; he hadn't volunteered.

She slunk back to the couch without changing the record. She must still be upset about her fight with Mr. Klein, or she wouldn't be so hypersensitive. Well, there was a bright side. David wasn't a pushy, opinionated male who wanted to usurp her fragile independence.

"Let's see," she mused aloud. "Begin with the fact that I wouldn't even consider Ted's offer if it weren't for the way Mr. Klein acted yesterday. After all, Strong is just another hardware store. On the other hand, Mr. Klein might fire me. Maybe he already has."

"That would make your decision easy."

He gave her arm an encouraging squeeze, and his words had a slightly persuasive tone. Maybe she was still hypersensitive, but was he really as neutral as he proclaimed? His next words confirmed her fears.

"Don't forget," he said, "this could be your big break, your chance to show you belong in management. It could be the start of your rise to the top."

"Maybe. And I always thought I'd jump at my big opportunity when it came. Do you know something? Mr. Klein doesn't deserve me." She shook her head slowly and sadly, yet a spark of determination entered her voice. The seed of a decision had just sprouted. "He really doesn't."

She was quiet for a moment before continuing. "There's more than just me involved here, David. If I left, the store would close within months, perhaps immediately. Mr. Klein would be all right financially—I know this from a few hints his lawyer has dropped about other investments—but the hardware store has been his life for thirty years.''

And my life for eight, she thought. She'd been a different person when Mr. Klein had hired her as an unskilled part-time clerk. Through all those years of change, healing and growth—Jason's affair, adjusting to single life, buying the town house, absorbing more and more responsibility—the only constant had been the hardware store. She'd been so hopeless, so incompetent, eight years ago....

She jerked her head in surprise, her mind focusing on the past. ''So that's why,'' she whispered.

David laced his fingers through hers. ''What do you mean?''

She was silent for a moment longer while she pondered her realization. Yes. It made sense. ''We have this stockboy. His name's Lamarr, and he's got three strikes against him—young, black and poorly educated. No, four strikes. You should see him, David. He looks so tough that no one in their right mind would hire him. But I did, and I've often wondered why. Well, I just realized he reminds me of myself when I started. My employment prospects were about as bright as Lamarr's. Oh, I might have been a bit more, how shall I say it, decorative—''

''Much more decorative,'' David interrupted.

Her lips shaped a silent kiss in his direction. ''Much more decorative, then. Anyway, Lamarr's probably a more competent worker than I was at the beginning. I learned everything I know from Mr. Klein and from the opportunities he gave me to teach myself, and Lamarr is my chance to return the favor. If I back out on my commitment to the store, the kid's back on the street, maybe for good. All because I'm mad at Mr. Klein.''

David squeezed her hand. ''I wish I knew what to say, but nothing I say will change things. Besides, I get the impression you've made up your mind and you just don't know it yet. But two things occur to me."

She smiled to cover the return of her wariness. "What?"

"You say that if you took the new job you'd still just be selling hardware. But—and it's a big but—you'd be a manager with a nationwide company. Even if you didn't stay with them, you'd have a great reference for your résumé."

"Résumé? I don't have a résumé."

"Then you have to start building references for one if you want to overcome the handicap of your lack of education. And you can do it. There's nothing stopping you but yourself. You're hardworking, intelligent—probably more intelligent than me, I'm sorry to admit. You've proven to yourself you can manage a business. Now you have to prove it to employers, and Strong might be the first step."

She pursed her lips and forced herself to nod. He wanted her to accept the job, then. Worse, everything he said made perfect sense, except for the flattery about her intelligence. His calm, masculine logic sliced her decision to shreds. With an effort she kept the disappointment out of her face and voice. "So you want me to take Ted's offer."

"I didn't say that. The decision is yours."

Her heart sank. So this was how David would manipulate her, by logically demonstrating the silly emotionalism of her position and then "leaving the decision up to her." It seemed she'd always had a manipulative man in her life—Papa, Jason, Mr. Klein. She didn't need another. Well, it was good she found out now, before she started dreaming of anything drastic. Like marriage.

As if sensing her unease, he lifted her hand to his mouth for a series of gentle kisses.

And if logic doesn't work, she thought with utter discouragement, he'll use sexual attraction. She eased her hand from his grasp.

"My second point," she heard him say as if from far away, "is that you care for people. You're worried about Lamarr. You're worried about Mr. Klein. Feelings like that aren't part of the bottom-line business mentality—and believe me, I know the business mentality."

Melody perked up and paid greater attention, each of his words jacking her spirits up a notch.

"I grew up thinking that being in business meant people had to be heartless, or at least tame their better feelings for the sake of the bottom line. I'm glad you haven't sold your soul like that." He enveloped her hand in both of his, and his touch was like a jolt of electricity. "I'm proud of you."

Too stunned for words, she stared into his beautiful face for a timeless eternity, not thinking about her job or his words but just *feeling*—soaring above her everyday existence to the lofty pinnacles of total communication, total acceptance, total lowering of barriers, total harmony with another human being. In that instant she knew she would love David Halifax forever, no matter what happened thereafter.

Words seemed paltry and inadequate to carry her emotional load, so she said simply, "Thank you." She smiled at this incredibly wonderful human being beside her. "And you're right. I have made up my mind."

"You're staying."

"I'm staying."

Silence stretched indefinitely through a moment that needed no words.

"The music's over," he whispered at last.

Melody nodded.

"I guess I'd better go," he murmured with what might have been a teasing expression. Did he know, then, of her desire to seduce him? "I have a choir to conduct in the morning."

She took a deep breath, then nodded again. This close-ness screamed for physical expression, so even if she hadn't already decided that tonight would be the night, the reve-lation of his wonderful, nonpressuring personality would have decided for her. "Before you go, David, I have a ques-tion to ask you."

"Yes?"

Bending her head to one side, she twirled a lock of hair around one finger. It was so difficult to come right out and say this. So much easier to show him with her lips what she wanted. "David..."

"Yes?"

"Would you like..."

A lopsided grin spread across his face. "Go on."

She couldn't do it, not in the face of that grin. She fin-ished her sentence in a rush. "Would you like to help me with a couple of passages from the Schubert?"

"*What?* Right now?"

"Sure. Now. I'll get my instrument. Be right back."

When she returned, David was stretched comfortably on the floor, his back against the couch. She noticed that he tenderly surveyed her calves as she prepared to play. *He* had the right idea, at least.

"Remember," he warned her, "this was your sugges-tion, not mine. A music lesson isn't high on my list of great ways to end a date."

There. He'd given her the perfect opening to wriggle out of this ill-considered performance. She merely had to in-quire what was a good way to end a date. Instead she ner-vously folded her lips over her teeth and blew. *Coward,* she chided herself.

Then she forgot about him, almost, while she played a short passage the best she'd ever done, past her previous, gasping limits and approaching true musicality. When she finished she felt too shy to look at him. She'd thought she wanted his honest opinion, but now she was uncomfortably aware that what she really wanted was praise, honest or not. Her head lifted just enough so that she could see him.

"Well," he began cautiously, "taking everything into account, that wasn't too bad. It's hard to play by yourself, and I'm sure you do better in rehearsals—"

"No," she interrupted, her gaze rising to study the picture hanging from the wall over his head, "that was the best I've ever played it."

"Oh. Well. Not bad." He paused. "I don't exactly know what you want me to say."

Her heart sank to her toenails. She should have known better than to expect praise from someone with David's standards. Why couldn't she just have kissed him? She said, her voice firm, "Why don't you start with how I can improve?"

A moment of silence greeted her suggestion. "Okay. But for heaven's sake, relax. I'm not giving you a grade. For starters lower your stand and sit beside me."

She wasn't accustomed to playing her oboe while sitting on the floor, and she tried several positions, then folded her legs under her. "I see what you mean," she said, chuckling as he slipped his arm around her waist. "This is much better."

"Of course." He moved his hand in a lazy circle from her waist up her back and then down to the sensitive swelling of her bottom. "Trust my professional judgment."

Melody glared at the arm that was sending lustful caresses through the pink pleats. "You're a professional at this?"

"Call it natural talent. Speaking of which, watch your breathing here and here...." He pointed to the music and gave her several tips, never ceasing to caress her back. She concentrated on his words as well as she could, then played again.

"Not bad at all." His carefully neutral expression had changed to enthusiasm. "Usually the hardest thing for amateurs is to play with feeling. I wish the other players in the Hyde Park Orchestra were as quick to learn what I want."

A pleased smile blossomed on her face. "Thank you, David. Tell me, what does the maestro want right now?"

One dark eyebrow rose, and his lips parted in unspoken invitation—an invitation she accepted. She leaned over him, her hair shrouding their kiss with a modest tent of privacy. He nuzzled her nose when the kiss ended. "Maestro says kiss me again."

"Oh, really? And is that the sort of instructions you were giving that violinist during the break last Wednesday?"

He laughed. "Give me credit for good taste. I only take advantage of the sexy ones."

As he raised his head to reclaim her lips with a passion that sent her pulse skittering, his powerful hand speeded her heartbeat still more by seeking refuge under the hem of her dress. With a restless, butterfly touch he moved his fingers with indecent slowness from her knee to the yearning flesh of her thigh, but too soon stopped—halted by the twin obstacles of their awkward positions and the unfulfilled limits of their former intimacies. The thrill of his touch continued to radiate throughout her limbs, however, leaving her nerves quivering with thwarted anticipation.

When his lips withdrew she felt the rapid warmth of her own breath reflected back on to her cheek from his. "Encore, encore," she whispered. She offered her mouth once more to the insistent probings of his, and her soul focused on the erotic dance in what was now *their* mouth. Blood pounded through her in a brisk accelerando that left her limbs frail and shaky. Her head sank against his chest, where her mind was filled with the roaring drumroll of his heart.

"One more time," he said huskily. "No, not that. I meant play the music one more time."

"David . . . Oh, all right." He was probably just trying to keep himself under control, she reminded herself with a sigh. These weeks of unreleased passion must have been difficult for him and she opened her mouth to tell him he need wait no longer. Again the words refused to come. Disgusted with her cowardice, she sat up instead and pressed the sliver of reed to her lips.

The throbbing pressure of his hand on her thigh and the still-pounding tempo of her heart doomed the music. She was remembering more the tormenting sweetness of his lips than his instructions about the tune, was aware more of the searing presence of his fingers under the pleats than of her oboe, was concentrating more on edging forward to drive his hand up her leg than on her breathing. Inevitably she played wrong notes, added extra notes and was forced to breathe in the middle of phrases. When David began to jiggle his hand against her sensitive skin, her playing deteriorated still more—first into a jumble of garbled notes and finally into a squawking whimper of air mewling unmusically through her sievelike lips.

Her eyes accused him. The quivering that had demolished the Schubert had been caused by silent laughter shaking his body.

"What are you laughing at?" Though she meant to sound stern, she had difficulty maintaining an aura of injured dignity after the pathetic sounds she'd just made. As soon as her words were out his silent mirth exploded aloud. She poked him in the ribs. "Maybe my playing was terrible, but you sure didn't help my concentration."

"I know," he gasped. "I'm sorry." And then his frame began to shake all over again.

"Everyone's a critic," she began, but the rest of her complaint was drowned under a rising tide of giggles. She placed her oboe on the table and stared at it sheepishly. She'd sounded ridiculous, all right. The noise of her giggles broke the last dam of David's self-restraint, and soon their laughter was a shared thing, a bond between them.

Playfully Melody poked at his side again, precipitating a one-sided wrestling match in which he merely defended his sides. "So you're ticklish, are you? Well, take this," she said. He twisted from side to side under her playful attack, allowing her this dominance while equilibrium was reestablished—shifting from amused teacher and absurd-sounding pupil back to equals enjoying each other's company.

When their laughter finally dissolved into breathless smiles, she was astride him, one knee on either side of his hips, fingers poised at his belly. "Had enough?"

"Uncle!"

She put her hands on the rug and shifted her weight forward to look straight down into his wide, dark pupils. "Listen, Halifax, we can either kiss or play music. Not both."

"Then let's kiss, Ross."

The power of her passion seemed to catch him by surprise, but he quickly responded with fervor. Her lips opened to the darting staccato of his tongue against hers, hers against his, each demanding and receiving the delights of the other's mouth. When the savage kiss finally ended she thrilled to the ragged quickness of his breath against her cheek.

Her lips still burned in the aftermath of his tantalizing possession when his fingers began a softer exploration of the features of her face. Her nose, eyebrows, cheeks, jaw and chin all glowed in turn under his touch. When a smooth fingertip traced the sensitive contours of her lips, she opened them to savor his taste and firmness. His mouth followed the trail already blazed by his fingers. She caressed with quick kisses whatever part of his face presented itself, tasting his masculine features in an effort to know his face in yet a new way. The rough furriness of his eyebrows. The soft pads under his eyes. The hard strength of his cheekbones. The faint, sandpapery grittiness of his beard.

And then he cradled her face in his palms so they could focus on each other. She caught her moving reflection in his eyes as he shook his head in wonder. "Milady," he breathed, "you are so gorgeous."

She smiled in a way that was both hungry and satisfied at the same time, recognizing the truth of his words at last. In the eyes of the man she loved she *was* beautiful. "So are you."

Closing her eyes, she stretched her neck taut as he began to draw amorous circles on it. Lower and lower his fingers crept, pausing to explore the pulsing hollow at the base of her neck before they danced over her wildly beating heart. She felt his deft hand at the top button of her dress, now the next button, and it indeed became a four-button night. And then her whole mind was absorbed by the wonderful sensations his touch aroused in the charged flesh of her breasts. Though his access was still hampered by burdensome layers of cloth, her blood poured music through her in a crescendo that swelled with each new nerve ending he touched on her yearning flesh.

Her muscles were growing feeble from desire. She weakly bent her knees, then sucked in her breath as she felt the powerful proof of his desire. She was torn between the need to keep her arms rigid to allow his continuing erotic discovery of her breasts and the need to sink against him and profess her full arousal to his silken lips.

Arms trembling in time to the fluttering of her heart, she maintained her position as his fingertips at last brushed a firm nipple. Pleasure waves rippled from the epicenter of his touch throughout her torso and limbs, pounding against her fragile muscle control till her elbows buckled and she collapsed against him. His hand, now trapped between them, gave her flesh a last, exquisite squeeze before slipping around her shoulders to crush her to him more firmly. Her fierce kiss hinted of desire gone past the point of no return, and he answered with a passion that was equally strong yet somehow still tethered by concern for her.

She rocked lightly on top of him, demanding more than their previous chastity had allowed. Her face pressing his firm chest, she lovingly monitored the steady increase in his heartbeat. With her body she urged his passionate caresses from her shoulders to the small of her back and over the rise of her buttocks. She didn't begrudge the time he massaged that soft flesh, but her blood sang as his hand moved once more down the outside of her thighs to her knees, then back up, underneath the dress, not pausing at their previous limits but up, sensuously up, till the strident warmth of his hand was muted by the thin silkiness of her panties.

Each forceful caress of his fingers slipping over the smooth cloth made her more aware of how close she was to losing herself completely in the sensations he aroused in her more-than-willing body. She wanted that loss, ached for it, and drove him toward it with tender kisses to his neck and ear. With a deftness that made it seem the most natural thing in the world, his hands pulled the elastic partway down her thighs.

When his fingers found her most sensitive flesh she was propelled into the wild winds of passion. Buffeted by the strong crosscurrents rising from his tempestuous touch, she progressed upward, with building tension, floating higher than ever she dared before and then higher still. The ultimate release left her limp and breathless with the beauty and wonder of what he could make her feel. She pressed herself tightly against him. As she drifted languorously back to earth, she was awed by the awareness that even this was not the limit of where David's love would take her this night.

When she could breathe again, she showered his face with rapid, whispery touches of her lips. He held her tightly but now motionlessly, waiting, searching her face. She marveled at his incredible control. Even now, when he desired her as much as she desired him, he nevertheless mustered restraint for her sake. Amazing.

She propped her chin on her hand for the simple pleasure of gazing into his eyes. She unbuttoned his shirt and slipped her hand across the warmth of his chest, delighting in his solid flesh.

He turned his head toward her wonderingly, questioning the message her eyes and hands were sending. "It's late," he whispered.

Melody nodded.

"I should be going. Unless," he said with awesome mildness, "you have a better idea."

Her hand probed farther across his chest, and she pressed her mouth to his aggressively. The beautiful words that had eluded her all evening slipped effortlessly off her tongue. "Why don't you spend the night?"

With a joyous laugh he wrapped his arms around her and began to devour her face with kisses. He communicated happiness to her in a rekindling of the excitement she'd felt so recently. Her breath caught the quickening rhythm of his, her pulse matched the pounding staccato of his, her desire intensified along with the roaring tide of his. In one smooth motion he rolled them together on to their sides and sat up. Another graceful move and she was in his arms, being carried effortlessly up the stairs to her room, one of her arms around his neck and the other working on the remaining buttons of his shirt.

The shirt floated unheeded to the bedroom floor and was soon followed by the new crepe dress, which would now be her sentimental favorite. She gazed into his eyes as they visually caressed the warm skin of her neck and shoulders, the lacy nothingness covering her heaving breasts, the smooth flatness of her abdomen and the translucent panties, which were still halfway down her thighs. Then she gloried in the cool airiness of being completely naked with him, in beholding the total perfection of his body for the first time.

"You are so incredibly beautiful, Melody. Perfect."

"Perfect, David." Then, because his name tolled like heavenly bells, she repeated it over and over as if she could never have enough of it—or of him. "David, David, David..."

Her heart pounded inside her chest as she felt the frantic ecstasy of his searing flesh against hers, his hand fully possessing her sensitive breasts, his leg pressing insistently between hers. His touch spread fires across her skin, the fires joining into an all-consuming blaze that centered in her abdomen. The passions aroused by his early caress, as wonderful as they'd been, now seemed a mere appetizer to the main course of his nakedness against hers. She memorized the urgent weight of his flesh, absorbed his manly scent, dissolved under the firmness of his need for her. His hands learned the private hollows of her body as she writhed shamelessly, helplessly. She was more than ready; she was frantic.

With one delicious thrust they were no longer two people in love; they were one. Moving as one, breathing as one, shuddering in delight as one, striving as one, gasping as one, tumbling weightlessly and endlessly to the ultimate pinnacle of enjoyment and satisfaction.

As one.

They lay panting she knew not how long, glistening chests heaving in unison as they stretched luxuriously among the tangled sheets. The lassitude and relaxation of utter satisfaction steamed through her veins and melted her body into a perfect fit for the crook of his arm. When she looked at his lean physique, she was filled with a contentment greater than she'd ever felt. Greater than she'd ever imagined.

And when she looked into his face she found an expression she'd never imagined, either. A dazzling mix of wonder, awe and love lent his features an inner glow that warmed her with its almost palpable radiation. The sinuous movement of his lips as he began to speak was like a Siren call, and she was amazed at how soon she was ready to repeat this shatteringly perfect experience. She slipped her fingers along his firm muscles, finding that he was ready, too.

"I love you," he breathed as he reached for her.

And I love you, she thought, though her mouth was suddenly too dry for the words to escape. Breathing heavily, she licked her lips and was about to try again when the abrupt jangling of the telphone intruded into their perfect moment.

She glared at the offending machine perched atop a pile of books on the bedside table. Glancing back at David's sexy eyes and sexier body, both proclaiming his readiness to love her, she hissed at the phone. "Rats."

He chuckled and trailed his hand from her neck to the rippling warmth between her thighs. "Go ahead. Answer it. Just get rid of whoever it is quickly, because I'll be waiting none too patiently."

When she stretched for the phone he demonstrated his impatience by capturing her hips in his strong grip and melting her insides with feathery kisses to her abdomen and thighs. "Stop that, David. I have to answer the phone. That's better. Hello? Yes, this is Melody Ross." Covering the telephone with her palm, she gasped. "David! I'm on the phone.

"Mr. Gold? Oh, yes, Mr. Klein's attorney. (David, stop it!) I'm sorry you couldn't reach me earlier, (behave yourself, David!) but I've been out most of the day, downtown and, uh, then, uh, somewhere else, ah, at a recital. (Oh, I love you, David!) Excuse me, Mr. Gold. What did you say? Oh, yes, please! No, not you, Mr. Gold. I'm sorry.... Uh, would you please repeat that?

"Oh, my God." She sat bolt upright and grasped the phone with both hands. David looked up at her with concern and a touch of frustration, but she scarcely saw him. "Yes, thank you for trying so hard to get in touch. I'll be there as soon as I can. Oh? They won't let me in. Well, thanks anyway."

David took the telephone from her limp grasp. The hands that cupped her face were no longer those of a passionate lover but of a solicitous friend. "What's the matter, Melody?"

She exhaled a long breath before answering in a subdued voice. "Mr. Klein. He's in the hospital. He collapsed at work today. David, he has cancer. He . . . he isn't expected to live."

Chapter Seven

"Herb's still in a coma," Robert Gold told her as they sat somberly in the tiny store office.

Strange. It felt as if it could have been any Monday—except, of course, for Mr. Klein's absence, Mr. Gold's unexpected afternoon visit and the hollow feeling in Melody's stomach.

Yesterday had been bittersweet. Bitter because of the taint of guilt that had paralyzed her mind, rendering thought and decisions impossible. Sweet because David had spent every waking and sleeping hour with her. He was her strength. It was he who had suggested she open the store as usual today. She had numbly agreed, glad for the comforting guidance of his advice.

"The doctors say he might drift in and out of the coma." Mr. Gold shook his head, as if he doubted even this much improvement. "It may be the best thing for him. At least he can't feel the agony of his stomach cancer."

"Cancer." The word felt ugly and unreal on Melody's lips. "I still can't believe it. I thought he had ulcers."

"That's Herb. Deny, deny. He couldn't have worked much longer, no matter how cantankerous he was. His doctor was after him to take out half his stomach and have chemotherapy, then take life easy. What did Herb do? He stopped going to the doctor." Mr. Gold shook his head. "And now they'll let only family members see him while he's in intensive care, though we've known each other since high school."

Melody was dully surprised that Mr. Gold was Mr. Klein's age. The small lawyer was so vigorous and spry that she'd assumed he was younger. The dark hair poking from under his hat, which he always wore to hide his bald spot, added to the illusion of middle age.

But then—and the thought still astounded her—Mr. Klein had been waging a desperate battle with cancer. Not ulcers. Cancer. No wonder Mr. Klein looked old. How could she not have noticed? And his overtaxed body had finally succumbed at the store, on Saturday.

Saturday. The day she'd frittered away downtown just to escape the telephone. Saturday. The day she'd contemplated treachery. Saturday. The day she'd refused to work. What part had her refusal played in his collapse? What agony had her fit of pique caused him, Saturday?

Not knowing what to say, she studied Mr. Gold's hand as it darted across the desk in her office—no, Mr. Klein's office!—to flip aimlessly through a heavy black ledger. All his actions were like that, fast and aggressive, like a hawk or eagle. Oh, he was pleasant, but she could imagine him pouncing on a witness with the intensity of a born predator. She recalled Mr. Klein telling her about this man not long after she'd started at the store.

"Anything the matter, Mel? You look like you're about to cry." He spoke with both surprise and concern, as if he couldn't fathom why she might cry.

Melody shook her head in a successful effort to drive the moisture from her eyes. "I was thinking about what Mr. Klein said about you the first time I met you."

His eyes narrowed. "And what is that? Or is it too impolite for a lady to repeat?"

"No, of course not. He just said 'Bob makes a good friend and a bad enemy.'"

"Hmph. What does Herbert know about being a friend?" He darted a nod at her puffy eyes. "If you cry for him, Melody, you'll be the only one who ever will."

Emptiness and horror welled up inside her—because she believed him. Yet coming from a lifelong friend and business partner, those words were the most terrible epitaph any man could have.

Bob's emotions paraded plainly across his face. Embarrassment and perhaps regret for having spoken so forcefully, followed by determination that showed the words expressed his true feelings. "In any case," he said, "I'm not here to reminisce about Herbert Klein. Knowing him, he'll outlive me." He paused. "Actually, I'm here at the family's request. Mrs. Klein instructed me to take charge of the store's books."

"Certainly." And then the implication struck her like a blow. "Don't you trust me?"

He squirmed, his gaze traveling everywhere but her face. "*I* trust you, Mel. From what Herb told me and from what I know myself, I trust you completely."

"But Mrs. Klein?"

His shoulders surged in a quick shrug. "When the cancer was first diagnosed, Herb gave Doris power of attorney in the event that he was incapacitated, and she just wants to get rid of this building as fast as she can. She's worried

about every cent, though I keep telling her the joint investments he and I made are worth three times this dump.''

His words sent her mind reeling. *Sell the store?* She seized
on an irrelevant detail to give her mind time to recover. ''I
didn't know he owned the whole building.''

''Two commercial spaces and five apartments upstairs.''
Bob waved his hands toward the cracked plaster and faded
paint. ''Every one as elegant as this. It figures you wouldn't
know. Herb played his cards close to the vest.''

''Plays.''

''Excuse me?''

''Plays his card, not played. He's not dead.''

''Of course.'' Mr. Gold twirled his hat around and around
in his hands. He was right, she realized, to cover his bald
spot. He looked old—old and tired.

''For now,'' he said gently, ''if you think you can run the
store by yourself, by all means do so. Call me if I can help.
Doris hasn't instructed me to shut it down, and I'm not
about to suggest it. But you should know that the Strong
chain has wanted to buy Herb out for quite a while, and now
that he's out of the picture, Doris is losing no time. She had
me contact them this morning.'' He smiled at her apologetically. ''Better start looking for another job, Mel. If you
leave before the deal is closed, I'll understand.''

She took several deep breaths. ''I see.'' The touch of David's strong hands would be so marvelous right now.... ''I
suppose I shouldn't be surprised.''

''But you are.'' Bob rose and picked up the store's led-
gers. ''I'm sorry it has to end this way, with a whimper. I'll
see to it you get a generous severance check.''

''And the other clerks?''

He fluttered his hand in a gesture of uncertainty. ''I'll see
what I can talk Doris into. They haven't been here as long,
though, nor done as much.''

Melody accompanied him to the door. She stood in the cold draft and watched him as he bustled down the sidewalk, his collar turned up against the freezing wind and first snowfall of the turning season. She leaned her head against the doorframe. "Rats." The chill seeping into her bones wasn't only from the crisp Lake Michigan gusts. "Damn, damn, damn."

The rest of the afternoon was bad. She tried unsuccessfully to contact David. How much easier it would be to have his sympathy and advice, to have him tell her everything would be all right, that he'd take care of her.

She spent half an hour in the office, staring at the phone, thinking and feeling miserable. True, she'd considered leaving here just days ago. But she'd decided to stay.

And now her life was unrecognizable.

First David. The change in their relationship was good—more than good—in the comforting way that it promised to revolutionize her existence. But add to that Mr. Klein's tragedy and now the imminent sale of the store. So much for her safe, sane existence. She'd be lucky to keep up the payments on her town house on the salary a high school dropout could make elsewhere.

"Oh, stop feeling sorry for yourself," she fumed. "You're a lot better off than Mr. Klein. And you still have the offer from Strong, so snap out of it."

After phoning for a Wednesday appointment with Ted Gleason, she made herself work out on the sales floor; there was nothing to keep her busy in the office. The snow kept business down, though, and she had time to think.

Too much time.

"Cellos, that's no better than you were six weeks ago." David ran his fingers through his hair, and his calm features momentarily dissolved into haggard frustration. "You're all alone here, so try to play it the way Schubert intended. The concert is three weeks away. Practice!" He pierced the unfortunate cellists with a withering glare that shouted his opinion of musicians who wouldn't, or couldn't, reach the musical ideal he heard in his head. He shook his head. "Everybody, take your break now. Back in fifteen."

It was always hard to get to David during the break. Melody jammed her instrument in its case. But she wasn't quick enough. A sloppily dressed violinist was already pointing quizzically at the sheet music he'd thrust in front of David's face.

She tried to stifle her disappointment. They'd spent Monday and Tuesday evenings together, but that wasn't enough. She could never have enough of him. Besides, she was still disgruntled that he'd been busy and couldn't drive her to this rehearsal. Important meeting or not, she preferred driving with him to driving with Noelle. She needed him with an intensity that sometimes scared her.

As a matter of fact, it scared her right this minute. Her life couldn't stop just because David was busy.

Greg Defosse, the first flutist, closed the lid of his instrument case and stretched his legs. He never said anything on his own, so Melody spoke first. "You're playing great tonight, Greg, especially in the Copland."

"Thanks. We'll be ready for the concert, don't you think?"

"Maybe the flutes will," Noelle interjected. "I'm not sure about the oboes."

"Relax. Concerts always turn out." Greg's stony features bent into a reassuring smile. "Unless, of course, they don't. By the way, a bunch of us are going to Benito's for pizza and a beer after the rehearsal. You two join us?"

Noelle grabbed his arm. "Is Chris coming?"

"I believe so."

"We'll come. Won't we, Melody?"

Melody glanced at the small crowd around David. "I'll let you know at the end of the rehearsal."

Noelle followed her gaze. "Oho. Do I detect a hint of sex in the orchestra?"

Greg discreetly turned to another musician, but Melody lowered her voice anyway. "If that's a question about what happened Saturday, forget it. I'm not going to blab the details of my sex life."

"You have a sex life now?" Noelle spoke too loudly and even she realized it. She glanced around, instantly contrite. "Sorry. I have a big mouth." She studied Melody's face, then smiled knowingly. "Besides, you don't have to say a word. I understand."

Melody felt the heat of a blush, which only seemed to make it harder for Noelle to contain herself. Miracle of miracles, the cluster around David dispersed, and Melody hastened away from the freckled oboist.

She snuggled up to the cozy wool of his sweater, for once not caring if others saw. He seized her lips in a quick, fierce kiss. "I've been wanting to do that all day," he said.

"Me, too." They wandered arm in arm to sit in the audience section of the hall. "How are the preparations for the *Messiah* coming?" She was pleased at the calmness of her voice. That blasted performance at Rockefeller Chapel was the reason he hadn't driven her to the rehearsal tonight.

A crooked smile touched half his face, and he sighed, "So-so."

"I see." In other words, until the performance was under control he'd be busy, just when she needed him most. Well, he had his own life to live—but she couldn't resist trying. "How about my place after the rehearsal?"

"Temptress." The warmth of his eyes sent a shiver swirling down her back. "But I've neglected my work already. As much as I'd like to spend the night with you, I'm afraid I've got things to do." He snaked his arm over the back of the seat to caress away some of the hurt from his words. "To-morrow night, I promise, though I may be kind of late."

Her answer was a fervent kiss. He hugged her affectionately before sitting straight and businesslike. "Now, tell me about your meeting with Ted Gleason."

His voice was subdued, as if he was reluctant to ask. That wouldn't surprise her, since sensitivity was one of the best of his many stellar traits. She kept her answer level and unemotional. It took an effort.

"He was very frank. I'll give him that much. I almost believe that in his own way he's an honest man."

David didn't say anything, but she heard his sigh of dread anticipation.

"He claimed," Melody continued, "that he has little discretion in running his store, because the regional manager is always looking over his shoulder. Furthermore, he already has an assistant manager." She hesitated. "Ted claims he was told to offer me a job as a way of scuttling Klein's."

David showed no surprise. "Sounds like a typical businessman."

"That's not all." She took a deep breath before continuing. "He said the offer was legitimate at the time because they would have found a position for me somewhere. But he's been informed that now that the company is negotiating a purchase, I'm no longer needed." She paused to force neutrality back into her voice. "He says he's very sorry, and if it was up to him he'd hire me into management without question. On his own, though, he only has authority to hire sales clerks."

David's strong fingers massaged her shoulder. "So what did you say?"

"I told him no thank you." She chuckled without humor. "I also told him what he could do with his clerk's job and added a few other unrepeatable suggestions." Her eyes became glazed as she stared unseeingly at the bright stage. "It's funny. Years of living in a man's world turned me off to profanity. I fancied I was above it. But a few days of adversity have me cussing like a steelworker. Just goes to prove my strong moral fiber, my unflinching composure in the face of trouble."

"Don't blame yourself, Melody. Remember, none of this is your fault. Mr. Klein would have collapsed even if you had been there Saturday, and you went out of your way dozens of other times to help him. Give yourself a chance, and I'm sure you'll do better than a clerk's job."

An image of Mr. Klein sprang into her mind, clutching his stomach in pain, suffering through Saturday when she should have been there. Exactly how guilty should she feel? Probably a lot less than she did.

"I imagine you're right," she said. "At least I hope you are. I'll start looking into other jobs."

He laid a reassuring hand on her shoulder. "You said you didn't want to sell hardware. Well, this is your big chance to break into another field."

She scanned his face sourly. Words like that came easily to him; he already had what he wanted, including an even better job lined up a year in advance. His confidence suddenly seemed overbearing. Her precise and unemotional voice hardened into barely concealed anger and determination. "One thing is certain. I won't work for an outfit like Strong Hardware or a worm like Ted Gleason. David, I was just a pawn manipulated by a corporation. To them I was *nothing*."

"That's the way business is," he said contemptuously. He gave her shoulder another squeeze. "Don't worry, Melody. Everything will turn out the way it should."

She wished she could believe that. "Talking helps. No, I take that back. You're what helps."

"Thanks, milady. But I'm afraid I have to get back to work and so do you. We've taken way longer than fifteen minutes."

After the rehearsal she bade David a wistful farewell before heading through the slush to Noelle's car. She didn't really want to go to the restaurant; she wanted David. But at least she wouldn't mope till bedtime, alone.

And in a way she looked forward to talking to the other musicians, because aside from David and Noelle she knew hardly anyone. Many of the people in the orchestra seemed shy, like Greg. She smiled as she thought of Greg. After years of living a mile from the university, he was the first professor she'd known.

The conversation at the restaurant was different from what she was used to, more cultured and intelligent, but—revelation—she could hold her own with them. The only uncomfortable time came when the talk swung to the conductor. Opinion about David was divided. Some, like Noelle and the bass player Chris, felt he was too hard on them, struggling amateurs that they were. Others, like Greg, welcomed his uncompromising toughness as a means of improving the orchestra.

Melody could understand both sides—she struggled more than most after all—but her loyalty was with David. She kept her mouth tightly shut.

Noelle obviously enjoyed herself, sitting next to Chris with many a beaming smile in his direction. Before the evening was over, her hand was stroking his shoulder. Melody began to fear she'd be stranded; she knew Noelle's priorities would place a one-night stand with a man above driving her home. Melody was ready to leave long before her friend and had to stifle a few unladylike yawns before they finally walked through the cold wind to the car. With each step she wished that her companion were ten inches taller, dark haired and male.

"Melody," the redhead announced, "I've decided sleeping around is getting boring. I'm not going to do it anymore."

A laugh slipped out before Melody could stop it. "Just like that?"

"Yeah. That's the best way to make decisions, on the spur of the moment, without thinking."

As they settled gingerly onto the cold vinyl seats, Noelle spoke again, an uncharacteristic discouragement subduing her usual bubbliness. "I wasn't always like this, you know. In the first week after the divorce I slept with more men than I had in my entire life." She ended with a whisper. "I'm getting tired of it. So tired."

Melody reached across and took her friend's hand. She was surprised by this sudden melancholy, considering Noelle's merry flirting with the bass player. "Is it Chris?"

Noelle smiled shyly as she pulled away from the curb. "Well, I didn't claim I was going to join a convent. I don't know if there's a chance for Chris and me, but yeah—I'd like to settle down for a while."

"That's wonderful, Noelle."

"Easy for you to say. You have Davey, and you know everything will turn out all right."

"I do? Noelle, you have no idea what's been happening—"

"You're right," Noelle said with a halting wave of her hand. "I guess you don't know the future any better than I do. But I'm scared." Her voice wilted to a cracked sigh that hinted at a depth of loneliness under the facade of easy frivolity and sociability. "I don't usually feel this way at the beginning of a relationship. The problem, I guess—if it is a problem, which of course it is—the problem is that I care for him, and the more I care for him, the more he can hurt me.

I want more than a quick affair. But I don't know what *he* wants.''

"What he wants..." Melody's whisper echoed her friend's words.

"I could make a total fool of myself by depending on him for more than he can give. So should I fling just my body at him, or my heart, too?''

Noelle's words reverberated through Melody's soul. How much should she depend on David? In the last few days she'd come to live for their moments together, yet the red-head's words sparked the realization that there was another reason for her desperate clinging.

Her world was crumbling, her security vanishing like her oboe's ephemeral notes, which, once played, died to silence and lived only in memory. Being the kind of person she was, she needed security, especially in the midst of chaos. And being the kind of person she was, she seized on David as her anchor. But could their relationship bear that strain?

All sorts of problems might come between them. Even if she wasn't overly dependent on him, their relationship might not last out the month. For all she knew she was just a casual romance, a welcome diversion for a temporary newcomer to the city, and she'd be a fool to count on him. She'd be a fool to build a dream world around him.

A wave of guilt washed over her. She was being unfair to David. Unless she was totally mistaken, his emotional intensity left no room for casual affairs. But still, he'd made no commitment to her, nothing solid enough to anchor her life. It was too soon for that. She was rushing things again.

Again? Why had that word come to mind?

Suddenly she pitched forward and buried her face in her hands. Of course. She'd rushed things with Jason, too. Instead of asserting her independence, she'd traded it blindly for the illusory security of happily ever after. Everything was supposed to work out all right after she'd said "I do." It hadn't. Being married had made her no more of a person. Less, in fact. She'd paid for that mistake for the better part of a decade, and yet as soon as turmoil reentered her life, she clung to a man again. Dangerous. Very dangerous.

She let out a long sigh as she looked at the melancholy face of her friend. "Noelle," she said sadly, "you're right. The more deeply you care for a man, the more he can hurt you." A hollow ache of loneliness settled into her chest. "Even if he doesn't try."

She stared silently through the windshield the rest of the way home, wrapped in a comfortless cocoon of uncertainty.

"Hi, David."

"Hello, Melody."

Her gaze caressed his lithe grace as he hung his coat on her coatrack. The mere sight of him triggered a pounding in her heart and head, and she felt alive for the first time all day. "It's late. How was your practice with the soloists?"

"Pretty good." As he turned he became aware of her scrutiny. A spark leaped between them, igniting the kindling of their desire. As they strolled from the vestibule they began eyeing each other, sending unspoken messages of attraction and agreement.

"Do you think the *Messiah* will be ready on time?" Her eyes said, In other words will you have time for me? It's been two whole days since we made love....

"Performances can always be better, but I think it will work." *I'll make time,* his eyes answered.

"I'm glad."

And then she was entangled in the strong web of his arms as he kissed her with the fervor of a man starved for affection. The throbbing in her temples grew with the slowly accelerating touch of his body against hers, extinguishing all concerns about their relationship, extinguishing all thoughts whatsoever. Neither words nor thoughts could match the rippling waves of desire his hands sent through the very fiber of her being as he and Melody littered the path to her bedroom with their clothes. His body filling hers was beyond mere thought, so she just let the experience happen, savoring every delicious sensation as she was devoured by his passion. His love transformed her into an unthinking bundle of erotic delight being carried higher and then higher, blazing new trails of passion toward the summits of ecstasy and fulfillment, where they basked together in the serene glory and wonder of being in love.

Later Melody lay as still as possible so she wouldn't disturb her sleeping lover. She'd felt weary before he arrived, but he'd refreshed her with his love. Her mind gradually began to function once more, churning with the multitudinous details she wanted to tell him or ask his advice about. She was considering a closeout sale at the store to bring in as much as possible for Mr. Klein's hospital bills. She wasn't positive it was a good idea, though, and she wanted David's opinion. His family was in business, after all. He'd probably have some good suggestions.

Then there were the want ads. She wanted to go over with him the job listings in today's *Trib* so he could help her define what she had to offer an employer. Melody smiled fondly at the man breathing quietly beside her in the darkness. Without him she'd surely have panicked by now. He gave her a reason to go on and the strength to persevere.

Gently she stroked the dark, silky strands of his hair that had fanned out on to the cool pillow. Even in sleep the contact of his arms with her side stirred her flesh. How good it had been these few mornings to wake with him beside her, feeling a warm, loving presence as she began the day; how much better it would be to wake beside him every morning. Then her life would be complete. Problems couldn't touch her, then.

Her fingers froze in the act of stroking his locks. Her spine grew cold. Her heart seemed to stop pumping. Her mind slunk back from the dizzying, terrifying direction of her thoughts.

No!

Her world might be crumbling, but that was no reason for her to crumble as well. She was strong enough to handle her own problems. She had to be, or else who was she? Her head wavered from side to side, trying to shake off the debilitating narcotic of passivity David's presence roused in her. Especially now, when her life was changing, she had to be strong.

The shaking of her head woke him. He mumbled something incomprehensible and reached for her.

A helpless horror gripped her as she felt words forming in her throat. She had to speak quickly, before his touch swept away the little strength she possessed. "David," she whispered hoarsely, "I think you'd best go now."

His body stiffened. She sensed him studying her in the dim light. After a second he raised his head. "I must have been having a nightmare," he said. "I dreamed you asked me to leave."

"Just do it. Please!" Bolting upright, she pressed her hands into her cheeks and slid them roughly against her skin till her fingers twined together at the back of her head, hiding her face in a self-made shroud of elbows. David lay motionless for a long time.

David, I love you. Please go. The thoughts whirled through her mind no matter how hard she tried to stop them. *I need you too much, oh, please, say something, no, don't say anything, I couldn't stand it, just go. I love you, go.*

He sat up finally and swung his legs off the bed. As much as she tried to stop her mind, she couldn't obliterate her mental image of the harsh set of his jaw and the rigid tension of his muscles. "Melody," he murmured, "is there anything I can do for you?"

"No! I have to do things for myself. Don't you understand?"

A sharp click and the sudden blood red of light through her eyelids told her he'd turned on the lamp. He grasped her elbows and forced them away from her face. She yanked the sheet up to her chin, refusing to meet his gaze.

"I don't understand," he said. "What are you talking about?"

"Just go."

He smacked his hands against his thighs. "What did I do? Tell me! Come on, Melody. Talk to me. Don't shut yourself away from me like this."

"Please," she whispered miserably, "go."

He waited for her to say something more. When she didn't he picked up his clothes and padded to the hall. He stood there for a long time, then ended his waiting with an explosive oath. "I know you're under a lot of strain, Melody, but still . . ." He gave her another chance to speak.

Silence.

Then, amazingly, his voice grew gentle. "I'll call you tomorrow, when you're rational."

The tears began crawling down her cheeks only when she felt the front door slam.

Chapter Eight

I'll be there before you start waving your baton. I promise."

David didn't answer immediately. He stared instead toward the members of the Hyde Park Orchestra milling on stage during the break. A horn player started to approach him, but something in David's face made the woman retreat.

"Melody," he said levelly, "you've never heard me conduct a real orchestra, not one like the Chicago Philharmonic, and I wanted to make it an evening to remember. Dinner at a quiet little restaurant, you backstage with me before the concert, the reception afterward."

"It sounds marvelous," she replied quickly, as if the speed of her response could somehow atone for the insensitivity of her message.

"There's a *but* coming. I can feel it."

"No, David, it really does." And it did. She wanted to share every moment of his life, the lows as well as the highs. She longed to know his every thought, to mingle her soul with his, to merge minds as they did bodies, but she was scared. Why must he want so much more intimacy than she could give? He wanted her time, her thoughts, her feelings, her fears, delights, anxieties. He wanted all of her.

And that she couldn't give and still keep.

With a surge of annoyance prickling along her spine, she steeled herself to withstand his loving demands. This conversation, or variations, had replayed and escalated over the past few weeks till it grated on her nerves like fingernails rasping across a chalkboard. "I have to work late, David, but I'll leave in plenty of time to catch a train for your concert. I want to be with you. It's just that things are moving so fast between us."

"Fast?"

She hurried on. "I have to work on the closeout sale." A note of desperation crept into her voice. "It's not as important as conducting the Philharmonic, but it's my job."

"Among the things you haven't mentioned is that you were having a closeout sale." To her it felt like an accusation, despite his mild tone. He opened his mouth as if to ask more, much more, but he buried the words and even managed a smile. "Okay. I won't push you. I guess that's my end of the problem. I'll leave a ticket for you at the box office and send someone to bring you backstage afterward." His eyes narrowed the tiniest bit. "That is, if it's all right with you."

She wanted to stroke his cheek to reassure him that she wasn't trying to hurt him, that he just expected too much, that she did love him. But all she did was nod.

Faint violin echoes accused Melody's ears from inside the concert hall. Not only was she frozen from standing in this

elegant but thin gown on a train platform that was exposed
to frigid lake gusts. Worse, she'd missed the beginning of
David's concert, and the Orchestra Hall ushers wouldn't let
her in till the first piece was finished.

It would serve her right if he was furious. Unforgivable of
her. Stupid. Pigheaded. She shouldn't have tried to mark
down the paint prices before she left. Her numb hands
scarcely obeyed her will as she dragged a comb through her
wind-damaged hair.

I'll be there before you start waving your baton. Damn.

Ringing applause roused her from her somber thoughts.
As the blue-uniformed usher led her to a seat close to the
stage, she prayed David wouldn't turn and see her sneaking
in late. Her face flamed. Maybe he hadn't noticed her absence. She wished the men between the aisle and her seat
weren't such gentlemen. She'd rather crawl over their laps
on hands and knees than have them rise like signal flags,
shouting to the concertgoers in all the balconies that she
didn't even care enough to arrive on time.

The music began again as she smoothed the black gown
over her lap. She checked her program; it was Prokofiev.
She tried to relax and use her new perspective to study the
interplay of instruments in the merry, unfamiliar symphony, but instead her gaze and thoughts kept wandering to
David. It was hard for her to believe the imposing figure in
long black coattails was the same patient man she loved.
Was this swaying brown hair the same hair she ran her fingers through as they made love? Were those diving and
swooping arms the same arms that held her in a warm, protected embrace?

It couldn't be. While she felt proud of his easy mastery,
she also felt estranged. She wasn't part of this world. She
applauded loudly at the end of the Prokofiev, but she felt
like an outsider, a mere member of the audience, hopelessly cut off from him.

The intermission added to her feeling of isolation. If she had come with him as he asked, they might have made arrangements to meet. But she had no one but herself to blame for having to wander the corridors alone among the buzzing couples.

She weaved through the lobby to a pay phone, then muffled her ear with her hand. "Hello. I'd like to check on the status of one of your patients, Herbert Klein...room 814.... He what? Not intensive care again...well, thank you."

The second half of the concert went past in a haze. Judging by the audience response, Melody wasn't the only one who found David magnificent. The crowd clapped and bravoed through four curtain calls, then buzzed with comment about the brilliant new conductor, David Halifax.

An usher came to bring her to the reception for orchestra patrons. The man led her through the plain yet glamorous world of backstage to a large room hung with red velvet curtains, filled with people wearing mink stoles and diamond tie clasps. They were clustered around a towering figure: David. His eyes flashed, and his darting movements sparkled with triumph and excitement.

"Melody!" He ran and whirled her around in the gleeful bear hug of a man intoxicated with life.

"You were marvelous, David. If people's hands weren't sore, they'd still be clapping."

"Of course. That's the only reason my audiences ever stop." His laughter was different than usual, more vivid and wild, as if a new facet of his personality had come to the fore. "Come meet the governor."

She stood rooted to the spot despite his tugging. "What governor?" she whispered.

"Of Illinois."

His exuberant tugging grew stronger, till Melody was reeled like an exhausted trout into the company of not only the governor but the deputy mayor, two state senators and their wives. She kept diligently silent till the group dissolved and a grandmotherly lady with fewer jewels than most came to congratulate David. Melody fell into small talk with the lady—yes, the champagne is excellent for a domestic; no, she hadn't met David in Boston—though she kept glancing at David as he charmed a gaggle of matrons. She was both awed by the respect he garnered for his artistic success and a bit amused, as well; she noted that the majority of the people introducing themselves to him were women, and despite the sophistication of the women's designer gowns, many a pair of eyes grew round as they followed his height up, up, up.

"Well, Melody," David said during a respite from wellwishers. "I see you've met Mrs. Drewston, the chairman of the Chamber of Commerce."

Melody blinked. *Chamber of Commerce?* The woman beside her seemed so, so *everyday*. Well, she should have known she was the only mutt in this dog show.

One by one the guests left. David's eyes still glowed, and he positively chattered as he led her to his small but wellappointed dressing room. A velour love seat against one wall and an oak dressing table against the opposite wall framed the open doorway to a private shower. The effect of the tasteful furnishings was somewhat spoiled by the harsh glare of the bare bulbs that ringed the dressing table mirror.

Now that she was alone with him, David's mood was infectious. She laughed gaily as she bent to smell a bouquet of roses on the table. "I gather you're happy with the concert."

"It was fantastic. Wonderful. Extraordinary. Nights like tonight are why I'm a conductor. I mean, I go along doing my everyday work, thinking I enjoy conducting—and I do—but occasionally the music springs abruptly to life and pours its magic into my soul." He paced the small room, unable to contain the magic inside him. "I don't know if I can explain. Words can't capture the feeling. It's as if I'm no longer just conducting the music, but I am the music. I'm not David Halifax anymore. I'm Serge Prokofiev, listening in awe to the miracle of his own genius. I'm Stradivarius, transported by the beauty of his violins. I'm the crisp blare of the trumpets. I am the music. The music is me."

A shiver rippled down Melody's spine. "I think I understand. I mean, I know it isn't the same thing as your music, but that's sort of how I feel when we make love."

The fire in his eyes flared. He wrapped his arms around her and kissed her with a fierceness that sprang perhaps more from music than from desire. But before his lips left hers, she felt his interest quicken and his desire harden, and she found herself dissolving under the smooth insistence of his hands on the bare flesh of her back.

He pulled away briefly to pierce her with a wild, hungry half smile before reclaiming her mouth. The delicious, demanding touch of his tongue on hers overpowered her senses so thoroughly that she was unaware he'd pulled down the backless gown's short zipper till she felt the ease with which the material began to slip from her shoulders, pushed by his forceful caresses.

"David," she began, but further words were drowned under the torrent of his passionate lips on her. Her blood was beginning to turn to honey, but he was already pulling the dress from her arms, too soon, too quickly. She glanced at the door and spoke breathlessly. "Is the door locked, David?"

"No one else is here." His luminous eyes caused goose bumps as his gaze paused passionately on her shoulders and breasts. She stood there, holding the dress by one sleeve as he checked the door. "Damn. No lock." When he touched the door it swung open an inch. Melody hurriedly pulled the gown in front of her, though no one could have seen. "Hand me the chair."

She stood as if frozen, not at all sure she trusted this place. Undecided as to whether she should help or stop him, she watched as he grabbed the chair from the dressing table and jammed it under the doorknob.

"We shouldn't be doing this here, David. Someone might catch us."

As if to emphasize her words, a bray of laughter erupted from the other side of the door, followed by several sets of footsteps. She ran her fingers through his brown hair. "Can't you wait till we get home?"

"No," he said simply and forcefully. Then he paused. She saw the effort on his face and in his whole body as he reined in his passion for her sake. His next words came slowly. "But I guess I must. I understand, Melody, and I won't force you to do anything against your will. Ever."

Grand words. But his eyes amended the message. *Make love to me,* they urged.

A tender smile spread slowly across her features as she stood silently, listening to the pounding of her heart, watching the strong, masculine set of his shoulders. He looked stunning in a tuxedo, like a conquering hero in his hour of triumph. In the end she heeded neither his words nor his eyes but the steadily rising tempo of her pulse as it spread sultry warmth throughout her body.

When she lowered her arms the dress slid with an intimate whisper to the floor.

As they drove south, away from Orchestra Hall and its magic, Melody stretched with the unself-conscious languor of a satisfied cat. Tonight had taken her by surprise. She had ridden an emotional roller coaster, ending with a hurried, impromptu lovemaking that had been the most surprising of all. "Quickies," as Jason had called them, had always left her frustrated and totally unsatisfied. With David, though . . .

A fond smile whispered across her face. With David lovemaking was perfect. Every time.

She wondered dreamily if that would always be true or if the magic could ever leave them. No, she decided. She couldn't imagine a time, as long as blood still ran through her heart, when his touch would fail to spread sharp pangs of desire.

"Thanks for driving me to the hospital to see about Mr. Klein," she said. He had offered to let her drive, as a matter of fact, but she preferred to sit and bask in the warm afterglow of his love.

He caressed her shoulder delicately. "Don't mention it. I'm too keyed up to go home right away, and since you say the hospital's just off the expressway, it won't take long."

"I still appreciate it. The trip takes an hour and a half by bus."

"You realize," he said softly, "they won't let you see him this late at night, especially if he's back in intensive care."

"I've got to try."

"I understand." His voice deepened with sincerity and urgency. "And I want to help you in any way I can, if you'll let me."

"I know."

"If you know I want to help, then let me help. I know you're going through a tough time, but you don't have to go it alone." He shot her a look of concern tinged with regret. "Lately it seems we only communicate physically, when we make love. Melody, I wish you'd talk to me the way you used to. Share your problems with me."

When she said nothing he stared at her for such a long time she grew worried about running into another car. "Why weren't you there for the beginning of the concert?" he asked.

Melody cringed. She'd been so glad he hadn't mentioned it that she'd almost begun to believe he hadn't noticed. Her guilt returned in a rush, making her fumble over her words. "The store. I . . . I got so involved marking down the paint that I didn't notice the time." The excuse sounded lame even to her.

"Sure." He stomped on the gas pedal, sending the Burgundy Flash surging forward with a startling suddenness that pushed her into the seat back. His fingers, usually so loving and delicate, curled grimly around the steering wheel. "The real reason wouldn't have something to do with how you feel about me, would it? I have this terrible feeling you're trying to ease out of our relationship and that one day soon you'll disappear completely from my life."

The lump in her throat made speech difficult. She hadn't realized how much she'd hurt him already. "David, I love you."

When he finally answered, the razor edges of pain and anger in his voice were somewhat blunted. "It's hard when you love someone more than they love you."

Her mind whirled at the unimaginable prospect of a love greater than what she felt for him. Was this the problem, that she was incapable of loving? Was what she felt a cheap imitation of what the rest of the world meant by love? That would explain so much about her life: a defect in her heart. "David, I . . ." A quivering sigh erupted from the depths of her soul. "I never meant to hurt you. It's just that . . . well, everything is turned end over end, and I feel I have to guard my independence."

"Your independence? Melody, I want to love you, not control you."

"Love is a kind of control, you know. Right now, I need—"

He interrupted her brusquely. "What about *my* needs? I've been patient with you, more patient than I thought possible. Day and night for weeks I couldn't think of anything but going to bed with you. The wait was worth it, though, because for a few precious days after we first made love, we shared something so perfect that not even Mozart could have captured its beauty. I had never felt closer to anyone in my life, and I was addicted to the feeling on the spot. But ever since then you've shut yourself away from me. You won't talk about anything important. You won't let me help you or even give you moral support. Being patient doesn't seem to work anymore. You give me your body but not your mind, and *I need both*."

She was crying by the time he finished. Words and thoughts escaped her. She simply cried. At first he offered no comfort, but then she felt him gently touch her shoulder. She took his hand in her own and pressed it fiercely to her cheek, held it as if she would never let go.

"You win," she said when her tears had washed away the worst of the pain, leaving behind a curiously lighthearted sense of relief. "You want me to talk? I'll talk. You want all the gory details of my problems—well, here they come. I hope your shoulders don't get too wet from all the crying I'm about to do.

"First," she said, "I've combed Hyde Park for jobs. There aren't any good ones. At least none I'm qualified for. Second, there's nothing promising downtown either, though maybe a decent job will turn up there eventually. Third, the bank manager is very sympathetic but very sorry. Under the terms of my mortgage the advances I've paid shorten the time I have to pay, but in the meantime I have to keep up the payments. Furthermore, one of the prices of my unusually short-term mortgage is that it can't be renegotiated. He says they won't foreclose immediately but..." She swallowed the lump in her throat, hoping he wouldn't notice how close she was to tears. "Fourth, I do have a temporary job lined up until after the Christmas holidays."

He shook his head. "I asked for this, didn't I? Well, at least something good is happening. What's the job?"

She stared out the windshield at the endless stretch of taillights ahead of them. "Cashier at the grocery store," she said tonelessly.

David said nothing, and she was grateful. He knew her dreams and ambitions. He knew the job meant humiliation, and no words could change that. She snuggled into the protective custody of his arm, wishing the world and all its problems would go away.

The massive, middle-aged nurse at the eighth-floor desk, whose name tag read D. Kowalski, R.N., adamantly refused to let Melody see Mr. Klein. "All I can tell you," the woman said, "is that he's back in a coma. He's being monitored by machines." Then she looked scathingly at Melody's cape and elegant gown. "When *my* father was dying last summer, I did more than visit him one single time, at the end of a fancy night out."

Melody cast her a startled look, and Nurse Kowalski grew contrite. "I'm sorry," she said. "I know it's none of my business. It just bothers me to see an old man like him so alone."

"I'm not his daughter. I'm a friend. Well, an employee, at least. My name is Melody Ross."

"You're Melody?" Nurse Kowalski's swift look of empathy surprised Melody. "He was muttering your name over and over before he went into the coma."

"*My* name?" She shook her head in confusion. "There must be some mistake."

"No mistake, Melody. Look, I really shouldn't do this, but I'm going to fudge a bit and put in the register that his daughter arrived slightly after visiting hours and saw him for five minutes."

The intensive care ward, where hope was not quite abandoned yet certainly strained, had the darkness of gloom. Despite the pervasive electronic hum of medical machines,

Melody almost felt she should tiptoe to maintain the near-deathly stillness. Mr. Klein was a mere parody of himself, with a colorless face and his emaciated body nearly invisible under the blankets. As she touched his cool fingers she tried to blot out the antiseptic smell of the room. She shifted from foot to foot, not knowing what to do. Finally she leaned across the bed and put her head close to his face.

"Mr. Klein," she whispered haltingly, "I know you don't like me to be emotional, so I'll try to keep this as business-like as I can. Which may not be very businesslike, I'm afraid. Well, I'm trying to close out the store the way you'd want. Your clearance sale is doing pretty well. Al Jevaert must have spent all his profits for the year, stocking up on this and that. You'll have a few extra dollars for your hospital bills."

She stopped to search her purse for a handkerchief. She wasn't going to cry, she wasn't. The image of Mr. Klein's scornful face whenever she had let her emotions show kept the tears painfully inside. "I'm sorry, Mr. Klein, but either I have to tell you how I feel or the dam's going to burst and I'll start blubbering. I—I feel terrible about not being with you that Saturday. I'm sorry. I hurt for you, and I miss you."

Her fists were clenched from the effort of talking calmly. She paused to collect herself before continuing. "You've been like a father to me, you know. More than my own dad. Even if you never loved me, you at least gave me the chance to grow. Mr. Klein—Herb—thank you."

Her next words were so quiet even she wasn't sure she said them aloud. "I love you."

She turned to go. As she did, one quick sob escaped her, and she whirled back, hugged his shoulder and kissed him tenderly on the cheek.

Later that night he died.

* * *

Melody took a long look around the lonesome, lifeless store. The shelves were half empty, the ceiling fans as still as death. In the twilight, she imagined spiderwebs already covering the room with a blanket of desertion.

And then she slowly pulled the door closed for the last time. This was it.

Mr. Klein's death had postponed the sale to Strong Hardware until the reading of the will tomorrow. Bob Gold had advised her that Doris Klein would be signing the papers immediately after the reading, so the store should close for good today. It seemed as if Melody should feel sad or relieved or nostalgic; she should feel *something*. But she didn't. Numbly she locked the door on a chapter of her life.

She'd been pleased but only half surprised when Mr. Gold had requested her presence at the opening of the will. Ever since Bob had mentioned that Mr. Klein had written a new, secret will three months ago, around the time she'd talked him into getting the computer, she'd wondered if the machine wasn't intended as her legacy. It was the kind of unsentimental gesture typical of him, and it would explain his attitude toward the computer, as if it was her exclusive property that he wanted nothing to do with.

Melody lifted her head as she turned resolutely away from the store. She'd survive, and on her own terms. Somehow she'd survive.

A cold winter rain spoiled her brave exit, however. She hadn't realized how miserable the weather was till she was outside in it. She was almost tempted to wait in the store till the rain stopped or turned to snow. But no; the store was gone, and she could never go back.

By the time she got to the corner she was chilled despite her umbrella. A car would be so wonderful at a time like this. David and the Flash began to materialize in her mind, but she shoved the picture away. He was a narcotic to her battered self-image, a drug that she must take only in moderation or become hopelessly, mindlessly addicted.

On her own terms.

"Hey, Mel!" Eric, the janitor of the building she was passing, beckoned to her from the open glass door of a vestibule. "You trying to drown or something? Come on in and wait it out."

She hesitated. In the vestibule she wouldn't have to cope with all the store's memories. Besides, Eric had gone out of his way to be civil lately. A trickle of ice water dribbling down her back spurred her decision.

Eric put his hand on her elbow as she went through the door, and she was momentarily reminded of when—was it really only a few months ago, or was it in a previous incarnation?—he'd been drunk and abrasive in the store. The day was etched in her memory. It had been just before her first date with David.

When she was in the small, tiled vestibule, Eric went back to work fixing a door buzzer, one of a row of buzzers arrayed above the brass mailboxes. His wet black hair glistened and stuck out at odd angles from under the rim of his green work hat. She watched through the glass as the rain rebounded high off the sidewalk and street.

"On days like this," she said, "I wish it would just snow."

Eric snorted. "No way. This is a corner building. At least this stuff I don't have to shovel."

She smiled feebly. Among janitors the complaint was common to the point of triteness. Well, this might be the last time she'd ever hear it.

Eric turned to look into her eyes. "Mel, I'm going to miss you."

She sighed, suddenly regretting the impulse that had drawn her into the vestibule with him.

"Yeah, you're one sexy lady." He took a step toward her. "Many's the time I imagined me and you together in bed—"

He never finished. Suddenly a shadowy figure blackened the dim light from the street. A split second later a man burst through the door and seized Eric by the collar.

"Freeze, turkey!"

Melody's hand flew to her mouth as she recoiled from the violence of the scene. Fear drove Eric's face a vivid red, and the white of his eyeballs was visible all around the circles of his irises. The intruder lifted the janitor from the floor then drove him against the mailboxes.

By standing immobile she'd lost her chance to escape. She felt no fear, only a dreamlike sense of unreality, and the world seemed to shift to slow motion as she stretched her arm toward the doorknob with sickening leisureliness while at the same time the invader swiveled to face her. This couldn't be happening. Not to her, not now, not on top of everything else. The intruder was coming toward her. Scream. She should scream....

"Lamarr!" Pent-up breath exploded from her.

Her ex-stockboy's lip scar was curled into a vicious leer, and she had to remind herself that this was the same lad she'd taught and supervised for months. Had he gone crazy?

"I'm gonna kill this sucker. Just give me the word, Mel. If he so much as laid a hand on you I'm gonna kill him."

When she found her voice she assured Lamarr that she didn't want Eric killed—though it was sweet of Lamarr to offer, thank you. The madness slowly drained from the youth's tense body.

A giggle, part relief and part amusement, bubbled through her as she turned to the janitor, who cringed in the corner of the vestibule. It was terrible of her to laugh at him when he was frightened, but he looked so funny, like a bad actor overdoing a melodrama. Besides, recalling all the times his hands had strayed, she felt as if things were even now. It was easy for her to talk him out of calling the police. She batted her eyelashes once, and that was it. What a fool.

Rain or no rain, she headed home, Lamarr at her side. "I feel like a fool," he admitted sheepishly.

That statement was like a grizzly bear admitting a weakness for sniffing wild daisies, she mused. Or maybe not. Maybe her preconceived notions only made it seem that way. Had she ever probed beneath his scarred face and tough exterior to see what he was like?

"I don't think you're a fool," she said. "Not that I'd recommend you make a habit of doing things like this. And stay well away from Eric in the future."

He gave an exaggerated shrug of his massive shoulders. "No problem. Won't have much reason to come to Hyde Park no more anyhow." He shook rivulets of icy water out of his eyes and pointed to an old, once-fancy convertible parked just ahead. "Give you a ride home?"

"I'd be a fool to refuse." Even Lamarr had a car, and she didn't know if she'd ever be able to afford one now.

Lamarr explained with an apologetic shrug and a pointing finger that the roof leaked onto the passenger seat and she'd have to sit in the back. Leaning forward and laying her chin on the front seat, she said, "It's funny. This is the last day of work, and it's the first time I've ever talked to you about something other than hardware." And immediately she was at a loss for words. But she had to say something. Anything.

"What are you going to do now the store's closed?" Rats. How could she ask him that, of all things? Probably steal hubcaps or sell cocaine.

His quick, confident reply caught her by surprise. "Plumbing. A guy over in Woodlawn runs a nonunion plumbing outfit. Most of the people there can't afford union plumbers. I did a few jobs for him already. I'll be kind of an apprentice. As long as pipes keep busting, I got work."

She smiled as she imagined the startled expressions on people's faces when this plumber came to fix their faucets. "Good for you, Lamarr."

"Yeah, well, it's because of you." His forehead creased into an embarrassed frown, and he hunched over the steering wheel. "I'm no good with words. I can't say too good what I mean. But you gave me a start, a chance. You taught me. You're a good lady. That's why I been watching you every day till you get past that turkey's building, just in case he tries anything. Ever since that day you told me he got fresh."

Melody was amazed, and she didn't know if it was because he cared enough to guard her welfare or simply because this was the longest speech she'd ever heard him make. "Well...thanks." She pursed her lips. He claimed he was no good with words, yet she was the one who was tonguetied. "I'm touched. I never knew...."

His whole body swayed from side to side in pleased bashfulness, and she realized that this was how he spoke. Not with words, which came hard, but with his body. Actions, like guarding her from the indignities of a creep like Eric, were his language.

"Thank you, Lamarr." She leaned forward to give him a peck on the cheek. "Thank you very much."

A dream tore her from sleep the next morning. When she tried to remember it, the details evaporated and she was left with only an impression of terror as she watched someone with a caricature of her own face building a crude wall between her garden and David's balcony, cement block by cement block.

After blinking a few times she was able to read her clock. Eight fifty-three.

It didn't matter. No hardware store today—or ever—and the reading of the will wasn't till eleven. She pulled a pillow over her ear and tried to escape to the oblivion of sleep.

Last night had been the worst. The last time she'd picked up the phone to call David was well after three o'clock. If she were with him, she had thought, he'd shield her in his arms and the future would seem manageable even if it wasn't. And because she needed him so intensely, because she needed the comfort of his presence more than she'd ever needed it before, she had put down the phone each time and suffered alone.

Eight fifty-four. She lay there, staring wide-eyed at her clock from under the overhang of the pillow, just as she'd done last night. If she'd had any whiskey in the house she would have been tempted to lose herself in its artificial anesthetic. Was that how her father and brother felt when they reached for another bottle of beer?

Eight fifty-five. Last night had made her realize that digital LED clocks were instruments of torture, with their glowing, satanical numbers sadistically blaring each and every minute of worried sleeplessness.

Eight fifty-six. She sighed. Oblivion would not come to release her from the confusion engulfing her life.

Eight fifty-seven. David, David . . .

Eight fifty-eight.

Eight fifty-nine.

With an angry cry that was muffled by the pillow to a mere whimper, she threw back the covers and sat up. The clock wasn't the enemy. Self-pity was the enemy, an enemy she had defeated before and would defeat again. Determinedly not thinking about the past or future, she forced herself through her morning chores with an intensity that turned her shower into a ritual cleansing, the toast she meticulously buttered into an offering worthy of sacrifice to the gods, and the train ride downtown into a paragon of mind-less meditation.

Nonetheless, her determined gait masked her nervous-ness as she walked across the thickly carpeted plushness of Mr. Gold's law firm. The gilt-framed paintings on the wall were originals, the furnishings massive oak. Melody felt underdressed. What was one supposed to wear to a reading of a will? She hoped her peach-colored dress wasn't too feminine. She meant Mr. Klein's memory no disrespect.

Bob Gold's working office contrasted sharply with the ostentation of the lobby. His bookcase was disarranged by constant use, his desk blotter latticed with cryptic scrawls and reminders. "Ah, Melody, I'm glad you came a few minutes early. Herbert left some papers for you, and you can read them before we begin."

He opened a filing cabinet with a metallic whoosh and began flipping through papers. "Herb was an interesting man," he commented as he searched. "He knew he was dying, of course, and his reaction was to spend his last months rewriting parts of his diary for the people closest to him. All the things he never told us while he was alive, he saved for after his death, when we couldn't talk back. Did you know he kept diaries?"

She shook her head, wondering with a stab of guilt if he'd had a chance to write about her desertion that Saturday. "No. I knew very little about him, really."

"That figures." Bob pulled out a thin manila envelope and slid the drawer closed. "Herb recopied—with changes, I'm sure—a selection of pages pertinent to his relationships with certain people. His wife and daughters, his nephews, myself—and you."

He tapped the envelope against his hand and looked her steadily in the eye. "I should warn you, Melody, that Herb was a rather vengeful man and maybe you won't like what you read. I haven't read your file, of course, but Doris is livid about hers, his daughter, Gretchen, refused to even come today because of what he wrote in hers, and I'm mad as hell about mine. Do you know he wouldn't even let me write up this will? Had one of my junior partners do it instead. If that schlemiel had ever come out with his suspicions about the sale of that damned apartment building on Minerva, instead of letting them poison our friendship, we would have stayed friends. I mean, we both lost money on that deal, but I didn't cheat him, and besides.... Oh, never mind."

He handed her the sealed envelope as he stood to leave. "You can read the file in here. I'll be in the conference room if you need me, and I'll let you know when the proceedings begin."

She heard the rustling of his feet on the carpet as he moved to the door behind her. She didn't turn, only stared at the deceptively normal-looking envelope in her hand.

"And Melody," she heard him say just before he closed the door, "try not to judge poor Herbert too harshly."

Chapter Nine

The envelope seemed to burn her fingertips. After a buildup like that, she was almost afraid to open it. She hesitantly pulled out a few crisp, stationery-quality sheets covered with neat, careful script. At least there wasn't a lot to read. Taking a deep breath, she picked up the first page, dated eight years earlier, when she'd first begun working at Klein's Hardware.

Tuesday, March 18

The new girl knows nothing about hardware—so insecure she checks with me before each breath. Her eyes cringe like she expects me to jump on her for the tiniest mistake even if she doesn't know it's a mistake. Like today, when getting a stepladder she knocked a 50 lb. box of one-inch finishing nails onto the storeroom floor. I was going to yell, had my mouth open. Damned if I know why I didn't. She almost had a heart attack when I got down on my hands and knees with her to pick them up.

She's ten years younger than my Gretchen. Maybe that's why I didn't yell, her age and vulnerability. I would have yelled at Gretchen, though. Gretchen needed yelling at. Still does, not that it would do any good.

Maybe that's it. Mel needs understanding and patience, and with her it might do some good. Interesting to find out, at least. With some self-confidence she could be someone special.

Monday, January 3

All day Melody didn't smile. Puffy eyes. When I locked the door at 5:30 I caught her wiping away a tear. Jason was drunk for the first time in their marriage and ruined her holidays, she explained, and then began crying for real. Put her head on my chest and started to cry. Something about unemployment tearing Jason apart— blaming her for the lack of presents under the tree and for the rent being due.

And there's nothing I can do about it. Here I am, getting a second chance at being a father, and there's not a damn thing I can do to help her. So frustrated I pushed her away and told her to stop crying. What else could I do? Tell her I loved her and have her call me a dirty old man?

Unbearable if that happened.

Melody put down the sheets. Mr. Klein's feelings for her were astounding, to say the least. He loved her?

She'd just begun to read the next sheet, dated several months later, when the receptionist called her to the elegant conference room.

Melody felt ill at ease there. Mr. Gold's harsh epitaph writhed through her melancholy thoughts; none of these uncaring faces had shed tears for Herbert. She was the only nonfamily member present, and the hatchet-nosed Doris Klein stared at her as if she were an unwelcome intruder. Melody wondered uneasily if any of Doris's diary pages alluded to Herbert's feelings for her. That would explain the glare. Uncomfortable and bored, after a while Melody tuned out the legalese Bob was spouting and sought refuge in the next page of Mr. Klein's diary.

Wednesday, August 22

Mel should leave that husband of hers. She's much too good for him. Jason came around the store today and talked to her in the storeroom, and he held her and kissed her. The creep. Then she came to my office just as nervous as when she first started and asked for an advance. His doing. When I told her no, she looked even more nervous and upset, and that hurt. I'd give her the money gladly, but not him. He's like my darling daughters. Spoiled. Daddy works hard for years. Do they appreciate the struggle? Ha. But when they're on their own they expect to start with all the things it took me a lifetime to get. Jason's dad was a steel company executive or something, but that doesn't give him the God-given right to live like an executive too.

Mel's not like that. She's more like me—a builder, not a parasite. Good kid. I wish *she* was my daughter.

The next few pages of the diary spanned the last six years of her time at Klein's. Bob was still droning multisyllable words about real estate holdings going to the wife and stocks to the daughters, so she continued to read.

Thursday, October 16

Mel told me she filed for divorce, and Jason isn't going to contest it. About time, what with him living with that horse-faced blonde. Bad taste, on top of his other faults. As soon as he gets a job that pays more than Mel, he dumps her. Idiot.

I was proud of her. Not so much for the divorce but for the strength in her voice when she told me. Divorce was inevitable, but I was worried it would hurt my darling. Now my worry is that I'll lose her. She's such a crackerjack at math, maybe I'll train her to do the books—not that I need help with them. Even if she doesn't stay here she needs more job skills. Least I can do for her.

Tuesday, September 11

Mel needs a man, someone who loves her enough to let her live out her ambitions. That light in her eyes when she faces a new challenge always surprises me, even after knowing her for years. Like today I said I was too busy to make out the order for electrical supplies, and she almost pounced with her offer to do it for me. Hope I haven't given her too much, though. Oh, well, I'll check her order against what we really need before it goes out, and if she's way off base I'll talk to her about it. Makes more work for me this way, but as I said, Mel needs me.

Wednesday, November 23

Mel asked if I'd help her move to her new town house. It hurt that she was so hesitant about asking. She knows how I feel about her, yet she looked as if she expected me to yell at her or something. My stomach's really bothering me lately, so I said no. She'll understand. She always does. Another ulcer, I imagine. Suppose I should go to the leech. Hate those guys, though.

Wish Mel would get married—to a good man this time. Be so much happier with a good man at her side, someone to look after her.

This is ridiculous. I'm too old to do this father-of-the-bride routine again.

                                    Tuesday, July 17
Don't know about that girl. Today Mel canceled my account with Louis Burbank Tools, and she didn't even consult me first! Louie and I go way back—I had him over for supper just five, six years ago. About as close as I've come to losing my temper with her, but I didn't say anything.

Now I'm sorry I left those night school brochures where she could see them. "How to Run a Small Business"—ha! If this new distributor isn't a *lot* faster and cheaper I'm taking charge again myself. Been getting antsy anyway, with nothing important left to do at my own store. Thought she was developing business sense, then she pulls a dumb stunt like this. Can't let her ruin the place now that Strong is down the street. No room for mistakes anymore.

Melody's mind was swimming when she laid the paper in her lap. Never, not once, had Mr. Klein said a word about any of this. Mr. Gold's voice was a mere background rumble as she picked up the last sheet in fingers that trembled—because the final entry was dated the night before she'd stormed away from their quarrel.

                                Thursday, November 9
There's some good news, at least. The sales figures are good. Business is still down a bit, but Mel's cut ex-

penses way down. Glad I decided to keep the place rather than sell out to Strong Hardware, like Doris wants. Work fills my days, gets my mind off what's growing inside me. At work I'm with Mel. Much better than staying at home with a wife who treats me like I'm already dead.

Mel doesn't need me at the store anymore, of course. She's got a lot of good ideas, and I'm no longer sure where she gets them. Not from me. My store has entered the modern world, leaving me behind. To rot.

Shyster Bob asked me today if I had any regrets. Of course I do, but I wouldn't give him the satisfaction. I regret I treated Mel so rough she couldn't love me. And that I've never kissed my darling girl.

Had to stop just now. Pain. How much longer? Not much, please. Better call Mel. She mentioned a date with some guy, but she'll come in tomorrow. She wouldn't let me down.

In my whole life she's the only person who never let me down.

As Melody put down the last page, her eyes filled with tears. *The only person who never let me down.*

She wasn't aware of the covert stares of the other people in the room. She scarcely heard Bob's voice droning, "The building goes to Doris. And to my beloved Melody Ross, who has singlehandedly kept the hardware store going...."

When he stopped with a startled intake of breath, she was vaguely aware that he was staring at her, staring at the tear trickling down her cheek. His birdlike features softened, and he cleared his throat loudly before continuing in a voice that was filled with surprise and other, less easily identifiable emotions.

"To Melody Ross, I leave Klein's Hardware Store."

Mr. Gold watched her for a reaction, but it was almost as if she hadn't heard his words or the gasp from Mrs. Klein. He watched the slow course of the tear down her face, cleared his throat again, and wiped quickly at his own eye with the back of his hand. "It's yours, Melody. All yours."

As soon as everything was over, she asked Bob if she could use a telephone in private. He led her down the hall to the office where she'd started reading Mr. Klein's diary. In the lobby she glimpsed Ted Gleason and an older man in a flashy checked suit that accentuated his ample girth. Probably the regional manager Ted had blamed for his deceit. The man reminded her of the used-car salesman who sponsored the late movie on TV. He was talking with Doris Klein, who pointed venomously at Melody.

The number she dialed rang five times before a weary, defeated voice answered. Melody said, "Hello, Papa. How are you?" She wrapped the phone cord around and around her finger, suddenly unsure why she had this urgent need to talk to her father. "No, I'm fine. I just wanted to say hello.... No, really, there's no problem. Uh, Papa, do you—do you love me...?

"It's not a silly question, Papa. Sometimes people assume other people know how they feel when really they don't, and the words that could make everybody feel better never get said.... I know I'm not making much sense, but do you? Come on, Papa, answer me! It's important."

The last trace of her composure melted, and tears streamed freely down her cheeks. "I love you, too, Papa. Thank you for saying it.... No, I'm fine. I guess a daughter just likes to hear the words every fifteen or twenty years.... No, that's all. That's enough, believe me. Bye, Papa. I love you!"

Only after she hung up did she realize she'd forgotten to mention her inheritance.

When she emerged into the lobby, dabbing at her red, tear-streaked face, she was met by Ted Gleason and his companion, who had the small, predatory eyes of a shark. "Melody," Ted said with a subservient gesture to the other man, "I'd like you to meet Rory Henderson, the regional supervisor for Strong Hardware."

"Yes, you mentioned him to me."

Ted's face stirred hardly a muscle, but his eyes pleaded with her, so she didn't elaborate. She shook Henderson's hand with distaste. So this was the man who'd hatched the plot to hire her simply to scuttle Mr. Klein, then withdrawn the offer when she really needed it. Not wanting to seem weak and emotional in front of him, she tried, with some success, to stifle her sniffles.

After a few insincere words of condolence, Henderson got to the point. "I'll be honest with you, dearie. We were prepared to close a deal with Mrs. Klein, but since you, for some reason—" he winked suggestively "—inherited the place instead, we're ready to make you an offer. I think you'll find this amount more than generous."

She glanced abstractedly at the figure on the memo pad he handed her. With a snort she started to give it back. Though it was more money than she'd ever hoped to have at one time, it didn't even match the value of the remaining inventory. When he reached for the paper, she yanked it back on impulse. He must think she was as much a sentimental sap as she looked right now. Or maybe he was counting on her sorrow. She'd show this vulture....

She knew the precise value of the inventory. Because she didn't like Mr. Henderson or his tactics, she tacked on an extra ten thousand for the store's good name and for revenge. She scribbled a figure on the memo pad and thrust it against his ample paunch. Even though he'd never give her that much, she'd show him she wouldn't be taken advantage of.

"You can't have the computer. Herbert would want me to have it. But if you want Klein's Hardware, this is what it'll cost you. Otherwise I'll drive *you* out of Hyde Park."

Ted hid a smile behind his hand when Mr. Henderson's face went red. "This is preposterous, dearie," he protested in an oily voice. "That store is worthless to a little girl like you now that Klein is gone—"

Ted interrupted, then motioned his supervisor down the hall for a conference. She couldn't hear what they said, but Ted kept pointing at her.

It was nice of Ted to stand up for her, but she couldn't keep the business going, she realized wearily. Too much of the stock had been sold in the closeout sale, and Mrs. Klein had the proceeds. Besides which, Melody vaguely recalled that Mrs. Klein had inherited the building, and she was sure the store would have to move. That cost money, as did restocking the shelves. Even if she could get a loan, the interest would plunge a bloody red knife through the store's fragile balance sheet.

Rory Henderson was subdued when he walked back toward her. Well, if he refrained from calling her dearie, she'd settle, on his terms if necessary. But if he called her dearie once more, she'd punch him. So help her she'd punch him in his fat gut, once for Herbert and once for herself.

Henderson looked warily from Ted to Melody before he spoke. "Ms. Ross, I think we can meet your price. It will take a day or so to have the papers redrawn. Is Mr. Gold your attorney?"

In a daze, she nodded. There was no one else she'd rather have, and she was sure he'd represent her.

Henderson nodded stiffly. "Fine. I'll phone him tomorrow. Come, Gleason."

As the two men walked away, Ted turned briefly to flash a thumbs-up gesture and a quick smile.

* * *

The air in the crowded room under the stage crackled with the tension of amateurs with preconcert jitters. Melody sucked on her reed and glanced around the room. The man sitting on the stack of backdrops on her right sawed furiously on his violin, his bow tie undone and a thin line of perspiration beading his forehead. Only Greg appeared as calm as usual.

As Melody fit the three pieces of her instrument together she was sure that she was the most nervous of all. For one thing, this was her first performance since high school. For another, her reed wasn't working properly.

But overriding those petty concerns was David.

She hadn't talked to him since the reading of the will. She'd saved the good news of her inheritance till tonight, because she'd had so many things to contemplate over the past three days, such as the details of Strong's purchase and her excitingly impulsive purchase yesterday. But of all the changes storming through her life, the most powerful was the realization that people did love her; people cared. Mr. Klein. Lamarr. Noelle. Papa. Even Ted Gleason had looked after her interests, for heaven's sake. She wasn't alone in life.

But facing life staunchly alone had been her style. From the age of twelve she'd been the uncomplaining heroine handling whatever problems came her way, caring about people but not depending on them to care in return. *Afraid* to let them care in return.

And David. She'd been even more afraid of his love. Afraid, she now realized, to trust or even believe in his love. He deserved better than that. Well, she would make it up to him. She had a lot to say to him tonight, and the weight of her words were a burden that made her shoulders tremble. Their relationship was salvageable—it had to be salvageable—but she had to stop shutting him out and start explaining how she felt.

How exactly did she feel? That was what she'd spent the best part of three days figuring out: vulnerable, anxious, scared. But hopeful, at last hopeful.

She stuffed the reed in her mouth and picked up her sheet music, oblivious to the chatter and music around her. It would be hard to open her armor. She would explain that he'd have to be patient with her, because she couldn't change herself overnight.

A cool snake of doubt slithered down her spine. Did he have enough patience left to help her grow? What if they couldn't work things out?

No! She was doing it again. David was a remarkable man. He loved her. She loved him. She would trust and believe in him, no matter how hard. For years she'd been sick, the wounds of her mother's desertion by death still festering; the bruises of her ineffectual yet stern father still vivid; scarred by her reckless choice of an immature husband she'd loved but not liked; ill with the disease of not seeing or trusting in love.

And David could cure her.

Through the chaos of noise her ears seized upon a metallic scuffling on the steep stairway to the stage. David. He stopped halfway down the stairs, and her heart leaped at the sight of him. His bow tie and ruffled shirt lifted him out of the ordinary world and into the romantic realm of heroes of yesteryear. His pose, with one foot resting on a higher step, reinforced the impression of an intrepid commander inspecting his troops before battle.

She found herself edging her way through the throng toward the base of the stairs. How could she summarize all her thoughts into a brusque, loving greeting, one that conveyed both love and her resolve to improve their relationship? Just as she opened her mouth she recalled the last time she'd seen him in—and out of—his tuxedo, and her words evaporated into breathlessness. "Uh, hi."

"Hello."

So curt, she thought.

"You look nice, Melody."

She swallowed, recalling how she'd worn the same long black gown, too, that night at Orchestra Hall. "So do you." She kept her eyes firmly raised. "I have to talk to you."

A flicker of unease danced across his features. "I'm not surprised. Well, save it till later. Right now we have music to make."

His expression stabbed into her heart. So, he expected her to end their relationship, or something equally dire. Had she let things degenerate so much he no longer trusted her love, either? Under other circumstances she would have reassured him with a kiss, but the narrow, winding stairway made that impossible.

"It's not what you think," she said. Several musicians pressed against her back, taking David's appearance as the signal to go onstage. "Later, David."

In front of an audience comprised mostly of friends and relatives, the orchestra members tuned carefully to Noelle's hesitant A and then waited tensely for David to stride to the podium. The applause that greeted him was enthusiastic; news of his Orchestra Hall success had preceded him. He raised his baton, and for just a split second his eyes locked on to hers.

The first half of the concert was brilliant. Under David's masterful guidance Schubert's Unfinished Symphony came to life, imbuing each orchestra member with a portion of its timeless beauty and grace, which spurred them to play beyond what they had dreamed possible. Melody was shaken by this involvement in something greater than herself, something that transcended her yet depended on even her contribution. Practice at home was nothing like this. Rehearsal was nothing like this. And, judging by the startled, rapt faces of the musicians around her when the last note was engulfed by thunderous applause, she realized that performances weren't usually like this, either.

It was David's doing. Her eyes treasured his well-dressed beauty as he bowed to the orchestra, his brown hair fringed with a spectacular silvery halo by the spotlights.

After the intermission, Melody filed onto the stage for the second half of the concert. Once again David caught her eye for an instant, and her mind was warmed by memories of his now-comprehensible elation after the Chicago Philharmonic concert—and of the transformation of that elation into vibrant passion.

Unfortunately, the magic deserted them. The oboe parts were more prominent in the second half, and the oboes, along with the cellos, were the orchestra's weakest links. As Melody had feared, confidence deserted her whenever her part was exposed. Knowing she could play better, she was embarrassed.

Noelle fared still worse. During the suite by Aaron Copland, she mangled the tricky rhythms in an exposed passage, confusing Melody so thoroughly that she stopped playing. Abruptly deprived of moral support, Noelle stopped as well, and a gaping hole ripped through the music. The confusion spread as other players were suddenly uncertain where their parts fit into the overall picture. Noelle's face turned the color of her hair.

With a fierce frown David waved the orchestra to a halt. The audience buzzed as he directed them to start again at letter G. The cohesive confidence of the group was shattered, and the concert limped to its conclusion.

Afterward Melody walked with Noelle through the unseasonably warm December evening the short distance to Greg's house for the orchestra party—or wake, as the case might be. She saw in the dim light of the streetlamps the strain filling Noelle's face. Melody laid an arm around her friend's bulky coat. "I stopped playing first, you know."

Noelle nodded wordlessly.

"If you don't feel up to it, we don't have to go to this party."

Noelle shrugged and tried a laugh. "Don't be silly. Chris will be there, and I wouldn't miss it for the world. Let's go have fun, fun, fun."

Greg's place was one of the large old houses bordering the campus to the east. His wife, a matronly woman whose easy, cheerful manner contrasted sharply with that of her husband, met them at the door with directions to a bedroom-turned-cloakroom and to the table that served as the bar.

Noelle downed a vodka screwdriver as if it were straight orange juice, immediately refilled her glass and then faced the party with such an impressively cheerful smile that probably only Melody realized how false it was. She stayed with her friend till Noelle and Chris got together. A tentative romance was blossoming between them, and he was the best medicine for her.

And then Melody all but forgot about Noelle as David entered. Though she was part of a small group dissecting the evening's disaster, her gaze and her mind continually strayed to his towering form as he moved from musician to musician, exchanging pleasantries and congratulations. When he drew nearer, she disengaged herself from her group and sat on the huge raised hearth so that when he sat beside her they were relatively alone among the standing crowd.

"Hello, Melody. Nice concert."

"Please, spare me the meaningless fluff. The Copland wasn't so nice."

"Don't fret about that. It's just an amateur concert. There's not that much riding on it."

Her glance strayed to where Noelle stood laughing too loudly at one of Chris's jokes. "That doesn't make it any easier to feel responsible for a debacle."

He followed the path of her eyes. "Don't you know, Melody, it's always the conductor's fault when things go wrong?"

"But it wasn't you who stopped playing—"

"That doesn't matter," he interrupted. "To the audience I'm responsible. And the audience is right, since I'm also in charge of personnel." He looked at her carefully. "How close are you and Noelle?"

"We're becoming good friends."

He nodded, and she saw his body shift as if, having finished orchestra business, he would leave. She spoke quickly. "I have big news, and I expect you to help me celebrate. I bought myself an early Christmas present yesterday. A car."

"Really? That's wonderful." She savored the pressure of his body as he leaned over to hug her. "Tell me more. What kind is it, how old is it, and how did you scrape up the money?"

The light in his eyes and his arm on her elbow gave her confidence in the future. With a bit of encouragement he made it obvious he still cared. "It's a dark blue Mustang with a white vinyl roof, and it's brand-new. It has a police special five-liter engine. We'll have to drag race sometime."

His musical laughter sent tingles along her nape. "You weren't kidding when you said you admired a fast car like the Flash." He studied her with a look that spread the tingles down her spine. "I have a hard time picturing you behind the wheel of a muscle car. It doesn't fit your image."

She shrugged. "My image is in dire need of overhaul anyway." Greg brushed against her knee as he threaded across the room. This wasn't, Melody realized, the best place for an intimate discussion, so she said no more.

"Don't keep me in suspense. Why did you decide you could afford a brand-new car?"

She teased him with her best Cheshire cat smile. "Mr. Klein," she said slowly and dramatically, "left the store to me." She was gratified at David's show of amazement. "Not only that, but I've already wreaked revenge on Strong Hardware by selling the remains to them for a totally outrageous price."

He started to speak, then stopped. "I'm speechless," he managed to say at last. "Melody, no one deserves a break like this more than you. Congratulations."

"Don't I deserve a kiss, too?"

His lips sent her pulse skidding wildly, driving her hands around him with more passion than was appropriate for this kind of party. She broke off the kiss and glanced around, embarrassed. A brunette from the French horn section was the only one who seemed to have noticed, and she winked. Melody's romance with David wasn't exactly a secret, but nonetheless she sat straighter, determined not to start tearing his clothes off him just yet. "So, when can we have that drag race? Tomorrow? The next night?"

His face clouded. "It will have to be tomorrow night." He hesitated, and she sensed important words coming hard. "Melody... I'm leaving the day after tomorrow."

"So soon?" She knew his European tour was right after Christmas, but she'd thought he wouldn't be leaving for at least a week.

His big, sad eyes made him look like a small boy who'd lost his puppy. "Afraid so. My family invited me to spend Christmas with them and—" his eyes flashed, but more in sorrow than anger "—I didn't think there was much reason to stay here."

"I understand," she said quickly. But she didn't, not really. She needed every possible minute to prove she could be the lover he deserved. He would be gone so long. A month without David... Well, that meant she'd have to make a faster start on improving their relationship. She rubbed her shoulder against him and arched her eyebrows in what she hoped was seductive invitation. "My place or yours tonight?"

Surprise danced in his eyes. The French horn player, she noted with a tinge of embarrassment, had seen Melody's expression and smiled a crooked, knowing smile. "I don't know if I can survive this new image of yours," David said. "First a fast car; now a lascivious leer." He grew thoughtful, then rubbed his hands together playfully. "This could be a very interesting evening. My place?"

She nodded, embarrassed further by the telltale blush she felt creeping up her neck. But everything would work out between them. She knew it. "Your place."

They smiled at each other for a long time. Eventually, though, he rose. She stood up beside him. "I'm afraid," he said, "that I have to circulate. At an orchestra party the conductor belongs to everyone, no matter how beautiful the oboist is. When the party's over, though, how would you feel about leaving with the maestro?"

"I'd be honored."

He took her hand for a gallant kiss that was entirely in keeping with his gallant looks.

Just then, as if she'd been waiting for their private discussion to finish, Noelle stepped over to them. "I don't mean to interrupt," she said in a slightly slurred voice, "but I'd like to apologize for my mistake in the Copland."

David shook his head. "You don't have to apologize. I know you did your best."

Noelle took another sip from her glass. Melody put her hand on her friend's sleeve, wondering how much of the redhead's courage in apologizing to David came from the alcohol that had put a flush in her cheeks and heightened the giggly quality of her laugh.

"Thanks," Noelle said. "I'm surprised you feel that way. As a matter of fact I was afraid the big-shot conductor would kick me out of the orchestra, or at least give Melody the first oboe parts for the next concert."

David looked at Melody with a sudden solemn firmness, then back at Noelle. "Just enjoy the party, and we'll talk about it later. I'll phone you," he said to Melody.

A queasy feeling seized her stomach. He was going to do it; he was going to expect her to play first oboe. Her immediate reaction was panic. She'd be subjected to pressure she'd rather avoid. But then her friend's stricken expression registered, and Melody pushed the selfish thought aside. She tightened her grip on Noelle's arm as she faced the masterful man she loved so much, the man whose word was law and who seemed to have already decided to hurt her best friend. She forced her voice to a lighthearted banter. "David, she just apologized. You can't bump her down to second chair after she apologized. Isn't there a law against that or something?"

He smiled quickly—too quickly—and nodded. "You may be right. In any case, I know there's a law against getting too serious at parties, so don't worry. We'll talk about it later."

"Now!" The stricken expression on Noelle's face had evolved into anger. The people near them turned, curious about the rising passion in her voice. "I never have been able to do anything right as far as you're concerned, have I? Well, if you have anything to say to me, say it now."

"Noelle," Melody began. The other woman never took her eyes off David as she shook off the restraining hand of friendship.

"If that's the way you want it." David kept his gaze level, but he sighed. "Melody's playing first oboe for the next concert. You're down to second."

"Wrong, Mr. Halifax. I quit!" Noelle whirled and walked a surprisingly straight line toward the cloakroom.

Melody reproached David with a glare. "That was a cruel thing to do. She felt terrible enough without you kicking her when she was down."

Frustration and annoyance swept across his face, then disappeared without a trace. "I didn't set out to make her feel bad, but the quality of the orchestra is my responsibility and I'm not about to shirk it. Telling her now wasn't my idea, either. What did you want me to do, lie to her?"

"No. No, of course not. I'm sorry for snapping at you. Well, she still feels terrible. I'm sorry about later, David, but I think I should drive her home and make sure she gets to bed safely." She looked back at him after a few steps. "Tomorrow night's still on, isn't it?"

His strong features softened. "Of course."

"Good. Because I still have things I want to say." She almost added the words *before you leave me*, but that wouldn't have been fair.

She took one last, heart-wrenching look at him before she turned and left the party.

Chapter Ten

David's living room ceiling was a rough stucco embedded with glittering metal flakes. When Melody squinted and moved her head from side to side, the dim glow from outside the sliding glass doors and from the gas-burning logs in the fireplace bounced off the flakes, creating the illusion of sunlight shimmering off a rippling pond. She needed sunlight in her life, illusory or not, so she concentrated on the rippling glitters.

Not for long, though. The sultry warmth of David's body distracted her, and she soon found herself watching the hypnotic rise and fall of his chest. She shifted on the white bearskin rug. He'd surprised her by spreading it with great fanfare after they'd gotten back from dinner. The fur was soft, but the floor underneath was hard. She didn't understand how he could sleep.

Her discomfort on the rug summed up the evening. They had both tried hard. Too hard.

The rug was supposed to be a humorous yet romantic allusion to all the dramatic love scenes played out on such rugs. It was an expensive gesture, she was sure, despite the holes in the leather backing he'd shown her when she'd fretted about the cost. She knew and appreciated that he was trying to set a romantic tone, yet it was too much. A single long-stemmed rose would have sufficed. Besides, the rug was uncomfortable. If pioneers had made love on bearskin rugs, it was only because they'd never heard of waterbeds.

But she had tried too hard, as well. Everything she'd done had seemed forced and awkward. Her prolonged laughter at his every joke. The expensive dinner she'd insisted on paying for. The ride home on the Outer Drive when she'd driven her new car too fast. The detailed accounts she'd given of Mr. Klein's will and the sale of the store—accounts that told all yet left the important things unsaid. Everything between them had been awkward, as if they were a couple of strangers out to impress each other.

Even, she thought miserably, their lovemaking had been awkward, as if they were both concentrating on the long weeks of separation facing them rather than on each other. The one thing that had remained miraculous even when she'd been most rigid and aloof had for once been less than magical. She felt unfulfilled for the first time with him, and only a short while ago she'd thought that could never happen.

The lack of release didn't bother her. Before David had entered her life, what had she had? Besides, the warm comfort of his body was pleasant in itself. No, what bothered her was that it had happened with *him*, and she wasn't sure how to cope with that.

Moving slowly so as not to disturb him, she sat up and looked for her clothes in the dim light. Her pink dress—the wonderful, sexy pink dress she'd bought especially for him and he'd taken off her so many times that it was almost an aphrodisiac in itself—lay rumpled on the far side of his sleeping form. She spotted her bra closer at hand and pulled it from beneath his shirt.

As she fastened the clasp, his eyes fluttered open. He watched silently for a moment, then spoke with a voice edged with hard intensity. "Going somewhere?"

His cold tone froze her heart. He was angry and trying to control it. But why? Surely their lovemaking hadn't been all that disappointing to him.

The anger in his voice made her miserable. This was the evening she'd vowed would start a new era of openness, yet she'd made a mess of it. Details were all she'd discussed, not feelings. He still knew nothing about her fear of letting herself be loved or of her resolve to change. She'd been unable to tell him that if they'd met a year earlier, when she'd known who she was, she probably wouldn't have had as much trouble opening up to him. She hadn't discussed how the upset in her life had triggered all her unspoken fears of trusting someone's love. And now, in the face of his anger, the words clogged in her throat.

"No," she whispered, "I'm not going anywhere. You are."

The dim light cast shadows on his face and turned his eyes into unreadable pools of blackness. "Yeah. The trip's been looming over us all evening." He ran a fingertip along the top of her bra, then dipped it under the soft fabric to tease her rapidly swelling nipple. "I can't get it out of my mind that this is the last time I'll see you for a month. The thought is driving me crazy."

Melody wove her fingers through the silky roughness of his hair. With startling swiftness the gentle friction of his hand on her breast was igniting the tinder of her passion, sending licking tongues of flame directly to her melting abdomen. As he lazily moved his hand to inflame her other yearning breast, her lungs began working faster, pumping more oxygen to the mellow fire inside her. Now that he was ready to talk, she was ready to make love. It figured. That was the way the evening had gone.

"You aren't saying anything," he whispered with a return of tension. "Please, Melody, talk to me. Don't leave me to imagine what's happening inside your head."

Breathing heavily, she grinned as she traced a vein on the back of his hand, urging him to deeper caresses. "At the moment not much is happening in my *head*, thank you."

His deep laugh showed he was both relieved and delighted at this reason for her silence. However, he also removed his hand. Melody swallowed her disappointment. She wanted—no, she *needed*—to feel the crashing climax of their passion one more time before he left. The memory of a perfect union might help to sustain her through the long drought.

He wanted to talk, though. Well, there was a lot to say. She stroked his hair again. "I'm sorry about tonight, David. I'm not sorry we got together, or made love," she hastened to explain. "It's just that I wanted tonight to be perfect, and it wasn't."

The shadowy corners of his mouth bent into a half-suppressed smile. "You noticed. The only time we've been this awkward was the first day, when you were frantically trying to pretend you weren't watching me undress."

"I was not watching you undress!" She poked him in the ribs, though she was glad he'd interjected a light note into the conversation. "You should know I wouldn't do such a thing."

"Do you mean my body doesn't turn you on?"

The quick glance she stole at the curly hair of his chest and the solid masculine hardness of his thighs turned into a long, loving stare that answered the question better than words. She had to swallow before she could speak again. "I love you, David."

"And I love you, milady."

She snuggled against his warmth. "Oh, David. Where did we go wrong? We started out so well, and now look at us."

She was startled when his chest swelled in a tense, extra-deep breath. He dug his fingers into her arm, causing un-intentional pain. "Don't say that," he grated. "You talk as if it's over between us. I won't let you talk like that, I won't let you think like that and I won't let you act like that. Understand?"

She nodded, shocked by his vehemence. Her image of him was one of serene confidence, urbanity and patience. Great passions burned in him, but he expressed them through music, not physical anger. "You're hurting me," she whispered.

"What?" After a moment of befuddlement he looked at her arm as if he hadn't realized he was touching her, then hastily released it. "I'm sorry. I didn't mean..." He looked around wildly before he turned on his side, facing away from her.

So he, too, was taken aback by the depth of his feelings—feelings that had for an instant shattered his control. Poor David, she thought. He was used to ruling his animal urges, channeling them into his drive for excellence. She hadn't realized till just then the depth of his pain. Well, the hurting would stop. It had to.

"I'm sorry, too," she said. "I'm sorry because I lied. Well, not actually lied. I just didn't mean it the way it sounded when I said I didn't know where we went wrong. I do know. It's me."

She pressed her breasts and cheek against his back. "You see, David, so many things have happened lately to destroy my sense of security. No, not just my sense of security. It's my sense of who I am. So many of the labels I've used to define Melody Ross have been swept away that I'm no longer even sure who I am. I wanted to grow, but I didn't want to be torn apart like this."

David said nothing, though his intense stillness told her he was listening. Could he understand? He, who was so sure of his goals and his future? Somehow she had to make him understand. She put her arm on his shoulder and gently turned his unresisting body to face her. "And then there's you, David. You're one of the biggest upheavals of all. A good upheaval, a wonderful upheaval. But still, something different and unexpected, beyond what I'd believed could ever happen to me. You're so wonderful, you scare me. You've got to understand, all my life I've aimed toward survival. Nothing lofty, just surviving hours of washing and cooking after a hard day in school, then surviving marriage and divorce and loneliness. Surviving with no one to look after me but myself. When you jogged into my life, I wasn't ready for a luxury like you and I didn't know how to handle our relationship without losing myself in you. I'm a survivor, but you threatened my survival just by being you."

She wiped at the tear gathering in her eye. This wasn't the time for weakness. "David, I love you, but—"

"But," he interrupted sharply, "you can't love me. Is that what you're trying to say?"

His quick words showed such total lack of understanding that they took her breath away. Her first reaction was to leave, before she said anything to make matters worse. Leaving, though, would hardly demonstrate her determination to improve their relationship. Absurd thought. She laughed humorlessly at her own stupidity. But, a ruthless corner of her mind wondered, was it really stupidity, or did the urge to leave stem from some deeply buried part of her that valued lonely survival over all else?

"Did I say something funny?"

"No," she said quickly. "I'm sorry." The rigidity of the control she felt in his body frightened her almost as much as his earlier outburst of temper. "David...I want to improve things between us. I'm not doing a good job, but that's what I want." She kissed him tenderly, nibbling softly at his lips, and she felt some of the tension ease from his muscles. Soon he was returning her kiss with flickering touches of his tongue. The urging of his hands drew her to the virile strength of his chest. By the time the kiss ended, her heart was pounding next to his.

"Come with me," he whispered into her ear.

Her heart pounded still harder. "What did you say?"

"I said come with me." His arms stroked persuasively across the sensitive flesh of her back and bottom. "I want you beside me like this while I'm in Europe. I want you to meet my parents, Martin, even Jennifer. I want you to attend every one of my concerts and then read me the reviews afterward. I want you to stroll the Thames and the Zuider Zee on my arm. Come with me, Melody."

Her mind swam. Europe. David. His parents. London. Amsterdam. Paris. David!

She sat up and laughed nervously. "I can't go with you."

"Why not?"

"Well..." Yeah, why not? She felt there were reasons, but she had to ransack her mind for them. "Well, you're leaving tomorrow morning, and I couldn't possibly be packed and ready by then. You don't understand the things a woman has to organize for a trip like that."

He snorted a dismissal of that argument. "So take a later plane. Meet me in Boston at Christmas. If even that doesn't give you enough time to pack, fly there just before I leave for Europe at the end of December."

Go with him to Europe.... Certainly travel was one way to spend some of her newfound wealth. A change of scene would do her good, as well as give her the chance to consider how she might use the rest of the money. She'd always wanted to see New England, though she'd imagined seeing it in fall rather than winter. Europe wasn't terribly high on her list of places to see, but she'd enjoy herself. She'd be with David, after all.

Yes, she'd be with David, and at every stop on his tour she'd have to face a bunch of strangers as his *traveling companion*. Not his wife or manager or anything legitimate. Traveling companion. Would bellboys smirk? Probably not. Maybe no one else would show they knew she was his kept woman, either, because times had changed. But they'd know her relationship with David was blatantly sexual. A wave of goose bumps swept over her arms. Even if people were unfailingly polite she'd still imagine their thoughts about what she and David would do together back at their hotel.

Did that matter? Melody swallowed and looked fondly at the big man beside her. They were, after all, lovers, and she wasn't ashamed of it. How could she possibly be ashamed of him? No. It was herself she'd be ashamed of, at least in the beginning. Private affairs should be kept private, not paraded publicly across two continents. Times may have changed, but she hadn't, and their relationship was under enough stress without adding the strain of embarrassment and shame.

David stirred impatiently beside her.

"I love you," she whispered. He squeezed her hand in reply.

She lowered her head in sudden shame. Those three words hadn't come from her heart but from her head, as a tactic to forestall his impatience. She had cheapened the most wonderful words in the universe. Nothing she did or said seemed right anymore, but she didn't understand why. She just didn't understand.

She did understand one thing, however. Right now she couldn't lock herself into a subservient position with a masterful man like David. It wouldn't work. If for no other reason than that she was too scared. She might take a trip with David as an equal, but not when he'd be the busy star and she his excess baggage, his mistress.

"Damn it, Melody, would you say something?"

She took a deep breath. When she spoke she was surprised at the calmness of her voice. "I can't go with you, David. I'm sorry."

He was still for a dozen heartbeats. Then the breath hissed out of him like air going out of a tire. Even in the dim light he appeared sad and deflated. "I'm sorry, too."

After that neither of them spoke. She listened to the faint rumbling of a commuter train, to the distant echoes of the happy laughter of strangers outside somewhere, to the lonely, mournful sound of his breathing and to the painful thumping of her shattering heart. She listened till she could stand it no longer.

Breaking the silence was difficult, but preferable to this awkwardness. She cast her voice as low and loving as possible. "Would you pass me my clothes, please?"

It was as if he hadn't heard. But then, slowly he gathered up her dress, panty hose, slip and underpants. He sat on his haunches and waited, a dark, hulking silhouette against the glow of the city coming through the glass doors.

"No!"

His cry made her jump. She raised her hands to ward him off as he reached menacingly for her. His fingernails scratched along the delicate skin of her chest as he grabbed her bra and jerked the stretchy material so that the straps bit painfully into her back before tearing away in his hand. Naked, she cringed as he surged to his feet and loomed darkly over her.

"You're not going anywhere," he rasped.

She watched with a madly thumping heart as he stalked to the glass door and slid it open. A frigid blast of winter emphasized her nudity as she saw him raise his hands over his head. Even then she didn't understand what he was doing. He'd suddenly become inscrutable, as if he'd transformed into someone she'd never met.

She couldn't believe it when he tossed her clothes into the December night. Her mind refused to register it. His movements had a nightmarish quality as he reached for the panties, which had draped themselves over the wrought-iron railing, and savagely knocked the intimate garment away with his hand.

Still sitting, she edged away from his advancing shadow till her back came up against the roughness of the couch. Cold fear spread through her body. This wasn't the man she knew and loved. It couldn't be. Her mouth was as dry as desert sands so that it took all her energy to croak. "David . . . have you gone mad?"

The nightmarish apparition paused to consider her words. "Yes," it rumbled at last.

His hands bruised her arms before slackening to a less painful grip. "Melody," the shadow said in a voice that began to sound faintly like David again, "we may only have till morning. I'm not letting you out of my sight till the last possible minute."

Then he dragged her to his bedroom before she could even decide whether to resist.

After he deposited her none too gently on the bed, she crossed her arms to cover at least part of her nakedness. She looked up at him warily, realizing more thoroughly than ever his superior strength. She prayed she read correctly that he was regaining control of himself, even if only marginally. What could she do to help him repress this demonic anger? "David," she said calmly, "if you want me to spend the night, just ask."

"No more words. I can't keep you with words. Maybe I can with actions."

He seized first her resisting shoulders and then her lips for a fierce, demanding kiss. His skin seemed to burn against her sensitive breasts, and his lips and tongue plundered her mouth with a savageness that overlay yet did not obscure his deep love. She shrank from his touch at first. Then she slowly felt the roughness, but not the insistence, leave his hands as they caressed the nape of her neck, her shoulder blades, her side from armpits to waist and at last the swelling of her breasts. He moved on top of her, and she felt a sad joy as she found herself responding to the burgeoning influx of tenderness in his touch. And then, miraculously, almost as soon as her pleasure began, it surged through her veins in an awesome explosion of need. The sensations only he could arouse consumed her totally, leaving her trembling body as nothing more than a quivering receptacle for the pulsing, pounding pressure of his love. Without conscious thought she oscillated her hips against his, threw her arms possessively around his neck, wrapped her legs around his hips to urge him to even deeper fulfillment. And then, when she could stand no more, she cried out with overwhelming, almost painful pleasure. She gloried in the feeling of oneness as she abandoned herself completely to the mind-numbing glory of being a partner to his love.

He collapsed beside her. Emotionally and physically spent, they regarded each other wordlessly. David's eyes held a confusion of sadness and hope, but at least they were *his* eyes rather than a stranger's. Together their labored breathing gradually returned to normal. A satisfied lassitude crept into her veins. She saw his eyelids flutter as he struggled to keep them open, but she never saw them close for the last time. She was asleep before he was.

Melody awoke, dazed.

And then, with a rush, the memory of the evening filled her mind with fear and love. Disengaging her leg from his with as little disturbance as she could, she tiptoed from the room.

A strange heaviness engulfed her as she examined herself in the mirror over his washstand. Her lips felt as if they were swelling from the unrestrained power of his kisses. Her whole body ached, though whether from his roughness or her own extreme tension, she wasn't sure. A long breath escaped from her throat in a shudder as she rubbed her arms where he had grasped her.

Her fists clenched and unclenched rhythmically. Sure, David had been upset. Sure, he was afraid of losing her. Sure, she'd handled her part poorly. Sure, he'd been pushed beyond his limits and hadn't meant to hurt her. But he still had no right to forget his strength. And he certainly had no right to throw her clothes out the window....

Her clothes. Oh, God, her clothes.

She was trapped here. She clenched and unclenched her fists faster, more fiercely. How dared he? Not caring whether she wakened him or not, she stomped past his room and into the living room. She spotted the heavy bearskin and wrapped it around herself, unwilling to be nude in his apartment any longer. The dead white hand of the animal flopped onto her shoulder, and she bared her teeth at it, daring it to comment on her predicament.

She felt around in the darkness till she found her shoes. They, at least, were still here. They hadn't been dumped into the winter night by an inconsiderate lover. Going over to the glass doors, she searched unsuccessfully for her clothes. They were probably in the garden, hidden from sight by the floor of the balcony—unless some pervert had already stolen them.

Pacing like a tiger from fireplace to couch and back, she rubbed the tender spots on her arms as she glared in the direction of the bedroom. Some lover.

Vaguely aware that she was making a momentous, fateful decision she would regret but was necessary, Melody crept to the back door of the apartment. It squeaked when opened; she pulled on the knob slowly and carefully. Before stepping outside, she adjusted the fur around her as best she could. And then she was gone, closing the door on yet another chapter of her life.

The wooden stairway was bare of frost; luckily the weather was mild for December. If she'd been fully dressed under the bearskin she would have been hot, but as it was, the frigid air slipped under the hem of her impromptu coat and insinuated itself through the gaps no matter how carefully she overlapped the leather in front of her. Still, it was better than nothing, and a lot better than a single long-stemmed rose. She smiled grimly.

The menacing shadows of the alley made her pause between David's and the neighbors' garages. She hated dark places like this, and even more so in the middle of the night. Her heart pounded in her chest as she reached for the gate. The rusty hinges shrieked in protest.

Probably the noise drew their attention. At any rate, two teenagers and a small dog standing a short way down the alley turned to look as she came through the gate. Melody recognized one of them, a girl of around eighteen from a town house down the block. The other youth had his arm around her. It must be a date ending with walking the family's schnauzer, Melody realized. And she would have to head toward them to get to her own yard. Her face grew hot. She was thankful polar bears made for big skins. For all the couple could tell, she was fully dressed.

Mustering what dignity she could, she stepped into the brighter light of the alley. The teenagers were pointing at her now, saying something indistinguishable that nevertheless made Melody's ears flame. Pulling the fur around her as tightly as possible, she ran toward her high garden gate, her movements fanning her burning shame into a frenzied conflagration. As in a dream her legs seemed to run through molasses in slow motion. With each agonizing step the fur around her legs bounced high, embarrassingly high, yet she had no free hand to hold it down.

The boy's loud, mocking laughter pummeled her ears. The girl's look of shocked amusement etched itself into Melody's brain. There goes my reputation, she thought through the red fog of her mortification. She was just a step from the gate when even the dog began yapping, calling still more attention to her predicament.

Melody wasn't aware of opening the gate, but somehow she was leaning against the inside of it, breathing heavily. A few guffaws reached her before she heard the girl shushing the dog and tactfully urging her boyfriend away from Melody's humiliation.

Melody remained rooted helplessly in place till their footsteps dwindled to nothing, feeling the hammering of her heart, tasting a salty thickness at the back of her throat as if she'd just finished a marathon. Her eyes were accustomed to the dark, yet she saw nothing through the turmoil of her emotions.

The first thing she became aware of was that David's windows remained dark. So, his sound sleep still guarded her from pursuit. That wouldn't last forever. She couldn't lean against the cold gate all night, but neither could she summon the energy to walk.

"Move, damn it," she whispered shrilly.

Her muscles obeyed the hysterical command, she was grateful to discover. One step. Pull the foot from the sucking, boggy mud. Another step. Now another.

Her pink dress was easy to spot, hanging upside down as it was from the tall fence, but when she jerked on it, the skirt wedged between two slats of wood and tore. She surveyed the damage clinically. A ragged, foot-long gash was torn

from the hem. Well, she wouldn't be wearing this dress for
David anymore.

But she was lucky, she realized after she rounded up the
rest of her clothes, that the dress had landed on the fence
instead of in the mud. She carried the cold bundle of clothes
on to the patio outside her kitchen door.

Like a thunderbolt, a terrifying realization struck her.

Her keys were in her purse. In David's apartment.

The clothes slipped through her fingers. This was too
much. Pounding her hand futilely against the door, she felt
tears spill over her cheeks. So much humiliation already tonight, and now this. It wasn't fair!

But after only a minute she glanced up at his window,
afraid her pounding had wakened him. No. She wouldn't
give him the satisfaction of discovering her like this. With a
muddy hand she brushed away the tears. She had a spare
key hidden on the trunk of one of the cedar bushes at the
front of the town house. When she got it she'd be warm and
private again.

There was no passageway in her yard to the front, though.
She must use the alley—either that or cut through the yard
of David's building, which she couldn't bring herself to do.

First, though, clothes. Moving close to the fence, she
made a crude tent by hanging the bearskin from the top of
the fence. Under the awkward shelter she pulled the dress
over her head, shivering from contact with the frigid cloth.
The rest of her wet, unwearable things, she dumped by the
kitchen door.

She should feel better now that she was decent, but all she
felt was cold. Cold to the core of her soul. She rubbed her
arms vigorously, though it made little difference. She was
chilled, seriously chilled.

She glared at the sightless eyes of the bear, then slipped
the rug over her shoulders again. "If you tell anyone about
this," she hissed, "I'll take a lawnmower to you." Her

spirits rekindled by the feeble bravado, she peeked over the fence before opening the gate to the alley. The coast was clear.

At first she heard nothing but the squish of her soaked shoes. But then, as she slunk down the shadowy alley, the distant noises that haunt a midnight city assaulted her frayed nerves. A dog barked, and she ran several steps before realizing the schnauzer wasn't at her heels. A door slammed, and she looked around wildly. Step by terrifying step, she forced herself onward, each movement of her feet a hard-won victory of determination over mindless terror.

When she got close to the streetlamp that marked the end of the alley, she ran gasping to the illusory safety of its circle of light. "You'll be fine," she whispered. "The hard part is over now." She pulled the skin tighter, but it couldn't stop the chattering of her teeth or the single, violent shiver that shook her spine.

The streets were deserted at this time of night, and she saw no one till she was nearly at the front door of her town house. When she saw the hulking form of a strange man walking toward her she hurried, hoping wildly that she could get inside before he reached her. Don't run, not quite. Don't draw attention to yourself. Faster.

She wouldn't make it, she saw. He'd begun eyeing her. Oh, God, he needed a shave. That observation seemed highly significant, though she wasn't sure why.... His beady eyes shifted furtively when he noticed her watching him. A series of shivers tore through her. She was painfully aware of the rip in her dress. Her uneven breathing. Her dirty, tear-streaked face. The polar bear on her back. If she'd looked normal, maybe he would never have noticed her. But now that he had...

Only a few more steps. She tried to run, but for some reason her legs wouldn't obey her. She fell, pain thudding sharply into her knees. When she looked up, the man was approaching, not as if to pass but as if to accost her. With a gasp she stumbled to her feet.

"Lady," he began as she lunged past him. His eyes were bleary and red. His breath reeked of beer. He reached for her, touched her shoulder, but she twisted from his grasp and he ended up holding only the bearskin.

She dashed behind the enclosing barrier of her cedar hedge. No time to relax. Her mind was so clogged with cold and terror that it was difficult for her to count to three. On her second try she got it right and reached among the branches of the third bush for the key, which hung from a nail in the central trunk. Please, she begged her unresponsive fingers, don't drop it.

She had to hold the key in both shaking hands in order to guide it to the lock. Just then she heard the lonesome, threatening clop of the man's footsteps, coming back toward her.

A sob knifed through her as her chilled hands missed the lock by half a foot. She tried for a second time to get the key in the lock, but her hands shook so badly that the key clattered noisily to the cement. And still the threatening footsteps drew slowly nearer.

Gasping, she reached for the key. As she straightened, the footsteps stopped, directly behind her. Her gaze flicked up to the front windows of David's apartment. She wondered wildly if he'd look out the next morning and be the first to discover her torn and lifeless body, hidden behind the hedge.

With energy born of desperation, she took off her shoe and hurled it at the man.

The missile bounced harmlessly off the bear's snout. The man stared at her with narrowed eyes. "Damn weirdos," he slurred. "Streets ain't safe for decent citizens no more." He dumped the bearskin on the sidewalk and slowly backed away, muttering unintelligible words.

Melody's frozen hands finally unlocked the door. Once inside, she closed all her curtains and blinds, turned up the thermostat and started the hot water in the shower. Her teeth chattered wickedly as she inspected herself in the mirror on the bathroom door. Her hair was a mess. The tremors that rippled through her frame were clearly visible. Dirt smeared her face like war paint, marred here and there by the streaked paths of tears.

As steam from the shower began to cloud her image in the mirror, she stripped off the dress. With calm deliberation, she seized the hem on each side of the tear and stretched her arms as far as possible. Then again and again. She grabbed scissors from a drawer and cut through the hem over and over, her calmness dissolving into a frenzied orgy of destruction as she exulted in the savage ripping motions of her muscles.

Lost in a swirling fog of steam, she hacked and tore the pink dress till not a single piece larger than her shattered heart remained.

Chapter Eleven

Melody awoke slowly, a pillow over her ear to block out—to block out what? The question tickled at her mind, thrusting her imperceptibly to wakefulness.

Oh, yes. Reality.

And David. A stab of pain brought her still closer to life.

It was now two weeks, four days and—she lifted the pillow for a bleary glimpse of the clock—seven hours since she'd last seen him, that night at his apartment.

Since then she'd done nothing but spend money. She had shopped relentlessly, joylessly, burying her grief and anger under a pile of receipts. It was a way, at least, of keeping her days full and her mind occupied.

She pulled the pillow tighter, trapping her own breath in a hot and stifling prison. "Think about what you need to buy," she mumbled into the pillow. She'd bought a lot of expensive Christmas presents: a chic wool suit that was rather demure for Noelle's tastes; outrageously expensive toys for the niece and three nephews she rarely saw; and, for Papa, a wheeled cabinet filled with an assortment of automotive tools. But Christmas was over; New Year's was over. Holidays lent her no easy excuse for shopping.

The house, then. It had seemed that she always needed things for her house. She'd already bought a framed landscape for the living room, a pair of bedside tables and a dozen records, none classical, to go in a new record cabinet. The only other thing she could think of was a new shower curtain—and a shower curtain wasn't sufficient reason to face the world.

Clothes? Clothes should have tempted her the most, gorgeous finery such as she'd desired since adolescence. But somehow the racks of dresses designed to attract a man depressed her. She had bought clothes, but recklessly, with an abandon and lack of taste that appalled her, mindlessly intent on self-destruction through overconsumption.

Nothing. She needed nothing.

Nothing from a store, at least. She realized with utter certainty that she couldn't drag herself to go to the Loop yet again. She *couldn't*. Better to just stay in bed.

She closed her eyes.

But then, with a sudden horror that jerked her to full wakefulness, she realized that her hand had stretched out and was searching the cool, empty sheets beside her.

Jumping from bed to an activity, any activity, she spent an hour choosing a spot for the computer from Klein's and plugging in its myriad cords. Only then did she realize the futility of her actions. All her programs concerned Klein's; none were relevant to her present life. But nothing seemed relevant without work and David. Especially David. For the first time she allowed herself to wonder if she'd lost him forever or if when he returned from Europe...

No. She retreated from the thought, diving instead into totaling her purchases. After a few minutes she was perversely disappointed to discover her buying binge had cost her only three thousand dollars. Rats. She couldn't even wallow in wealth properly. Worse, when she finished the calculations there was nothing else she needed the computer for—not that she really needed a four-thousand-dollar machine to add up a few bills.

Nothing else needed doing, either. The Mustang was being serviced at the garage, so she couldn't drive aimlessly. Nothing to do but sit and brood. She got out her oboe, but before she played a note she did the unthinkable: she smashed the delicate tip of her best reed against the wall.

She phoned Noelle, but as expected, the younger woman was at work. Too bad. Any doubts Melody had ever felt about their friendship had disappeared during this Christmas of mourning and loneliness—mourning that was mutual, since Noelle's affair with Chris had come to a fiery conclusion when he'd supported David's decision about the first chair, rather than Noelle. If anything Noelle had reacted worse than Melody. Instead of shopping, she ate—and she was a more self-destructive eater than Melody was a shopper.

The gray gloom of depression seeped further into Melody's unoccupied thoughts. In desperation she put on her coat and boots to do the one thing that had shielded her from thinking, ever since that horrible waking nightmare. She went shopping.

She didn't need much from the grocery store, but she nonetheless managed to kill an hour and a half. As she waited in line she watched the check-out woman ringing in purchases and chatting cheerfully with the customers. "There but for Herbert Klein stand I," she whispered. Still, the woman was at least doing something and doing it well. Her fingers flew over the register with a practiced ease that Melody found herself almost envying. She caught herself considering the cashier's job she'd been offered here. It would keep her busy....

"Get serious, girl," she muttered. She smiled self-consciously at the cashier, who looked at her inquiringly. Really, she wasn't *that* desperate for something to do.

Was she?

As she carried her bag out of the grocery store she paused in the middle of the open mall to wave to Lou, the owner of the record store. The poor woman had ended up suffering through another Chicago winter rather than retiring with her husband to Arizona as she'd hoped.

Melody's hand stopped in mid-wave. With a sudden, dizzying rush of certainty that made her feel foolish for not having realized it before, she knew what she would do with her inheritance and her life.

Three weeks later the smell of fresh paint lingered at the edge of her consciousness as she stood nervously in Melody's just before it opened for business in the old site of Hyde Park Records.

It had been a hectic three weeks, hectic enough so that she was able to ignore David's imminent return. It had been an exhilarating three weeks that had filled her mind with ideas and possibilities.

Sometimes it had been a terrifying three weeks, too, so that she had to force herself to take each little step, just as she'd forced each step down the alley. How ironic, she thought as she checked her watch for the third time to see if it was nine yet. Just when she realized that she wasn't all alone in life she dashed into a venture where success depended on her alone. Her store. Her baby. Despite Papa's repainting of the subdued canary walls and Al Jevaert's repairing of the multicolored pastel record shelves, she was alone. It was a rather nice aloneness, though, except for the out-and-out loneliness caused by Bob Gold's warnings. As she rechecked the till for change, she recalled the meeting in the lawyer's office.

"You thought you had a fortune," he had said. "Well, what Herb left you is peanuts for starting a business of your own. Most small businesses fail within two years, usually because of undercapitalization."

She told him she planned to use the town house as collateral on a loan. She'd sell her car if necessary.

"Half that store's income is from the Christmas season, and you missed it. January's a ridiculous time to open. Besides, have you done any market studies to determine whether there's a future?"

Melody's would be the closest record store to campus, she had replied with more confidence than she felt. If she catered to the student trade, the place could be a gold mine.

"I hate to see you risk everything, Melody. I could direct you to safer investments—"

"No," she had interrupted, "you don't understand. It isn't the money. This is what I've always wanted to do. I just didn't realize it."

And now her store was about to open. Taking a deep breath, Melody smiled professionally at her reflection in the glass door. Amazing. In her new navy blazer and beige skirt, she actually looked like a businesswoman. She turned to her clerk. "Welcome to Melody's," she practiced saying.

For the grand opening her clerk wore the demure gray suit Melody had gotten her for Christmas. The suit and the subdued nervousness in her eyes made the redhead seem more down-to-earth and substantial than usual. Noelle had leaped at Melody's hesitant job offer and had bubbled with ideas for sales promotions. Now that the time had come to unlock the doors for the first time, though, she looked as scared as Melody felt.

Melody hoped her own nervousness wasn't quite as apparent, however. "Ready?"

Noelle rubbed her palms on her slacks. "I . . . I guess so."

And so, with only high hopes and two record store neophytes standing between Melody and bankruptcy, her store opened for the first time.

Her first paying customer was Lamarr—buying, of all things, an album of Baroque oboe concertos. When Melody asked him if he liked Baroque, he just shrugged in embarrassment. He stayed, wearing his plumbing clothes and glaring at every patron who left without buying anything. By midmorning Melody's was gratifyingly full, though to Lamarr's disgust more people were gobbling down the free coffee and doughnuts than buying records. Many of them weren't really customers at all but merchants welcoming Melody to their ranks. The local Chamber of Commerce president, whom she'd met at the orchestra party, greeted her like an old friend. It was a good feeling, having people go out of their way to meet her. Melody felt as if she was on the verge of becoming *somebody*.

And then David walked in. Her heart skipped a beat and her thoughts lost focus. She realized with a dizzying panic that she'd never considered the questions suddenly swarming through her mind. Where do we go from here? Where do I *want* to go from here?

If anywhere.

David didn't come to her immediately. Instead he threaded through the people in the aisles, pausing now and again to glance at records and tapes, never looking directly at her but coming steadily closer. His every move shouted to her how difficult this moment was for him. What would he say to her? What would she say to him? Melody stumbled absentmindedly through her conversation with a bearded university student who'd already had three doughnuts without buying anything. All the while her gaze kept darting to the slowly advancing form of her ex-lover.

"Hello, Melody." He'd finally reached her. His expression was carefully guarded, and he watched her face closely.

It was all she could do to keep from shouting, Why didn't I hear from you? Not even a Christmas card, just my purse tucked against the kitchen door the next morning. She couldn't say that, not ever, but she had no idea what she would say until the words finally popped out.

"Hello, Mr. Halifax." The levelness of her voice amazed her. She turned to the young man beside her, deliberately including him in the conversation so she wouldn't have to face David alone. "This is David Halifax, the famous conductor. You may have heard of him."

The impressed student looked at both David and Melody with new respect. He had indeed heard of Mr. Halifax, and could he please have an autograph? David signed the lad's napkin and then turned to Melody with such exclusive intensity that the student realized he was no longer welcome and wandered off.

"So, I'm back to being Mr. Halifax."

His voice held pain and an edge of anger under a heavily camouflaged neutrality. For the very first time she looked at that night through his eyes. She'd abandoned him without a word. Without even a note. How could he still love her? She'd been a fool to even allow herself a moment's hope. Only his sense of honor had dragged him here. Well, the least she could do was let him off easily.

"Yes, Mr. Halifax." She refused to look up at him, afraid of the hypnotic allure of his eyes. Her feeble willpower was disintegrating rapidly under the pressure of the looming, overwhelming aura of his towering height.

He said nothing for a minute. "Did you get my postcards from Europe?"

"No."

"You should soon. Overseas mail is slow." He stood immovable as someone in the crowd jostled him. There must have been something about the tension between them, because no one approached them. "I was very proud when I heard you'd bought this place. Melody's. That's an appropriate name for a record store. I'm sure you'll make a success of it." He sounded like the Chamber of Commerce president but more formal.

"Thank you," she said.

He cleared his throat and sighed. At least this meeting was difficult for him, too. That knowledge gave her a nudge of relief. Still, she just wanted him to go away and let her enjoy the triumph of the grand opening.

He reached a hand halfway across the gulf between them. "I really blew it that night, didn't I?"

She looked up at him for the first time, wondering if this was an apology. If so, it wasn't enough. Not nearly enough. Anger returned. Her eyes became smoldering embers. All the time she had shopped she'd hated him for being thousands of miles away when their chance for reconciliation had blossomed and withered without so much as a telephone call. And now, though the weeks had dulled the razor edge of agony, she was filled with blunt pain. Pain over what might have been and now would never be.

"Yes," was all she said.

He nodded, any pain that he felt carefully concealed under tight self-control. "You ran out on me, deserted me without even saying goodbye." He paused. "But still, milady..."

"This guy bothering you, Mel?" Lamarr had materialized at her side, arms folded ominously across his barrel chest, his snarl none diminished for facing a man half a foot taller.

"Huh? No, Lamarr, he isn't bothering me." Lamarr looked unconvinced, ready to pounce. "Really! It's all right!"

David smiled with a warmth that refused to cool despite the youth's fierce demeanor. "So you're Lamarr. I'm very glad to meet you."

Lamarr grunted. "You David?"

"I see you've heard of me."

"It's all right, Lamarr," Melody insisted.

But he paid no attention to her. "Look, man, you leave the lady alone, see? You hurt her enough already. You stay away from her. You understand?"

"Lamarr," Melody whispered, glancing around at the customers who had turned at the vehemence in the youth's voice. She put a gentle hand on his arm. "Please."

His glance darted from David to Melody and back again. "If you say so, Mel." But instead of leaving, he stepped still closer to David, his head turned up to a degree that unintentionally underlined the mismatch; physically not even Lamarr was on a par with David. "I'm watching you, turkey."

David looked from Lamarr to Melody. He nodded and though the motion was tinged with other meanings, Melody's fogged brain understood clearly only resignation. "I understand," he said.

For a few seconds Lamarr glared up at David. He turned to Melody with the satisfied look of a good deed accomplished. "He won't give you no more trouble, Mel. But if he does—" he glared back at David "—you just let me know." And then he left her, and she was more alone than before.

The moment was awkward. David still towered beside her, but she didn't know what to say to him. But still, milady... She couldn't ask him what he'd been about to say before Lamarr interrupted them. Could she?

"Excuse me, young lady," a matron shrilled. "I'd like to pay for these records now." She impatiently arched her brows in David's direction. "If it's not too much bother, that is."

"I'm more than glad to help," Melody answered with false brightness. David stood nearby as she rang up the woman's purchase. He said nothing and his face showed nothing—yet he was obviously waiting for something.

When she was finished she swallowed hard before opening her mouth. "You were about to say something, David?"

His eyes narrowed, and it took him a moment to answer. When he did, his manner became brusque and business-like. "Uh, yes. I heard you skipped the rehearsals while I was in Europe. I hope you won't let what happened between us make you drop your interest in playing. We need at least one oboist for the concert coming up."

So that was it. She shrugged. Two could play this game of sophisticates-at-end-of-relationship. "I'm pretty busy here."

"Knowing you, I'm sure you're working seventy hours a week. Still, I'd appreciate it if you'd consider coming back to the orchestra. We need you."

Now he only needed her lips for oboe playing. She was about to refuse, then stopped. "I'll think about it."

"Thank you, Melody." He seemed to read more into her words than she intended, for his face regained its usual color and vitality. "Thank you very much. I suspect it's more than I deserve."

"Don't get your hopes up," she said quickly. "If I do come, it will only be because I refuse to let you destroy my love of music."

"I understand." His smile was undaunted. "I'll see you next Wednesday."

"Maybe."

"Right." He nodded vigorously. "You might be busy so close to the opening. Maybe this Wednesday, maybe next."

She watched him cross the store and hold the door open for two incoming teenagers. When she saw the new customers, though, she whirled toward the wall, her face the color of Noelle's hair.

One of the teenagers was her neighbor who owned the schnauzer.

Slowly Melody's life settled into a new pattern—a pattern that didn't include David.

She had thought she worked long hours at Klein's, but Melody's devoured even more of her time. Just as well. That way she had less time to think and feel. Monday through Saturday she arrived an hour before opening to attend to the myriad details that needed her personal attention: studying record catalogs, familiarizing herself with suppliers, keeping computerized records of the music most often purchased, learning as much about music as possible so she'd be able to help customers and purchase stock intelligently. The chores went on and on.

Noelle's friendliness was an asset with customers. Melody was surprised by how relieved she felt as the redhead developed into a good saleswoman. After a while she finally figured out why her relief was so overwhelming.

Without even realizing it, she'd taken huge risks hiring an inexperienced friend, risks to both the store and the friendship. She hadn't stopped to think how sticky things would be if Noelle didn't handle the job well. However, following the grand opening, the two women had established unspoken agreements about the bounderies between business and friendship. Melody grew to respect the unexpected tact of her friend and employee.

She did return to the orchestra. Though she worked to exhaustion on Wednesday, she found her spirits and energy level rising as the time for the rehearsal approached. That was strange in several ways. Of course there was the strain of being close to, yet distant from, David. She was on edge just seeing him, hearing him, breathing the same air. It was both depressing and exhilarating. But on top of that was the pressure of playing the music. She'd missed all the rehearsals led by David's understudy, and what with the prominent oboe solos she was expected to play she was desperately in need of practice. As if sensing her frustration, David called to her during the break the first night she returned.

"Melody," he called as she crossed the stage in conversation with Greg.

Reluctantly she disengaged herself from the safety of the flutist's neutral company. Though she was aware of her cowardice, she kept a music stand between herself and David. "What?"

"Nothing. I just wanted to tell you how good you sounded in the Tchaikovsky. I feel you have the potential to become an adequate first oboist for this orchestra."

She just nodded, then hurried after Greg. *Adequate?* Oh well, coming from a professional like him, it was probably high praise. But he'd spoiled it by adding that bit about "for this orchestra." Was that supposed to be an insult? She played with extra care and gusto after that, trying to prove something to the arrogant, self-centered man she still loved.

February brought a surprising warmth that turned the winter's snow into ugly piles of dirt, then into slush, and finally into puddles that seemed to dribble forever into the storm sewers. The warmth also lured an increased number of students into the record store and even an occasional jogger.

David was dressed in his jogging suit when he strode into Melody's for only the second time. He waved casually, then walked to the classical section. Utterly distracted by his presence, Melody shuffled a stack of purchase orders at the back of the store while she covertly watched him. Her heart accelerated at the sight of his lithe grace.

She was almost able to stifle the sensations. The record playing softly on the demonstration stereo gnawed at the calm she pasted on to her face, however; "Afternoon of a Faun," the same music she'd played when they'd first made love. She wondered when she'd forget the electrifying magic of his body covering hers.

Probably never.

She was still half fighting mellow memories when he carried a large stack of cassettes and compact disks to the register. Melody looked across the store at Noelle, who feigned total immersion in helping a pair of browsing coeds. Melody knew David wasn't Noelle's favorite person—she blamed him not only for the demise of her relationship with Chris but also for hurting her friend and employer and driving her away from the oboe—but the least she could do was take his money. Fighting down a warm flush of annoyance that brought a slight tremor to her knees, Melody walked to the register.

"Hello, David."

"Hello, Melody. You're looking good."

"Thank you." A gray blazer complemented her frilly white blouse and loosely tied red scarf. It was her favorite outfit and she was glad she'd worn it today—and then was immediately upset with herself for feeling glad. It was over between them and she might as well get used to it. "You look handsome, as well."

"I put on weight over the winter." He patted his still-flat stomach without self-consciousness. "Back in Boston I can't usually start jogging this early. Who said Chicago has a lousy climate?"

He paused, and she knew she should pick up the conversation. But small talk about weather was too much for her to bear; this was David, not some unknown customer. She said nothing. Before the pause grew noticeably awkward, she nodded and started to ring up his purchase. How depressing and stilted their short conversations were. Really, it would have been better if he'd never come.

She totaled his purchase, then whistled at the sum. "Two hundred five dollars and fifty-nine cents. You're a big spender."

"I hope you'll accept a check. I have identification—driver's license, credit cards."

She glared at him. She made an effort to be friendly—or at least to talk to him—and he turned around and insulted her by offering identification.

He met her glare with a straight face, but when she noticed the long-lost twinkle in his eye she began to smile—a smile that turned quickly into a laugh. She laughed longer than the dry humor called for, but it had been such a long time since she'd shared a joke with him. Months. And come to think of it, they hadn't done much laughing toward the end, either....

"Before I answer," she said, "tell me one thing. Has your sister run the family business into bankruptcy?"

The twinkle in his eyes spread to a grin that seemed as relieved as her laughter. "On the contrary. My quarterly dividend check arrived yesterday, and I was surprised they found an envelope fat enough for it. Jennifer has a good head for business."

"Then I'll accept the check."

"I'd have bought more," he said as he filled the check with his precise script, "but you didn't have some of the pieces I wanted. I guess I'll have to get them in the Loop."

Across the store, Noelle's head shot up at these words and she began motioning vigorously behind David's back. So, she'd been listening to every word. The sneak. As if Melody needed any prompting when it came to business. "Nonsense," she told David. "My prices are as good as any store downtown. Tell me what you want and I'll order it."

"Well, okay. How long will it take, though?"

A cool shiver shot along Melody's spine. Back to reality, girl. In two weeks, right after the Hyde Park Orchestra concert, he was returning to Boston. His departure seemed suddenly imminent. "Three days. Maybe four."

"Fine." David reached into his back pocket for a list scribbled across the ledger lines of a piece of music paper. He scratched most items off the list before handing it to her.

When she took the list his fingers brushed her palm, and the gentle contact was like an electric shock. Throbbing sparks shot up her arm and throughout her whole body with such devastating effect that she had to hold on to the counter with the other hand to maintain her balance. Stunned, she stared at the simple yet confounding contact between his fingers and hers. A second later a dancing excitement followed the sparks, flowing like bubbling wine from his hand to hers before settling warmly in the pit of her stomach. Her legs seemed to melt from the sudden heat in her abdomen, and she leaned weakly against the counter. Her world turned somersaults, so powerful and unexpected was the animal arousal that swept through her. She slowly raised her head.

His eyebrows were arched in amazement. She thought at first he'd simply seen her traitorous body's overreaction to his touch. After all, it must be obvious to everyone; how could she experience such a tidal wave of physical emotion without it showing in her eyes, her mouth, her posture, her whole body? But no, she sensed that wasn't the reason for his expression. Something—lust, perhaps, or awe—flickered deep in the hazel pools of his eyes, and she wondered if he felt the same upheaval she did.

Was it possible? Suddenly she *had* to know. But how could she ask?

Their fingers touched for what seemed an eternity. At last they withdrew in unison. Breathing rapidly, Melody busied her trembling hands by pushing his music into a bag.

Amazed, disheartened and encouraged all at the same time by this powerful residue of feelings, she felt her tidy, newly built world tilt on its axis.

After all this time.

His face was shrouded in neutrality when she picked up the bag to hand it to him. What had *he* felt just now? Damn it, what had he felt? Her distracted mind allowed her fingers to slip. The bag dropped to the counter, spilling cassettes to the floor.

"Oh, I'm sorry, David. I'm so clumsy. I hope your cassettes aren't damaged. I mean, I don't know what to say." Squatting behind the counter to stifle her babbling, she fumbled with the tapes that had fallen.

"Rats."

The deep, warm voice came from right beside her. She jerked her head to see David kneeling at her side. Her pulse began pounding at being alone with him in even the meager privacy afforded by the sales counter. She shook her head in confusion. "What did you say?"

"I said *rats*. You didn't know what to say, so I said it for you."

She laughed quietly. Her eyes became filmy. "I . . . I've missed you."

"I've missed you, too."

They gazed at each other in silence till Melody thought she would burst. And when he finally took a deep breath it seemed as if that would be the end of it. Another opening squandered.

But suddenly his shoulders slumped. "Look, this is crazy. I can't continue to live as if I never loved you. I thought I could, but it's killing me. What we had was too wonderful to end with this kind of pain and awkwardness."

He paused, and Melody's heart seemed to stop while she waited for his next words.

He slowly extended his hand. "Friends?"

Without hesitation she shook his strong hand. "Friends." But inside she wondered if being friends wouldn't hurt just as much as being strangers.

"You look tired, Melody. Are you sure you aren't working too hard?"

"I love it." *I love you, too, David.* "At last I have something that's all mine." *I wish you were all mine.* "You don't know how good that feels." *Not nearly as good as it would feel for you to put your arms around me right now....*

"As your friend I worry about you working too hard. Do you ever give yourself a day off?"

"Day off? What's that?" *I'd only have time to think about you, David.* "Oh, maybe eventually I'll take a vacation. I always dreamed of staying in the Grand Hotel. We went to Mackinac Island in northern Michigan when I was a kid, but we stayed in a cheap motel instead of the Grand, and if the store works out, I'll actually have enough money to stay in luxury like all the kings and presidents who've visited there." *I'm babbling. Why don't you tell me to shut up? Oh, David, don't look at me like that!*

Abruptly she stood up and shoved the bag into David's arms. Noelle was standing on tiptoe, craning her neck toward the sales counter. The redhead at least had the grace to blush and shrug in apology. David said goodbye. As he left, Melody watched his sensuous canter till he reached the parking lot, not caring if Noelle saw her.

That spark—it was celibacy. Just celibacy.

David jogged by the store every day that week, totally confusing Melody. Their chats were always impersonal—about her work or music or the orchestra—but the whole time they talked, her body would be pouring the juices of love through her system, reducing her to a quivering bundle of frustration by the time he waved a cheery goodbye.

They never touched, which was a good thing. She was afraid even the feeling of his fingernail could make her melt into a little puddle on the floor. But they were apparently friends. Just friends.

Noelle's interest in their renewed relationship was intense. "He still likes you," she announced during a lull in business Thursday afternoon.

Melody shrugged. She really didn't want to discuss it. She didn't even want to think about it. Soon, too soon, David would be history. "We're friends. That's all. He's never made an effort to make us more than that. The romance is over."

"And what have *you* done to try to make you more than friends?"

Melody turned to pick up a pile of records. "Would you file these, please?"

Noelle took the records with a loud "Hmmph." Her orangish curls swayed as she shook her head. "Dumb, dumb, dumb. You may be a good businesswoman, but when it comes to men you're blind. You can't smell, either." She stomped off to the far side of the store with the records.

She said no more. After a minute Melody's curiosity overwhelmed her stubbornness. "Smell?"

"Smell," Noelle answered as if the delay had never occurred. "Haven't you noticed David stops by when he begins his run rather than when he's all sweaty? And how many joggers put on cologne before they run?"

Melody squelched an explosion of foolish hope. She wasn't about to let an accident of David's jogging route raise her blood pressure. "Whose side are you on? I thought you didn't even like David."

"Don't change the subject. We're talking about you and David, not me and David. You're both so full of pride and stubbornness that neither one will get down on your knees and beg for forgiveness. It's just silly pride keeping you apart."

Melody slammed another stack of records on the red-head's hand.

"Hey, be careful. Melody, I think he still loves you."

"Don't be ridiculous. How could he?" The words slipped out with more intensity than Melody intended. Embarrassed, she quickly picked up another pile of records.

Noelle shook her head, surprise and pity awash in her features. "Honey, everyone who knows you loves you. Me, Al Jevaert, your dad, Lamarr. I think even Mr. Gold has a crush on you. How could David help but love you?"

The words cut deep into Melody's mind, but she stubbornly refused to let Noelle see how close to the core she'd come. "In any case," Melody said, "he'll be leaving soon. It's over."

Noelle started to object, but Melody shouted, "It's over!"

After work that day she drove home on a roundabout route that took her by the beauty parlor where Klein's Hardware had been. She pressed the accelerator hard till she was past her old place of work. Things changed, leaving no trace except in memory—though there forever.

Maybe pain would pass, as well.

The next morning dawned warm but gray. As Melody parked the Mustang and crossed the nearly deserted lot, a cashier on her way to work waved respectfully. "Good morning, Ms. Ross."

"Hello." It was the same cheerful woman she had watched the day she bought the store. She didn't know the woman's name, but she was getting used to people knowing her.

"Congratulations on being elected treasurer of the Hyde Park Chamber of Commerce," the clerk said. "It's about time some women got in."

"Thanks. I was the only one willing to take the job, actually."

"Just the same, I'm rooting for you." The woman nodded and headed toward the grocery store.

Such recognition would ordinarily have made Melody glow with quiet pride. Today, however, she merely turned to watch a Via Rail train rumble south on the Illinois Central tracks. She wished she were on board, headed anywhere but to the inevitable loneliness of her own life.

She didn't notice anything as she unlocked the glass door proclaiming Melody's in large red letters. But then she wasn't expecting anything unusual, and her mind was distant. She locked the door from the inside, flipped on the lights and started to take off her coat as she turned around.

She froze.

David was perched nonchalantly on the counter.

He just sat there, utterly, maddeningly calm. She couldn't understand how he'd gotten there or why he was there or why he was dressed in tan suit and red shirt rather than jogging clothes. She stared in confusion at the key in her hand, then at him. "How did you get in?"

"Noelle let me in. She's waiting out in her car."

"Oh." That answered nothing. Noelle wasn't supposed to be here either, not till noon. And as for David, he never jogged at this time of morning. To the best of her knowledge he never even got up at this time of morning if he could help it. "I don't understand."

He reached inside his jacket and pulled out an envelope. "I have two airplane tickets. One for you and one for me. Our plane leaves in three hours."

"Plane? I don't—"

He held up his hand to forestall her words. "Hear me out. Please." He motioned her to the chair behind the counter and continued talking as she dazedly moved to sit down. "I'm going back to Boston soon. The closer my departure gets, the more I realize I still love you."

Melody swallowed hard. He still loved her?

"I realize our relationship is pretty messed up," he said, "but I always believed in my heart we'd get back together somehow. I didn't know how or when, but I always expected that one day I'd wake up and everything would be all right between us." He chuckled, a wondrously vibrant sound that caressed Melody's ears. "I guess what I actually pictured was you crawling back on your knees. Well, it was a nice fantasy, but you're too strong a woman for that." He nodded to her, and she acknowledged the sign of respect with a dazed smile. "Suddenly there's almost no time left for our relationship. I don't know if it's salvageable. I hope so."

"So do I," Melody said with a deceptive calm. He still loved her?

"Well." He smiled raggedly, hinting for the first time that his composure was also a facade. "Good. There's hope for us, then. The thing is, though, that we don't have much time to find out." He held up the envelope again. "That's why you're coming away with me this weekend, far from business and music and interruptions. We'll see what we can save from the mess we've made. We have a lot of talking to do and not much time to do it."

Melody was too stunned to answer right away. All this time he'd never given a hint of his feelings and now this....

He still loved her?

Incredible. Yet through the swirl of her surprise and confusion she saw their relationship clearly, more clearly than ever before. Yes, she owed it to him—and to herself—to see if their love had a chance. Yes, this took precedence over everything else. She took a deep breath. "Where will we go?"

David sighed as if he'd been holding his breath. He knelt beside her and put his arms around her with sublime tenderness. With equal gentleness she stroked his fine brown hair. It wasn't an embrace of passion but rather an embrace of delicate hope.

After too short a time he stood and straightened his suit. His voice was husky. "The Grand Hotel, where else? Dinners are formal, so bring your black gown. We'll stay Friday and Saturday and you can be back in time for work on Monday."

"The Grand Hotel? But David, the store—"

"Noelle agreed to work this weekend. Don't worry. I have everything planned."

"Noelle agreed? David, she wouldn't even wait on you, let alone conspire with you behind my back."

His eyebrows arched, and his fascinating eyes glinted in a rakish smile. "Call it the Halifax charm. Noelle can handle things here for a couple of days. Surely you aren't going to spoil a perfectly good conspiracy by worrying."

"No." She nodded decisively. "We go to the Grand Hotel in three hours. But David, I'll pay my share of the cost."

He started to protest, but she waved him silent. "I insist. And one more thing. I think we should have separate rooms."

His eyes flickered, and she hurried on. "I know I still feel attracted to you physically, and on top of that I haven't touched a man in months. I want this to be more than just a wild weekend, though. As you said, we have a lot to discuss, a lot to work out. Our future depends on this, and I think it would be best if we each had a room to return to—" she paused, then finished with a whisper "—if we want."

He grinned at her last three words. Leaning forward, he matched the hushed promise of her whisper. "I haven't touched a woman in months, either." Then in a normal speaking voice he said, "I was ahead of you on this. The reservation is for a two-bedroom suite. Any other questions?"

She shook her head. There wasn't time for questions. She had packing to do.

Chapter Twelve

Melody went with good intentions.

Probably they both did. Certainly they both wanted to resolve their difficulties. But neither of them had counted on the sensuous spell the venerable Grand Hotel could cast on reunited lovers.

Though northern Michigan was still in the final grips of winter, no cars were allowed on Mackinac Island. From the moment they stepped into the sled pulled by prancing, red-plumed horses for the ride to the hotel, Melody felt as if she were entering another world.

And she was: a world in which her worries and responsibilities could evaporate in the crisp, clean air and the sunshine of David's presence. She relaxed into the thick seat and simply *enjoyed*.

She enjoyed the cedar-lined road that expanded into a panorama of white lawn sloping lazily down to the broad moat of the straits. She enjoyed the delicate tickling of her hair blown against her cheeks by the sled's passage and the rhythmic crunching of the horse's hooves. She enjoyed the brisk aroma of the Lake Huron breeze and the sight of the huge hotel's three-story Grecian pillars, which seemed to stretch to the far horizon.

And most of all she enjoyed sitting by David's side, holding his hand under the blanket.

Discussion of their problems was postponed by mutual, unspoken consent while she delighted in the elegance of their suite. "It's marvelous." She spun around to survey the airy garden effect created by the large windows, grass-green carpet and rose-trellis wallpaper. "I feel like I've stepped into a fairy tale."

"And you're the beautiful princess," David said.

The raw emotion oozing through his husky baritone made her heart do a somersault. Slowly she turned, not caring whether he saw the sudden naked desire emblazoned on her face. There was no need for words. David held his arms out, and she went to him. Their pent-up passion transformed the embrace into a frenzied, life-restoring coupling on the couch of the sitting room, the supposedly neutral space between their separate bedrooms.

Afterward, when words were needed, they talked only of the present, as if the past had never been and the future never would be. Reality intruded only once, at dinnertime, when David made the mistake of asking how Melody's was doing.

"It's a bit soon to be certain," she answered guardedly. Ordinarily the store was her favorite topic, but tonight she didn't even want to think about her life in Chicago.

"That bad?"

"No, not at all. It's just that a new store doesn't make money in the first five weeks. There are all the start-up costs to cover, and I have a lot to learn. Plus I'm still in the process of getting my message across to the university students.''

David leaned across the table to cradle her hand in his. ''I'm sorry.''

''Sorry?'' She couldn't think what she had said to make him sorry. Maybe it was the comforting firmness of his fingers on her wrist that made thinking difficult. ''Whatever for?''

His eyes danced merrily, in the hauntingly familiar way they did when he tried to keep a straight face. ''I'm sorry the store isn't doing well.''

He didn't look sorry. In fact his eyes seemed to be enjoying a joke—but she couldn't find the punch line. Her face puckered into a puzzled frown. It was no use. She couldn't think straight with him touching her, and she reluctantly pulled her hand from his grasp. ''David, I didn't say the store was in trouble.''

''Not in so many words. You said, though, that it wasn't making money, and when a company doesn't make money, that usually means things aren't going well.'' He gazed at her with a fond, vaguely smug expression. ''You see, I did learn something about business from my family. You can't fool a Halifax.''

''All I said, Mr. Smart Aleck Tycoon, was that the store needs time. I haven't reached El Dorado, but I'm at least on the road. Ask me in a year how the store's doing and I'll give you a complete financial statement.''

Again a pleased smile fluttered almost imperceptibly around his mouth. ''But it's not a big money-maker, right?''

''Well...no.'' Why did she get the feeling that the store— her baby, her pride and joy, her namesake—was under attack? ''I'm not making much, but then I didn't expect to get rich right away.'' Her voice grew more emphatic. ''As it is, though, I'm thinking about hiring another clerk.''

''Sounds risky, if you aren't making money.''

"Beginnings are risky times." Why wouldn't he let it drop? She took a deep breath before continuing in a whisper turned fierce by the perverse pleasure lurking on his features. "I assure you, David, that Melody's will not fail. I won't let it!"

He hesitated, surprised by her vehemence. "Of course it won't," he assured her in a totally different tone. All traces of smugness disappeared, replaced by a sad seriousness. He looked at her like that for a few seconds, as if he were far away, and then sat back in a deep well of silence.

What had just happened? The entire conversation made no sense to her. Before they'd broken up he had complained she didn't tell him how she felt. Yet now, when she let her feelings out, he reacted in this mysterious way. What did he want from her?

Instead of delving into his mood, though, she laughed with forced gaiety and asked him if he'd like to inspect the museum of the hotel's history. Numerous celebrities, presidents and members of royalty had stayed here over the decades....

Brightening immediately, David agreed. They strolled arm in arm toward the lobby, struggling to prop up the fragile facade of carefree romance surrounding them.

But by Saturday afternoon the strain of ignoring reality was wearing them down. Friday night, after the incident in the dining room, it hadn't been difficult. Neither of them had felt the need for words as they had made love, first with the savage, unslakable thirst of people long lost in the desert and later with the tender, hopeful desperation of parents nursing a seriously ill child.

Yet now, as they ate dinner in the elegant hotel restaurant, they lapsed into longer and longer silences that were punctuated only by deep, yearning stares. This would be their last night here, and Melody was loath to reopen the old wounds while a single minute of carefree love lingered.

David returned her meaningful glances. He obviously felt the same. And still she waited for him to begin the confrontation that offered such possibilities, yet frightened her to the marrow of her bones.

Several times between bites of her veal cordon bleu Melody opened her mouth to speak. Do you think we have a chance? What would I have to do to win you back? Must you leave for Boston so soon?

But each time she closed her mouth without speaking. Like the first time they shared dinner together, she held her silence. She'd come full circle with David, starting with an uncomfortable dinner in silence and ending—*No*. Not yet, she thought. Just a little longer. Let us have dinner in peace. Please. Not yet. Peace.

Peace!

"Did you say something?" David was poised with his fork halfway to his mouth.

"No," she said quietly. She busied herself by cutting her veal into even daintier pieces. "Nothing at all."

"Oh." He took several more bites, then again stopped with his fork halfway to his mouth. "Melody—"

"Yes?"

He shook his head. "Nothing."

"Oh."

After another minute of silence, David pushed his plate away with a clatter of silverware. His gaze was frozen on to her face.

This was it. A heavy weight seemed to settle like a shroud over her body.

"It's not working anymore, Melody. As much as I'd like to pretend we haven't a care in the world, it simply isn't working. We have to talk."

She nodded. A stranger's voice came from her mouth as she stood up. "Let's go to the room."

"Don't you want to finish eating?"

She fortified herself with the last mouthful of her wine, ignoring the remnants of her meal. "I'm not hungry. Let's go."

They said nothing as they walked to their room. In the rectangle of light from the opening door the leafy rose wallpaper and green rug hammered at Melody. They had met in a garden and now returned. Full circle. They even had a whopper potato this time around.

A hot one.

She pulled her legs under her on the couch as David settled on the easy chair on the far side of the coffee table. The northern lights outside the window gave the room a murky gloom, yet neither of them turned on a lamp. Some things were easier to face in twilight.

"Well," David said at last.

"Well."

He squirmed on his chair. "This isn't easy, is it?"

"Did you expect it to be easy, Alistair?"

"Alistair?" He chuckled, then rubbed his chin with his hand. "No, I didn't. This is one of the hardest things I've ever had to make myself face."

Melody hugged her arms to stifle a shiver. "I feel it, too. I thought the difficulty would come in working things out, but I never dreamed how hard it would be to even start talking. So much depends on this, and there's so little time...." Her voice trailed off into a shrug.

"Yes, I see what you mean. That's not what I meant, though."

"Oh? What did you mean, then?"

He shifted to the edge of his chair and leaned toward her. The light from the windows turned him into an unreadable silhouette, so she could see no clues to his feelings. "I meant...well, Melody...will you marry me?"

"Yes."

Her quiet answer popped out before she even had time to think, and it was hard for her to tell which of them was more surprised. A stunned silence enveloped the room. Then David hurried to the couch beside her. He kissed her forehead tenderly, but she scarcely felt his lips. She was still in shock. "David, wait," she whispered as his lips began to roam across her face. "Stop. Please."

He pulled back, and her shock began to melt in the warmth of his gaze. How she would love to swim in the deep pools of happiness she saw in his eyes. Mrs. Melody Halifax...

She shook her head. Not yet. Her heart was racing wildly, but she tried to rein in its willful gallop. Maybe, but not yet. Nothing was solved between them yet. "David, we still have to talk."

"Sure," he answered happily. "Anything you want."

"That's better. David, you do realize what you're getting yourself into, don't you?"

"I sure do." He pulled her to him, engulfing her in the protection of his arms.

"I don't mean that," she said into the warmth of his shoulder. "I mean me. You wanted a degree of intimacy I didn't dare give you after Mr. Klein went into the hospital. Well, I'm afraid that when another crisis comes I might withdraw again, and then you'd react the same way, too." She wrapped a strand of hair around and around her finger, wishing he'd wipe that silly grin off his face and take her confession seriously. "I'm not good at confiding in people, David. I haven't had much practice. Rather than share my problems, rather than dealing with them, I've always buried them."

He removed his hand. "You're being too hard on yourself again. You're doing a great job of sharing your problems right now, with me. And you'll have me for the rest of your life. Depend on it."

She touched his cheek affectionately. "I drove you crazy, remember? I hope I'm changing so it won't happen again, but I've only just begun to learn to open myself up. I'm trying to change but... I guess I'm saying I'm scared. I love you, but I'm scared, and you have to learn not to get frustrated with me. You have to learn, too."

"Anything, Melody. Don't worry. Everything works out once you're married."

"I can tell you've never been married," she muttered.

"Your first marriage wasn't *us*. I'm not Jason. I'm me. I'll make the marriage work."

Her serious expression melted into a lopsided grin. "Have I ever told you that sometimes you're conceited?" To take the sting from her words she gave him a lingering kiss that left them both breathless.

He probably would make it work, she thought. She wanted to believe that. Commitments were important to him, and when he married her he would devote all his formidable energies to making it work. A sudden smile came across her features as the last of her doubts evaporated. She believed. What would it be like being married to a wonderful man like David? She was going to find out.

Safe and protected in the circle of his arms, she listened to his breathing. It gained speed rapidly as she raked her nails up his shoulder blades, across his neck and upward still into the sensitive scalp at the back of his neck. His hand sought her neck, as well, and they slowly guided each other's mouths toward union. His tongue gently parted her lips and began a dance of exploration and seduction. She flattened her breasts against his chest, her thigh against his, her lips against his, her hands against his back. Her insides began to turn to honey as she felt his lungs work more and more strongly, till she felt too weak to hold up her own head and only the incredible magnetism of his lips kept it upright.

When the kiss ended, they gazed into each other's eyes despite the gathering gloom. "I love you," he whispered.

Those three words rang through her heart like the trumpeting of angels, and their echo in her soul was a peal of laughter happier than anything she'd felt in months. "Sure," she said merrily, "you love me so much that proposing was the hardest thing you've ever done. You actually had the gall to tell me that!"

"Hey, have pity on me." His voice was cozy with love and happiness. "I'm a longtime bachelor. The matchmakers in my family gave up on me ages ago." A delectable shudder swept through her as he squeezed her tightly. "I can hardly wait to see my mother's face. Let's not tell them till we move to Boston, okay?"

The skin on the back of her neck abruptly cooled. The squeak that escaped her lips sounded as if it came from a different kind of creature. "Boston?"

"Yes, Boston. You know, that big city in Massachusetts. You sound like you've never heard of it. Maybe you'll decide to take some courses there, perhaps even work on a degree, the way you talked about doing."

She interrupted his happy chatter as if she hadn't heard a word. "Boston?"

She leaned over to turn on a table lamp so she could see his face better, then sat upright. The glistening reflection from the lamp seemed to give his large, soft eyes a sparkling innocence—a dangerously naive innocence, if he thought marriage would automatically smooth all differences between them. "You want to live in Boston?"

"Not necessarily. We'll have to talk about that."

She relaxed slightly.

"Actually," he continued, "I think I'd prefer Cambridge or Brookline. Maybe Newton."

Melody fought back the angry words that came to mind. She took a deep breath, then spoiled its effect by recalling his unilateral decision to move to Boston. She remembered how thoroughly he planned his life—and now, it seemed, hers. She couldn't keep the edge out of her voice. "Gee, I'm glad you're willing to discuss living in the suburbs or the city."

He recognized her irony, and his next words were cautious. "You're right. I apologize if I got carried away. Just remember that I'm used to living alone and making my own decisions. It'll take me a while to adjust."

A smile slowly stretched across Melody's face. Well, at least he recognized the problem and seemed willing to work on it. That was a good sign. He'd been single for all his life, and living with someone else would be an even greater novelty for him than for her. Still, she'd have to stand up for her rights, especially since decisions came so easily for him and with such slow agony for her.

That was for the future, though. Right now she had to get this Boston business cleared up. "Tell me," she said, "who's the new assistant conductor of the Chicago Philharmonic?"

He looked at her steadily for several heartbeats. "No one yet. They'll make their decision in the next week or two." He continued quickly, before she could comment. "How long will it take to sell the record store?"

"No!" The word tore from her throat with embarrassing vehemence, and she studied her hands till her emotions returned to a manageable level. "I mean, why do you just assume I'm going to sell the store?"

"My career is in Boston."

"Mine's in Chicago."

He gave a weary, almost apologetic sigh. "But the store's not making money."

Disturbing tremors of fear rippled along her nerves, threatening to bury rational thought under an avalanche of panic. She took several slow, deep breaths to still the accelerating hammer blows of her heart. "Is that what your family would do, walk away from an investment that wasn't producing a big enough return?"

He didn't answer, merely continued to look at her steadily.

"I see." The flowery decor of the sitting room, which twenty-four hours ago had seemed like something out of a fairy tale, abruptly turned malignant. The fairy tale had gone wrong, as if the cast were melting and dripping into ghastly caricatures. The flowers on the couch and drapes seemed to loom malevolently, like the roses that overwhelmed Sleeping Beauty's castle and formed a prickly, menacing shell. In that tale Prince Charming woke the princess with a kiss, as David had wakened her, but in real life Prince Charming seemed to expect a massive price for the happily ever after. "And you expect me to be like your family? Don't you realize I'm different from the Halifaxes? Am I that much of a stranger to you?

He slowly shook his head. "No, of course not. It's just a business, though, so I thought—"

She charged through the middle of his words. "Even if it is a business, the money isn't the important thing. What's important is that for the first time in my life I'm building something that's mine. Melody's is more than just a catchy name for a record store. That place is mine, and I am its." She ran her hand across her forehead, as if that could help her find the words for the truths inside her. "You're right. The store isn't yet a money-maker. That's precisely why I can't sell it now. I'd never know if I could have been a success. It'd be like asking you to quit conducting just when you were learning how, before you'd convinced yourself you could really do it.'' She shook her head in frustration, realizing she'd said the wrong thing. How could she expect a person like David Halifax to understand the uncertainty and self-doubt of a high school dropout who'd failed even at marriage? Could a fish understand a desert?

For an eternity David sat motionless, his face expressionless granite. Melody longed to reach her hand across the gulf that separated them, but she, too, sat as if carved from stone. A wild, surging, fear-driven pounding of her heart left her suddenly weak. With each passing beat the fear grew stronger, mounting into a panic that rose in her throat with a vile, sickly taste. Yet she sat and waited.

And then, finally, a hint of softness—or was it just pain?—twitched through the muscles of David's mouth, as if the effort required to keep his face rigid was becoming unbearable. ''I didn't realize,'' he whispered. ''I should have realized but I didn't. Forgive me, Melody.''

A sob tore from her throat. The forlorn sadness etched in his voice chilled her more than angry words ever could have; it was the sadness of resignation. She'd been afraid he wouldn't understand, but he did. She could tell by his words, his tone, his expression, his posture, that he did indeed understand what he'd asked of her. And, understanding, he would not ask again. She yearned to reach out to him, to touch him, but he was now further away than ever before.

''David,'' she began, ''the Philhar—'' The Philharmonic, she'd been about to say, is a fine orchestra, a world-renowned orchestra, better than the New England Pops. Surely your career wouldn't be ruined by one year as assistant conductor.

He answered her unfinished thought with an agonized closing of his eyes. When they reopened she saw more uncertainty and pain than she could stand.

A sunburst of understanding exploded in her brain, casting David in a new light that illuminated him as more human, more lovable—and yet at the same time more unreachable—than ever. She remembered their first date, when he had confided in her about the ghost of John Halifax, who haunted the Halifax men and drove them to strive hopelessly toward unattainable levels of success. David claimed to have escaped the ghost. True, he strove not for money. Yet she saw now that he hadn't escaped. David was still haunted by the ghost of old John as much as any man in his family. Maybe more, even if his goals weren't dollars and cents. David needed success the way other men needed food and water; without goals, without progress, without his carefully planned career schedule, he was less than old John and a failure in his own eyes.

Melody's eyes closed in silent, agonized prayer. David, she thought, for your own sake as much as mine—for the sake of freeing yourself—please, David, consider staying in Chicago. For a year at least. Even if you decide not to, consider it. I'm afraid you'll never be truly free otherwise—controlled by your strength rather than controlling it yourself.

His determination and vision were his strength, as well as his weakness. What would David Halifax be without his drive for perfection? She tried to imagine him as an assistant conductor ten years from now; it was a defeated David she pictured. Even though a year as assistant conductor would do him no harm, ten years would. The impulse to bend would have to come from inside him, not from her, or he might break. She couldn't do that to him; she couldn't ask that of him, demand that he choose between vocation and love. She simply couldn't. She loved him too much.

Just as he loved her too much.

The shock of defeat gave her voice the metallic, unemotional inflections of a robot. "David, I can't marry you. Not right now. I hope you understand."

He didn't seem surprised at her words, but his face slumped. "I love you, Melody."

"And I love you." As empty as she felt now, she knew she would feel still worse later—maybe in a few minutes, maybe in an hour, maybe for the rest of her life. Right now, though, the emptiness lent her a mindless calm to camouflage the deep despair that lurked inside her somewhere.

"Well," she said in the hollow silence filling the room, "I suppose we have alternatives. We could have a long-distance relationship. See each other every few months."

Her suggestion met with tortured silence.

"Or," she said, "we could arrange to meet here in a year to see if there's anything left for us."

He still said nothing. His beautiful, lively eyes had grown desolate and dark. If it weren't for his slight wince at the suggestion of a long-distance relationship, she wouldn't have known he'd even heard her.

"Or," she continued relentlessly, "we can break it off cleanly right now."

He bowed his head silently.

Strange, how their roles had reversed; now that everything was over she was the stronger one. But then, she'd had a lot more experience in not getting what she wanted. She rose from the couch and looked down at the handsome, haunted man she would love for the rest of her life.

"I'm sorry," he managed to say.

She reached behind her for the zipper of her gown. "Don't say you're sorry," she whispered. In one smooth motion she shrugged the dress off her shoulders and onto the floor. She held her arms out to him. "Just give me a memory."

David didn't look up at her. He was slouched like a man with no more reason to live. Slowly, painfully, he came to his feet, crippled and bent like Mr. Klein.

She lifted her arms higher.

Still without looking at her, he hobbled wretchedly to the door of his bedroom.

Melody kept her arms raised to him, despite the tears that flowed freely down her face, until his door shut with a sound like a death knell.

The violinist had draped his tie over his shoulder as he bent close to Melody's oboe to tune his instrument. "Thanks for the A, Melody," he said.

"Sure," she answered. "Break a leg."

"Oh, don't worry about me. I never get nervous before a concert." The violinist nodded and walked in the direction of the stage, tie still perched on his shoulder like a red and blue parrot.

Melody pulled the reed from her oboe and stuck it in her mouth cigarette-fashion to keep it moist. She scanned the wings of the stage yet again. No sign of David. If he didn't show up soon she wouldn't have time to tell him of her decision before the concert.

Her decision. Probably the hardest decision of her life. Harder even than the decision to get a divorce.

But it was done. She'd officially told Bob Gold to put the record store on the market, at a low enough price to ensure a buyer. And lo and behold, one of the junior partners in Bob's firm had already expressed interest. So it was done. She hadn't seen David since she'd limped out of their hotel room alone, a week ago. And now she ached to tell him before the concert, so ill will wouldn't poison the magic of the music they would make tonight.

"David," she muttered, "where are you?"

"Right behind you."

She nearly bit her reed in half. "You scared me, David."

"That's nothing compared to what you've done to me over the last week." His expression, however, held no hint of a tormented week. Instead he looked happy, indecently so. His fluent eyes spoke of excitement, eagerness, confidence.

"I have something I want to tell you," she began. Then she stopped. She'd had to work hard with a make-up brush to disguise the circles under her own eyes, yet David looked exactly the way he should look before an artistic triumph— not the way he should look after having a marriage proposal rejected.

Unless he was glad. Unless he had realized she wasn't worth the agony of regret . . .

No! She wouldn't fall into that self-denigrating trap again. *Never again.* She was worthy of David Halifax, and she would win him back. No matter what. Still, she hadn't counted on this barely subdued jubilation that gave his every movement a quality of importance and grandeur promising an extraordinary musical performance.

"You were going to say something, Melody?"

She couldn't do it. She couldn't break the magical spell that enwreathed the very air around him. Afterward there would be time enough. Right now, in the face of his excitement, her explanation could be neither short nor comprehensive.

"No, David. Nothing."

He accepted her words with a nod. His gaze darted toward the rapidly filling hall. "It'll be a great concert tonight. It has to be a great concert tonight."

"Of course," she told him with a calmness that cost her dearly. "But you once told me only relatives and friends came to these concerts. No one is critical of our mistakes, and nothing more than pride is at stake."

"My pride is very much at stake." He tapped his baton rapidly against his left hand. "It seems some of the amateurs in the orchestra object to the demands I make of them. Andy Blankhurst heard about the griping through his son. Since the Philharmonic's assistant conductor has to lead the Civic Orchestra, Andy got all concerned about my ability to handle amateurs. A couple of people from the Philharmonic are out there tonight, listening for every sour note."

"I see." The reason for his keyed-up state was suddenly clear. Her voice took on an edge of sarcasm that he was oblivious to. "If we don't play well, you might not get the honor of rejecting the Chicago Philharmonic. Well, good luck."

She turned away and didn't speak to him after that. She tried instead to calm herself. In her present frame of mind she'd be prone to errors, and pride forbade that she be the cause of his losing a job—even one he would never take. Regardless of her sudden doubts about her decision, she had to play as if nothing had happened.

But it hurt. It hurt to see him just as badly as it had hurt not to see him.

She managed to get through the first half of the concert without more than her usual quota of small mistakes. Greg even complimented her at the intermission on the short flute and oboe duet they'd played in the overture. That surprised her. Greg was sparing of compliments, so it meant she'd truly played well. Yet the evening felt like a bad dream.

The second half was worse. Not that she played any worse, but her mind kept slipping into the past. David jogging by her garden. David giving her driving lessons. David conducting the Philharmonic. David making love to her.

She was amazed she could play her instrument at all. The first piece whizzed past, and suddenly they were ready to play the last selection, *Swan Lake* Suite—their last beautiful music together.

David lowered his baton and the music began. Almost immediately Melody had a long, haunting solo, the longest she'd ever had. Thoughts of David lent an extra depth and poignancy to her playing as he gave her, the soloist, all his attention. His arm rose expressively, and she matched his motion with a delicate crescendo. She forgot about her instrument, forgot about her lips and breathing and simply poured out her love, her joy and tenderness and grief. She played inspired by his arms, inspired by his face, inspired by his love, and for one fleeting eternity their souls reverberated in perfect harmony. The music soared between them in heartbreaking melancholy and nobility, floating outward for others to hear as the testament of their love.

A tear gathered at the corner of her eye when their swan song was over. The principal violist turned and stared at her, startled by the unexpected perfection of her playing. A fragment of her mind marveled at the overwhelming touch of David's inspiration and magic. The keystone of his personality was his drive for the transcendence she'd just felt. Amazing. And so simple, really. Losing oneself completely in the music. Yes, David was her inspiration, her magic. Melody's lungs pumped fresh oxygen to her starved core, but her eyes never left David. He was worth any sacrifice. Losing herself to gain herself; oh, yes, there was a rightness to it....

The waltz began, and she tried to gather her wandering thoughts to concentrate on the music. She must be ready for the tricky duet with the flute. As she counted rests a quiver of insuppressible joy jogged the numbers momentarily from her mind.

Greg spoke softly out of the corner of his mouth. "The count?"

Startled, Melody wrenched herself back to reality. "Uh, eleven." Or was it ten? She was about to tell Greg she wasn't sure, but too late. He already had his silver instrument at his lips, he was breathing deeply, he was blowing.

And it was all wrong. He was a bar early. Lost in her reverie, she'd told him the wrong count. Greg lowered his flute in momentary confusion.

It was an exposed, obvious mistake. The cellists, easily confused as usual, hesitated and then stopped completely. David waved his baton with exaggerated precision, but the music fell apart rapidly. It was grinding to a total halt—and with it David's chance to turn down the Philharmonic.

Ashamed of her mistake, Melody had never begun her part of the duet. Now she did, loudly, not knowing whether she was right or wrong but only that she had to play as strongly and confidently as possible. David adjusted his beat to her playing and urged the others to follow her lead. After a few notes Greg began to play along with her. The violins followed. Eventually even the cellos got over their confusion and joined in.

Buoyed by having overcome this close call, the orchestra finished the suite with more verve and confidence than ever before. The audience applauded enthusiastically. After David bowed to them and had the orchestra stand up, the crowd kept applauding till he returned to the stage.

This time he threaded through the string section and held out his hand for Melody. Surprised and more than a bit embarrassed, she numbly let him lead her to the podium to confront a sea of anonymous faces. Together they bowed to the audience.

"Melody," he said as he bent with a natural grace she couldn't hope to match, "I phoned the Pops yesterday and told them I quit."

He straightened up and smiled benignly at the crowd as if he hadn't just changed her life.

She lacked his iron control. She stared at him dumbly, her mouth half open. Had he really said those words, or had her overwrought brain imagined them? "What?"

He turned to her with a humble expression, ignoring the clapping of the crowd. "If you, and the Philharmonic, will still have me—"

Melody didn't give him a chance to finish. She threw herself in his arms, making him stagger backward from the force of her love. Her mouth sought his with desperate passion, and she forced his lips open with her tongue to drink deeply of his love.

Only when she needed to breathe did she pull away long enough to realize that his arms were around her waist, lifting her feet off the floor—and that she was surrounded by hundreds of wide-eyed, laughing, clapping witnesses to the most aggressive kiss she'd ever given. But it didn't matter. It didn't matter, either, which of them ended up making the sacrifice, or whether they worked out a compromise instead. With a love like this nothing else mattered, as long as they had each other.

"Encore," Noelle yelled from the front row. The orchestra picked up the cry, then so did the audience. Melody gazed into David's wonderful face.

He shrugged his shoulders. "We can't disappoint the customers, now can we?"

"No," she breathed, "the customer is always right."

She closed her eyes for another kiss.

*   *   *   *   *

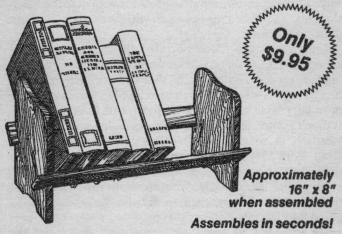

Silhouette Special Edition

THE O'HURLEYS! CHANTEL'S STORY

from
Nora Roberts

Skin Deep

Available September 1988

The third in an exciting new series about the lives and loves of triplet sisters—

In May's *The Last Honest Woman* (SE #451), Abby finally met a man she could trust . . . then tried to deceive him to protect her sons.

In July's *Dance to the Piper* (SE #463), it took some very fancy footwork to get reserved recording mogul Reed Valentine dancing to effervescent Maddy's tune. . . .

In *Skin Deep* (SE #475), find out what kind of heat it takes to melt the glamorous Chantel's icy heart. Available in September.

THE O'HURLEYS!

**Join the excitement of
Silhouette Special Editions.**

SSE 475

COMING NEXT MONTH

#475 SKIN DEEP—Nora Roberts
In book three of THE O'HURLEYS!, private eye Quinn Doran stakes out
Chantel O'Hurley's too-avid, threatening "fan." But his tougher case is
uncovering the warmth beneath Chantel's icy exterior.

#476 TENDER IS THE KNIGHT—Jennifer West
A spell had been cast that Juliet meet a man worthy of her tenderness.
And poof! armor-clad Rocco Marriani appeared. But could simple
conjuring conquer Juliet's private demons?

#477 SUMMER LIGHT—Jude O'Neill
A match between bohemian Wiley Ranahan and conservative Molly
Proctor couldn't possibly last forever. But after spending August basking
in his affection, Molly began wondering if summer love could linger....

#478 REMEMBER THE DAFFODILS—Jennifer Mikels
Knowing whimsical, unpredictable Ariel Hammond would eventually let
him down, sensible Pete Turner had left before she broke his heart. Now
he wanted her back, but had his practicality compromised their passion?

#479 IT MUST BE MAGIC—Maggi Charles
Upon meeting her volatile new client, Alex Grant, Josephine suspected her
rule about business and pleasure was about to be broken. But could the
magic of love make her deepest fears vanish?

#480 THE EVOLUTION OF ADAM—Pat Warren
For self-made Adam Kinkaid, to-the-manor-born Danielle Ames held the
key to high society. He thought he wanted in...until rebellious Dani made
him long for so much more.

AVAILABLE THIS MONTH: